# WE
# KNEW
# ALL ALONG

**Also available by Mina Hardy**

*After All I've Done*

# WE KNEW ALL ALONG

## A NOVEL

### MINA HARDY

**CROOKED
LANE**

NEW YORK

Published in the United States by Crooked Lane Books, an imprint of The Quick Brown Fox & Company LLC.

Crooked Lane Books and its logo are trademarks of The Quick Brown Fox & Company LLC.

Library of Congress Catalog-in-Publication data available upon request.

ISBN (hardcover): 978-1-63910-140-5
ISBN (paperback): 978-1-63910-536-6
ISBN (ebook): 978-1-63910-141-2

Cover design by Nicole Lecht

Printed in the United States.

www.crookedlanebooks.com

Crooked Lane Books
34 West 27th St., 10th Floor
New York, NY 10001

First Edition: December 2022
Trade Paperback Edition: December 2023

10 9 8 7 6 5 4 3 2 1

For anyone who's never had a book
dedicated to them before,
this one's for you.

# 1

W HAT DO YOU do when you look across the room and see the one man you've never been able to forget? You thank whatever god is responsible for push-up bras and the stomach flu that got rid of that last four pounds. You swallow the last of your complimentary glass of cheap champagne, and you take a deep breath. You lift your chin and turn away from him.

And then you wait.

It takes Christian Campbell exactly three minutes to cross the ballroom and tap me on the shoulder. I know because I counted each second passing on the big, ornate wall clock above the double doors leading to the hotel hallway. Three minutes is not a long time, but it felt like forever . . . and also not nearly long enough.

I don't turn around, not right away, not for as long as it takes me to breathe in and out and my heart to thunk a quadruple beat.

"Jewel? Jewelann Kahan?"

At the sound of my name, I turn, turn, turn. I slowly, slowly turn. A smile. A tilt of my head, brow a little furrowed, but only a little. It's a face that says I should know him, but I don't . . . quite . . . remember . . .

"It's me," he says with a thump of his fingers on his chest, over his heart. "Christian."

I take a few delicate steps back, feigning shock. Of course I know him. I'd been searching for a sight of him from the first moment I stepped through the doors into the ballroom. I hadn't even been planning to come to this stupid reunion until I saw on our high school's Connex page that he was listed as an attendee. There had been a list of the Labor Day weekend event schedule and the confirmed RSVPs, account profiles tagged for each one. I'd thought of C.C. many times over the years since I'd last seen him, but this was the first time I'd ever looked him up online. There was nothing to see but a gray silhouette and an empty profile.

"Oh," I reply simply. No gushing. No arms open for a hug, no turning my cheek for a fake air kiss.

He notices, all right. His crystal-blue eyes narrow for a moment, looking me over. Assessing. It's the way he used to look at me in high school, back when I powdered my fair skin to a ghostly pallor and dyed my naturally pale hair black, when I shrouded my curves in layers of black. I've never had a man look at me that way since.

"You haven't changed much." I instantly regret allowing him to get under my skin. I'd planned this night so carefully, from top to toe. I can't screw it up. I won't.

A slow smile tips his lips on one side. Sly but charming, and he knows it, the same way he knows I just lied. Christian has changed *a lot*, in all the best ways. The youthful spray of freckles across his nose and cheeks has become the tan of a man who spends his free time with outdoor sports, probably golf or skiing. His wheat-colored hair glints with silver at the temples, but it's still lush and thick. A few crinkles appear at the corners of his eyes when he smiles. The Christian Campbell of years ago had never been in need of a glow up, but he sure has grown up, and everything I'd swooned over when he was a teenage boy has been amplified now that he's become a man.

"*You* have," he says.

Butterflies.

Considering that it's Christian, they're probably moths, the kind with skulls on them. From that movie with Hannibal Lecter. Except, I guess the truth is, if Christian offers to eat me, I'm totally ready to let him.

He steps forward to press his lips to my cheek, his hands warm on my bared shoulders. His breath gusts over my skin, his voice rumbles directly into my ear, and I shudder as the fine hairs on the back of my neck rise with his words.

"You look amazing, Jewelann. Absolutely gorgeous. And still dressed all in black. You look better as a blonde, though. It suits you."

I don't mean to close my eyes, but I do, and I'm shot back all the way to our junior year when his words had been different but the sentiment the same. We'd been making out in my parents' carriage house with the lights off so they wouldn't know we were in there, his hands under my shirt but over my bra and his hard-on nudging my thigh for attention. Then I'd believed him, and a few years later he'd broken my heart. Crushed it, more than once. I have never forgiven him. I have never forgotten.

I believe him now, too, because he's right. I *have* glowed up. Bigger breasts and hips, courtesy of pregnancy and time, but a flatter tummy I've worked hard to get and keep. Reverting to my natural color hides the incoming gray and takes much less work and money than maintaining regular visits to the salon, but the blonde does suit me. I *do* look amazing, at least on the outside.

Inside, I'm still the same ugly mess.

The moment between us lasts for . . . well, a moment, before his hand presses the small of my back. My eyes open.

He brushes his lips on my cheek again, too close to my mouth. I'm the one who steps back. Not out of reach. Not that. But I do put some distance between us, and I make it obvious that it's deliberate.

I wish the look in his eyes was regret, but Christian's expression is too neutral to read. Pinned by his gaze, I can't move. What does he remember about me? What does he think about who I have become?

"You look good, really good. How've you been?"

I believe he means what he says, but I can't believe what he says means anything.

I don't have the chance to answer. Tiff Reade, one of the reunion committee members, has swooped down on us. She's hawking raffle tickets from a big roll she wears on her forearm. The prizes are gift cards for local restaurants or BOGOs for attractions you're supposed to take your kids to, except that my kid doesn't like loud noises or crowds, and too much fried food will make him puke. I buy an arm's length of tickets for five dollars anyway, although I know even that small, unexpected expense is going to nibble a bigger hole in my wallet.

"Use *his* arm," Tiff says with a grin and gestures at Christian. "It's longer. More tickets."

Gallantly, my former high school crush offers his arm. She measures off a strip of tickets and winks at me, then him, and hands them to me. She does the same for him next, but Christian takes four sets. He hands her a twenty and takes the paper anaconda of tickets from her. Quickly, carefully, precisely, he accordions them all into a thick but compact bundle and shoves them in the pocket of his suit pants.

"Who are you here with? Ken?" Christian asks.

He remembers my husband's name.

"Ken is out of town," I say.

My husband troubleshoots point-of-sale systems for small businesses. Mom-n-pop motels and convenience stores in the middle of nowhere. He's on the road three weeks out of four, these days. It wasn't always like that.

"That's too bad. It would've been great to meet him. And I promise"—he holds up his hands—"I wouldn't even tell him about what a bad girl you used to be."

"Maybe he already knows," I answer coolly, although of course Ken has no idea who I was before I met him. He doesn't know who I am now.

Where is that bad girl, anyway? Worn away by the years of packing healthy lunches and laundering the stains out of her husband's tighty-whities. She's buried beneath the weight of credit card debt and a house she keeps for a spouse who's hardly ever in it. She's struggling to protect a weird and socially awkward son from a world that would love to knock him down again and again. That bad girl has become a caricature of wife and mother.

But not tonight.

Do I imagine the gleam in Christian's ice-blue eyes? Wishful thinking? No. His interest is definitely there, and in that instant, I release a tension I've been clenching inside my chest since I first read his name as "attending."

Christian remembers *me*.

"Good to see you," I tell him, all easy-breezy. I squeeze his bicep, hard as a rock, through the sleeve of his black suit jacket. I move away from him, my eyes already seeking out someone else. Anyone else. I don't care about a single other person here, but I want Christian to think that someone, anyone, is more important to me than he could ever be.

This is the man who broke my heart, after all, and even though he'd been a boy when he did, I'm here tonight to make sure it's the man he's become who will regret it.

CHAPTER

2

I HEAD FOR A cluster of my classmates grouped around the
silver trays of appetizers placed on tables covered in black
and red cloths. Our school colors. There'd been chatter on
the reunion event page about dressing to match, and I see a
lot of red or black gowns and ties. One man stands out in a
bright crimson suit with a trendy cut, tight pants cropped
at the ankles. I don't recognize him, but I wave as though
I do.

My simple black dress is a classic look, approved by my
husband, who has opinions about things like that. He'd
never come right out and use the word "whore," but I know
that's what he thinks about too much cleavage, skirts cut too
far above the knee. I'd bought the dress at an estate sale to
wear to his company holiday party a few years ago. It's one of
at least two dozen black dresses I own, all in a similar style.
I doubt Ken would be able to tell one from the other, which
is kind of the point. He can't complain about me having too
many black dresses if he can't tell them apart.

Christian might be watching me walk away from him,
but I don't look back to check. I wave at a few more people
in the group. I live in the same town I grew up in, and

yet I haven't seen any of these people in years, some since our graduation twenty-five years ago. I know the woman in front of me, though. Lisa Weaver and I had been friends in elementary school, bonding over our love for sticker albums and hatred of white milk in cartons. We'd drifted apart in middle school, and in high school she joined the cheerleading squad in a desperate but successful bid for popularity. I'd taken the path toward a different cliché, thrift-store Goth. Looks like we both ended up in much the same place, though. Domestic "bliss."

"Jewelann! Don't you look great! Like something right out of an old black-and-white movie. So glam." Lisa's dark-eyed gaze moves up and down over my dress, takes in my upswept hair and the glint of my earrings, real diamonds that had belonged to Ken's mother. Her eyebrows lift the tiniest bit at the sight of my black heels with the red soles. "Oh, wow, I love your shoes."

I tilt my foot side to side. Nonchalant, although inside I'm gleeful that she noticed. "Oh, these? Thanks."

"'Oh,' she says, like you picked them up at Target." Lisa wears her hair in a natural wealth of soft curls that she's pinned back on the sides. Her deep red lipstick is perfect against her dark skin. She wears a red dress to match.

I resist the urge to tell her I bought them at an estate sale, still in the original box with the receipt. I spent less than half of what they originally cost. Less than half was still a lot. This is the first time I've ever worn them. They pinch my toes.

We hug. She smells of perfume, a scent I can't place. Her embrace shakes my arm so the cheap sparkling wine sloshes from my glass.

"Whoopsy." Lisa's laugh is raucous and reminds me of why we used to be such good friends when we were children. "Don't want to waste the bubbly. Such as it is. How long has it been since I've seen you, anyway? Are you still living in your old house?"

When my parents decided to move to Florida and offered the house to my brother Jonathan and me, I'd been the one to accept it, while he took the cash they offered instead. At the time, I'd thought I was getting the better bargain. Real estate always goes up in value, doesn't it? At twenty-three, I hadn't understood what a burden owning a house can be, how refinancing to put cash in your pocket ties you financially to a bunch of brick and wood and glass, how the choices you make inside its walls can turn a home into a prison.

"Yep. Still there. How about you? Are you still over on . . . ?" I don't remember where she was living the last time we spoke. Honestly, I can't recall *when* we last spoke.

She picks up when I trail away. "No, no. I moved over to a condo in Lincoln Park. Near the Fraze Pavilion. Loud as hell over there, between the concerts and the freaking high school football. But I'm too lazy to find another place. And since it's just me . . ."

Lisa's the one who trails away this time, but with an expectant look, as though I'm meant to fill in the blank she's deliberately leaving. When I don't speak up, she continues. "You know we only live a few streets away from each other. Why don't we ever hang out?"

"Oh, you know," I tell her with a wave of my hand. "Life stuff."

"It shouldn't take a class reunion to get us together," she says.

The glint of tears in her eyes alarms me. I'm not sure what to say in response to this surge of emotion. She's not wrong, but she's also talking as though we'd been bosom buddies, when the reality is that by the time we graduated from high school, she was passing me in the hallway without even looking at me. Pleated skirts and pom-poms versus black lipstick and torn fishnets. We hadn't had a falling out, but we'd done a bit more than simply drift apart.

"Let's grab a couple of fresh glasses of that terrible champagne while we catch up. Okay?" She's already waving toward one of the servers, and I have time to admire her perfectly polished, crimson nails. I haven't had a manicure or gel tips in months. Too expensive, and besides, working in the garden ruins long nails.

"Oh . . . I really shouldn't . . ."

"It's a class reunion. If that's not the perfect reason to get hammered, what is? I mean, c'mon. Look at this group! We all got so freaking *old*." Her laughter has an edge, but it's still contagious.

I accept a glass from the server and lift it toward Lisa's. "I always did get into trouble with you."

She laughs again. Leans in close. The liquor on her breath is much stronger than the bubbly they're handing out. She wobbles a little, and I put out a hand to steady her. Even in her heels, she's still a few inches shorter.

"That's saying something. You got in trouble a lot." Lisa steps back so rapidly I'm left cupping empty air. Her gaze goes to someone else across the room, and she waves as her eyes light up. She calls out a name.

"It's Beth," she says. "I'm going to go say 'hi.' You coming?"

Beth and Lisa had been cheerleaders together, but Beth and I had never been friends. They angle their bodies toward each other to giggle over gossip about our other classmates. I am not a point on this triangle until Lisa pulls me a step closer so she can tell me all about so-and-so's boob job, and Beth chimes in that the dentist husband of someone else has been schtupping the orthodontist husband of yet another.

I am . . . included.

I don't have any gossip to share; if anything, I'm sure there would be plenty of whispers about my family. My son, who attends school with the children of some of these people, but who stands apart from them. My husband, who's always on the road. And, of course, there's always the side-eye glance you get when you've been known to show up slurring to the preschool play. Mommies have long memories. I brace myself for the questions, but although Beth looks me up and down and takes in every inch of me, every hair in or out of place, even my expensive shoes that are nevertheless several seasons old, she doesn't ask me a single question.

There's a reason why I always got into trouble when I hung around with Lisa. She's always been a real force of nature, hard to resist. Before I know it, the three of us are laughing and clinking our glasses together. Beth waves over the circulating server with the platter of puffed pastry treats, and Lisa disappears, then returns from the bar with three more glasses of chilly golden bubbles. The drink tastes better now, either because I've already downed two glasses or she's upgraded us to something better, I can't tell.

"This is going right to my head." I lift the empty glass.

Lisa eyes me as she drains the last of hers. "Not a drinker?"

"Oh, she was never into *that*, were you, Jewelann?" Beth says, and that's how I know that she *does* know the gossip.

We share a look, but it's one of understanding. She doesn't keep that figure with Pilates and clean eating alone. We all have our own ways of numbing our pain. Mine used to come in a prescription bottle I lied to my doctor for, so I'm really in no place to judge.

"I got my medical card," Lisa says suddenly.

Beth and I look at her.

"Beats buying a baggie of skunk off Todd Villanueva behind the bleachers at halftime," Lisa says.

Beth laughs. "If by buy you mean *blow*."

Lisa waves a hand but doesn't deny it. Her eyes gleam, but not with tears this time. She gives a pointed look around the room. "I wonder if he's here tonight?"

"I saw him when I came in. Married, four kids, owns a car dealership in Columbus." Beth leans a little, closing our triangle. "Christian Campbell's here, too."

Lisa fans her face. "Ooh, la la. That would be Dr. Campbell to you."

"C.C.'s a *doctor*?" I shouldn't be surprised. He'd always talked about becoming a surgeon. How he'd have his own practice, a fleet of sports cars, a big house, and a bigger bank account.

"That's the rumor. A surgeon, no less. Plastic, maybe? Think he'd give me a friends and family discount?" Lisa asks with a laugh as she spins halfway around to seek out the sight of him. "God, he's hot, isn't he?"

"Hotter than he was in high school, even," Beth says and fixes me with another knowing look. "Didn't you and him have a thing?"

I pull a surprised expression. "Not really. We were lab partners our junior year. That's about it. We didn't really hang in the same crowd."

But sometimes, we got high and fooled around in my parents' carriage house. Sometimes he'd come over after school when my brother was at football practice and my parents were at work. Sometimes, he would call me late at night and whisper to me through the phone, as though even then, he didn't want to risk anyone overhearing.

The rest of the time, in public, in front of his friends and anyone else, he'd pretend he didn't know me.

"Anyway," I add, "he was dating Jen Tillis."

We all fall silent at that. Jen Tillis was the first of our class to die. Suicide, freshman year of college. Without social media to spread the news, it had filtered to everyone via word of mouth, and I wasn't sure I'd ever heard the whole story. I saw her parents now and then around town. Her mother hadn't aged well.

Beth turns to me. Her smile is bright and wide, showing a span of gleaming white teeth that stand out against the dark plum of her lipstick. Like me, she's in black, and like me, she's a blonde. We match without looking anything alike.

"So," she says over the rim of her glass, her eyes locking with mine. "When did you go blonde?"

"It's my natural color."

Beth's artificially shaped eyebrows go up, up, up. "You bitch. A natural platinum blonde *and* those fucking Louboutins? *Jay kay.* You look great. I hate you. Kidding, I'm kidding."

She's not kidding.

The arrival of several of their high school cheerleading squad friends is heralded by squeals. They all bounce up and down and hug each other, while their husbands sip whiskeys from squat glasses and stand at an appropriate distance without speaking much to each other. A few of the husbands are sizing me up. They don't know that in high school I wasn't one of the popular girls, like their wives. They only see me the way I am now, and I'm not ashamed to be proud of how I look in comparison to those high school beauty queens who've aged and broadened and started going gray. None of it's for them, though. This dress, the shoes, the hair, the jewelry, the lipstick . . . it's all for Christian. Except, when I turn casually to look for him across the room, he's no longer there.

I've missed my shot.

CHAPTER

3

I'D DONE SUCH a good job ignoring Christian that I've lost
track of him. Disappointment clogs my throat, and I want
to kick myself for ruining my night's big plans. I scan the
room, but a woman steps between me and a clear line of sight
toward the last place I saw him.

"Eli's your son, right? Eli Jordan?" She wears enviably
thick fake eyelashes that show off her deep brown eyes. Her
teeth sparkle inside the frame of her hot pink lipstick, and
twin spots of bright pink blush highlight the bronze apples
of her cheeks.

I have no idea who she is, but I smile as though I've been
waiting to talk to her all night. "Yes, Eli's my son."

"He's in Maya's class. My daughter. I'm here with Shawn
Lincoln, he's my husband. I was a couple of years behind
you guys. But you and I used to volunteer at the preschool
together." Her look is intense. Keen.

I remember Shawn from high school, barely, and I do not
remember her at all. She clearly remembers me, but I don't
want to think about the reasons why. Or what she recalls.
The years my son was in preschool are all . . . blurry.

"I'm Sheila," Maya's mother prompts.

I nod, looking past her to scan the room again. No Christian. Tension coils in my chest. I put on my best "mom" voice. "Sheila and Shawn. Of course. How've you been? It's been *so* long, right? Can you believe the kids are juniors now?"

"I find it hard to believe none of us are still juniors," Sheila says with a chagrined laugh as she waves a hand around at the rest of the room.

Why do we all love talking about the past so much? Why can't we ever walk away from it, leave it alone? I'm as guilty of it as anyone here tonight, but I try to steer Sheila toward memories of high school and away from the years our kids were in preschool together. We laugh about old teachers and hairstyles and phone calls on landlines, and we avoid bringing up old nicknames and rumors and memories of shame.

I am bright. I am sparkling. I am poised. I am vibrant. I am a vision.

I am a mirage.

It was all for nothing. I don't care about these people. Anything I could possibly want to know about them, I already do, because they post everything on Connex, and I scroll past the photos of their babies and their brunches and their boredom without leaving a comment. Lurking but never participating. I came here tonight for one stupid reason, and apparently, he's left early.

I've allowed Christian Campbell to take up too much space in my mind for too many years. Isn't the best revenge having a good and happy life that doesn't include him at all? Too bad I'm not able to exact that revenge if I can't even rub my good and happy life all over his face.

"Excuse me," I say to Sheila, "I think my husband might have texted me."

Ken has not, of course. He leaves for his trips without even waking me up, and he rarely checks in while he's gone unless it's to let me know when he'll be back so I can make sure to have dinner ready and waiting. When he's home, he's the perfect, attentive husband and father. Affectionate, slightly stern, full of advice. Right out of a sitcom. When he's gone, I might as well be single.

They call us to get seated for dinner, and it turns out that the singles are all at the same table. Me, Beth, Lisa . . . and Christian Campbell.

Relief floods me with the force of a river after a torrential rain and threatens to wash me away. He sees it in my eyes and smiles that slow and knowing grin again, the one that always made me hate and love him at the same time. How could I ever have thought that seeing him again wouldn't send me reeling?

"Hello again," he says as he pulls out a chair for me. He gives Beth and Lisa each an equally flirtatious look. "I guess I'm the lucky guy tonight, huh?"

"You're cheesy," Beth says, but fondly.

There's something between the two of them they think nobody else will see. I understand that, because that's how it had been with me and him, back in the days of black eyeliner and the back seat of his mother's Buick. Lisa sees it too. My heart gets tight, beating faster as though it's fighting hard against the squeeze of a fist.

"I thought you left," I say.

Christian slides into the chair next to mine. "Were you worried?"

"Of course not," I tell him, but he knows I'm lying again.

During dinner, Christian's knee bumps mine too often to be an accident. Somehow, he manages to get a few bottles of wine for the table so we can keep refilling our glasses without going up to the bar. He regales us with gross stories about med school, making Beth squeal with a disgust that sounds fake.

"So, you never got married?" Lisa asks shrewdly as she holds up her glass for him to fill.

Christian shrugs. "Nope. Dating in med school's too hard, much less trying to have a family. I figure I'll wait until I make it through my residency, get my practice going. Then I'll settle down."

"You'll be an old dad," Beth says.

"Maybe I'll marry someone who already has kids. Ready-made," Christian tells her smoothly. "Get myself a sugar mama."

"If you're going to be a plastic surgeon, why would you need a sugar mama?" Lisa asks with a laugh.

"Because med school is expensive," he replies.

They think he's making jokes, but I hear truth in his voice. When he turns toward me, his gaze sweeps over my face. He touches the pendant necklace nestled in the hollow of my throat, but so fast I don't even have time to pull away before he's turned his attention back to Lisa and Beth.

"Someone who can keep me in style. A classy divorcée," he says.

Beth chuckles, but her eyes narrow. If I noticed the way she looked at him when we sat down, you better believe she's noticed that touch he gave me just now. "What if you meet someone you're totally into, but she's not divorced?"

"Any woman can get divorced," Christian says, "with the right motivation."

An hour later, Beth slurs her words. Her eyes are red. Her updo is coming down from its pins. She's taken off her shoes to hit the dance floor while the DJ spins the top hits of our high school years.

I haven't danced like this since before I was married. I haven't drunk like this, either. When the music slows and couples pair off, I duck away from the dance floor and head for the restrooms, where I pee forever and then spend another five minutes at the sink, trying to get my head on straight.

The alcohol and mediocre hotel banquet chicken fight a battle in my stomach. I dampen a paper towel with cold water and pat my face carefully, doing my best to preserve my makeup. It's kind of a lost cause. I freshen my lipstick, baring my teeth at myself in the mirror. A good and happy life, I remind myself. One that does not include Christian Campbell.

Any woman can get divorced, according to him, but that's not true. A woman who depends on her husband financially can't simply leave him. A woman who has vowed to protect her only child from any more upheaval and trauma can't rip his family apart.

In the hallway, I pull out my phone to check for texts. There aren't any, of course. At sixteen, Eli is old enough to stay home alone. Old enough to get into trouble, too, except the sort of hijinks I got into at his age don't seem to be in Eli's wheelhouse. I hadn't been one of the "popular" girls, but at least I'd had friends. Eli's been teased and bullied as "the weird kid" since elementary school . . . and although my heart breaks for my son . . . he *is* weird. An outsider. Fretful. Easily pushed off balance. Friendless.

I sense Christian before I look up and see him.

"There you are. Don't tell me you're leaving already, Jewelann. We haven't had the chance to really talk. So many other people around," he says.

The reunion's supposed to go on for another forty minutes or so. I can hear the music still playing from the ballroom, but people are drifting out of the double doors and off into the night. I tuck my phone into my bag. He moves closer before I can reply.

"You look so good tonight." His voice drops low. He lifts a hand as though he means to touch me but holds back.

"I look good every night, Christian."

His eyebrows raise a little bit. His smile worms a slow tingle of heat through me. "How long has it been since we last saw each other? Ten years? Longer?"

"A few years longer," I tell him as he takes another step toward me.

"I guess we fell out of touch."

"Something like that." My smile does nothing to soften the hard edge to my tone.

Christian takes another step toward me. "Tell me you're not leaving yet."

"Tell me you want me to stay."

That's when, at last, he touches me. A single light press of his fingertip on my collarbone, tracing it from the center and up toward the sensitive space below my ear that always makes me shiver. He touches my pendant again. He remembers, I think. I have not become nothing to him. There's still something between us.

"You kept this," he says. "I won it for you at the St. Paul's church bazaar."

"I know." I cover it with my hand.

"It's just cheap junk."

"I know," I repeat.

We stare at each other.

"Stay," he whispers into my ear. "Please."

# 4

"THERE YOU ARE." Lisa comes out of the ballroom. She carries Beth's shoes hooked over her fingers on one hand and a raffle basket in the other.

"I guess we didn't win anything," Christian says. "Too bad."

Beth stumbles out after her, a hand on the flowery wallpaper to help keep herself upright. "After-party in Christian's suite, right? Unless *you* have a suite, Jewelann? Me and Lisa are sharing a double."

Tonight's gala is at a mid-level hotel chain famous for cucumber water in oversized dispensers displayed in the lobby and its free afternoon happy hours. The hotel is technically in Kentucky, although most of the reunion weekend's other activities were across the river in Cincinnati. We're about an hour away from our hometown of Kettering, but this is closer to the airport for people coming in from out of town. I hadn't gone to any of the other events . . . and hadn't anticipated needing a room of my own for tonight.

"What makes you think I'd have a suite?" I ask her.

"The bottoms of those shoes," Beth says with a snort, but under her breath as though I'm not meant to actually hear her reply.

"We'll go to mine," Christian says smoothly and puts his arm around her waist. The other goes around Lisa's. He pulls them both close to him while I stand apart. "Jewelann?"

This is not how I'd planned for the night to go when I put on this dress. Being invited up to Christian's room? Yes. Going there with two other women? Not in my imagined scenario. Yet there I am, riding up in the elevator to the top floor with Christian, Lisa, and Beth, and somehow we're all wrapped around each other with roaming hands and there's kissing and touching and laughing that I'm sure is giving the security cameras a really nice show. We manage to make it down the hall and into his suite.

This room has a bank of glass overlooking the Ohio River and the Cincinnati skyline. In the kitchenette, Christian has champagne in buckets of melting ice and crystal glasses. He pulls out a platter of strawberries and chocolates from the full-sized fridge. Through an archway, I see a king-sized bed with a bathroom beyond it.

"Swanky," Lisa says. "*Dr.* Campbell."

"Chin-chin," Christian says as we all clink our glasses.

Golden bubbles slosh over the sides. I take a careful sip, but no more than that. I was tipsier tonight than I've been in years, but I'm starting to sober up and I need to stay that way.

Beth is totally trashed. Lisa seems giddy, laughing and twirling in the center of the room, but she's not as far gone. At least she manages to keep her feet underneath her, while Beth topples over onto the couch. And Christian . . . he keeps pouring, but I can't manage to catch him drinking.

He puts on some music and pulls Beth into his arms for a dance in the center of the suite's living room. All the curtains are open. My own reflection stares back at me, faint as a ghost, with the ripple of the water beyond it. This is not the same river that flows through Dayton, minutes from my house in Kettering. That's the Great Miami River, but it does connect to the Ohio, one flowing into the other, all the way down to the sea. For a second, I imagine what it would be like to step through this glass, an Alice without her Wonderland. Can I jump far enough to hit the water? Would it hurt? Would I be awake when the water rushes into my lungs?

Behind me, Beth's transparent outline staggers toward Christian, melding their shapes into one for a second or so. I cross my arms over my stomach, one hand cupping my elbow, the other holding my warming glass of champagne. When I turn around, I see her kiss him on the mouth. The kiss is sloppy. Brief. When she pulls away, a look of repugnance crosses his expression, gone so fast I might've imagined it except that he looks up, his glance catches mine, and a small, sly smile twists his mouth. He knows what I saw.

"Come dance with me," Christian says and holds out a hand.

Of course, I do. When in my life have I ever been able to resist C.C.? In the first grade, he stole my favorite pencil eraser and when I threatened to tell the teacher, he promised to let me catch him at recess when we all played Prisoner. I hadn't been able to do it then, or ever since.

Until tonight.

Tonight is different. I see it in his eyes and in that warping smile, and in the touch of his fingertip again along my bare collarbone as he pushes away a strand of hair that has worked free of my stylish chignon. His hands fit on my hips, pulling me closer. The song is fast, but we dance nice and slow.

Lisa wrestles Beth up from the couch. She's protesting, her words a fuzzy mumble. Lisa scolds her, but with laughter. Their voices rise and fall. Christian nuzzles my neck. I close my eyes.

When I open them, Lisa and Beth are gone, and it's only me and him. The door shuts behind them with a loud click. Christian's teeth slide along the top of my naked shoulder. His breath is hot, but I shiver.

"Jewelann Kahan," he whispers into my ear. "You smell the same."

I pull away. "Jordan. My name is Jewelann Jordan now."

It would be so easy to forget that with his hands on me.

"J.J.," he says. "Welcome to the double initial club. I like it."

I take another step back from him. I'm not wearing a watch. My phone is tucked into my clutch bag, abandoned on the end table. I don't know what time it is, only that it's late. I have an hour's drive back home.

But I don't have what I came for . . . not quite yet.

"I should go."

"You don't have to go," Christian says. "We have a whole other bottle to drink."

I look at the buckets with their melting ice. "*You* haven't been drinking anything."

Christian tries to hide his surprise with another of his cocky grins, but I catch the flash in his eyes. "Guess I wasn't thirsty."

It's my turn to smile. "Oh, I think you're thirsty, all right."

Another flash in his blue eyes. Another slow grin. "Jewelann *Jordan*, you're still a bad girl. Aren't you?"

I am bold. I am seductive. I am the one in charge here, even if he thinks otherwise.

Christian pulls me close again, and we spin, spin, spin. I don't know if what we had before was ever *really* love, but I've always wanted him. I've always wanted him to want me. So I let him kiss me, and I let his hands wander up and down my body, and I even allow him to pull me into the bedroom.

"Take off your clothes," I command, "and get on the bed."

Again, surprise. Then a gleam of heat in his gaze. "Yes, ma'am."

His body is lean and muscled, but not in perfect shape. There's a softness around his belly easily hidden by the well-tailored clothes. He hooks his thumbs into the waistband of his tight boxer briefs and slides them over his thighs without hesitation. Christian is proud of what's underneath them. He tosses his clothes onto the floor without a second glance, a man used to someone else picking up after him, and a spark of jealousy flares inside me. Who's been taking care of him all these years?

He pushes himself back against the headboard, thighs spread, giving me a full view of what he's offering. I've seen it all before. I'd despise myself for the warmth of arousal stirring in my lower belly, except it's mingled with a heated glee at how easy it was to get him into this position. How *obvious* his wanting is.

"Now you," he says with a gesture. "But do me a favor, please. Keep those pretty shoes on."

My pretty, pricey shoes. Oh, I plan to keep them on, all right. I never planned to take them off.

I shake my head. "It's really late. I need to go."

"You're kidding."

I smile.

Christian scowls. "You didn't put on that dress tonight just so I couldn't take it off you."

"I'm a married woman, Christian. I can't do this."

"It didn't matter fifteen minutes ago," he says. "Or seventeen years."

So he *does* remember how long it's been.

My resolve might've weakened then, if I did not also remind myself of all the times his sweet nothings turned to sourness and naught.

I shrug, backing up. "It's late. It's been great catching up, but I really do need to get home."

"You . . . damn it, Jewelann." He tugs his wilting erection and sits up straight. "Cocktease."

I shrug again and turn away. Not rushing. I give him a full, long view of the sway of my ass beneath the soft and clinging fabric of this dress I did, in fact, pick out specifically so he could not take it off of me.

Is that a shout following me as I close the door? Something that sounds like my name? Maybe, but it doesn't matter, because for once I'm the one leaving Christian Campbell behind.

I make it to the car. My stomach roils and twists as I grip the steering wheel, taking in deep breaths, in through my nose and out my mouth. I'm nauseous. I'm giddy. I'm alternately hot and cold, armpits damp but teeth chattering. In the rearview mirror my eyes look wild.

Trying to calm myself enough to drive home, I sit in the parking lot for a good ten minutes with the air blasting against me. My head falls against the steering wheel while I take in deep, slow breaths that sometimes mutate into semi-hysterical giggles when I remember the look on Christian's face.

Revenge *is* sweet.

It's not until I'm pulling into my driveway that guilt slides its knife between my ribs. If Ken finds out I went upstairs to another man's hotel room, that I let him kiss me and touch me, that I'd ordered him to strip and saw him naked . . . it won't really matter that ultimately I didn't have sex with him. Any of that would be reason enough for my husband to pull the lever dropping the floor out from underneath me, leaving me to hang.

I get out of the car and stare at the dark windows, no lights left on to welcome me home. My husband will never find out, I reassure myself. After all, it's not the first secret I've kept from him.

What's one more?

# CHAPTER

# 5

SUN STREAMS THROUGH my window when I open my eyes. It's been a long time since I slept past eight, even on a Sunday, but I didn't get home until close to four this morning. I don't know if Eli noticed. When I got back, his room was dark and quiet, but that could have meant he was asleep or playing on his computer with his headphones on. He's not likely to be out of bed before me, anyway, so I take a few minutes to relax while I stare at the ceiling.

Remembering the feeling of Christian's hands and lips on me, his tongue in my mouth, I can't stop the small giggle that forces its way out of my mouth. I have to roll to bury my face in the pillow for a minute to get myself under control. Things had gone farther than I'd wanted, but it had felt so good to put Christian in his place, no matter how briefly, that I can't stop thinking about it. I'd never rejected *him* before. Few women probably did. I hope it stung him, hard.

Still, my revenge is bland as stale matzah, neither sweet nor sour. Yes, I'd left him naked and wilting in the bed he'd wanted me to share, but it hadn't been easy. Instead of the cold calculation I'd promised myself, I'm stuck with the taste of him still lingering on my tongue. Some doors, I think as I force myself up and out of bed, will never, ever close . . . and some never open in the first place.

I shower quickly, scrubbing away last night's flavors. A small headache throbs between my eyes, the barest of hangovers. I need coffee. Food. I yawn until my jaw creaks as I go over my plans for the day. There's an estate sale today, far on the other side of town, and the photos showed an array of designer shoes and bags that will probably be gone by the time I get there, but whatever's left will be fifty percent off, and surely I'll find something to bring home with me. Several somethings.

In the hall, I pause in front of Eli's door and listen for any signs that he's awake. Nothing. I press my palm flat to the door below the scuff marks in the paint from where he tore off the colorful wooden letters that had once spelled out his name. This room had been my brother Jonathan's when he was a kid. Ken and I share the room my parents had used. My childhood bedroom is at the far end of the hallway, door always closed to hide the closet full of clothes and shoes I never have occasion to wear, and the bins under the bed, and the dresser full of still more things I convinced myself I couldn't live without.

I rarely go in that room, but I have dreamed about moving back into it. Sleeping alone in the narrow twin bed with the creaking frame, cuddled beneath a mountain of afghans knitted by my grandmothers. My childhood was not perfect—I don't really think anyone's is, not if you're honest with yourself about it. But it was good. My parents were fun and loving and they took care of me and my brother. I was the bad kid, the one who turned my mom's hair gray, made them worry. I definitely was not the golden daughter I'm sure they'd wished for. I miss them both terribly, but at least with them both gone, I don't have to worry about continuing to disappoint them.

I dream about sleeping alone in a single bed too often for it to be anything other than some kind of desire that's less sub, more conscious. It won't happen, though. How could it? I haven't had a job since before Eli was born. Ken wanted a homemaker. A hausfrau. He wanted to be taken care of in a certain kind of way, and I needed to be taken care of in another. I've spent the last eighteen years giving him what he wants.

What about what I need?

There's an empty hole inside me that's been vacant for a long, long time. And what do we do when there's a blank space? We try to fill it.

For me, it was with weed. Then prescription sedatives. After that, it was home parties held by women who were not my friends but invited me anyway, hoping their parties would have enough sales for them to earn the bonus hostess item. Cookware, prepackaged spice mixes, diet powders, stretchy clothes in ugly patterns. When those women stopped inviting me, I switched to thrift stores and estate sales. I consoled myself by saying it's all so cheap, but every month the bills came in, and I promised myself I'd stop buying. I told myself I'd actually flip the stuff I bought because I thought I could resell it online. I bought things I didn't need and couldn't afford but also could not give up, so now here I am, pinching pennies until they scream and lying to my husband every month about where the money goes. I live in a house that should be worth half a million dollars, if it wasn't starting to fall apart all around me, and if I hadn't taken out a loan to make the payments on a storage unit stuffed to overflowing with things I cannot bring myself to get rid of. This is not the life I'd envisioned for myself. This is a life still trying, always trying, to fill up an empty hole.

Ken, on the other hand, was a pampered son, an only child of two only children. Adored by his parents. Family dinners every night, home cooked by Mom. A game of catch in the backyard with Dad afterward. Then a cuddle-up on the couch with some popcorn for a movie. The way he talks about growing up and the expectations he's always had for our family seem like something straight out of a dream. An ideal. *Idyllic.* At least until both parents died in a house fire when he was eighteen.

The thought of what my son would do if Ken and I both died right now sends a shudder all through me. The kid can barely feed himself a balanced meal, much less do his own laundry, pay a bill, find a job. He doesn't even have his driver's license, something I'd champed at the bit to get when I was his age, but he simply seems happy to think about "later."

This is my fault, of course. I'm the one who coddles him. I was the epitome of the Participation Trophy Mom. Gold stars for everything. Gold stars because of my guilt.

I knock on Eli's door. No answer. I knock again. "Eli?"

His door opens. He scowls, hair rumpled, oversized hoodie hanging nearly to his knees. "Mom, what?"

"I'm making pancakes. Do you want some?"

My son furrows his brow. His lips purse with thought. Pancakes are one of my specialties. I haven't made them in ages. They used to be a regular Sunday morning treat to sweeten the chore of attending Hebrew school, but since he became bar mitzvah three years ago, Eli's been more prone to sleeping in until lunchtime, and the pancake making has gone by the wayside.

Suddenly, I am desperate for him to say yes. I want to sit across the kitchen table with him and sip coffee and watch him cut his stack of pancakes into four equal portions, an X made with fork and knife. I want to chide him gently when he pours too much syrup, when he licks his fingers instead of using a napkin. I want to laugh over dumb knock-knock jokes we both already know the answers to but will still and always pretend are brand new.

"Not really hungry," he says. "I'll get something later."

It's not okay to let your son see how his rejection makes you crestfallen. A good mother does not allow her emotions to depend on the whims of a teenage boy who has grown too big to sit on her lap. She does not rely on him for her emotional support. I know I'm far from the best mother, but I try my best to be a good one.

I keep my response light. "No problem. Pizza for dinner later? Dad won't be home until Thursday."

Pizza grabs his attention better than the pancakes. Eli nods and sidles past me, heading for the bathroom at the end of the hall. He closes the door behind him with a firm click of the lock. I am shut out.

I make pancakes anyway.

Butter, syrup, fresh strawberries, and some whipped cream. Mindful of the reunion, I'd stepped up my regular diet and exercise routine over the past few months. Today, I can indulge.

As is typical when I let myself go, I gorge. The entire stack of pancakes disappears, washed down with strong coffee sweetened with sugar and lightened with cream. I sit back from the table, hands on my stomach, and close my eyes. I'm stuffed. I chastise myself. I feel worse about this gluttony than I did about last night's truncated seduction.

"Mom? You okay?"

I open my eyes and force a smile. "Ate too much."

Eli scans the kitchen, eyes going to the stove, then the empty platter on the table. "I changed my mind. But if you ate them all—"

"I'll make some more." I get up, stomach protesting the too-swift motion. "There's coffee, if you want some."

I'm not sure when he started drinking it. Probably when he started staying up until all hours playing his online games and reading forums. I began my own addiction to indulgence in high school, spending hours at the local diner, drinking coffee by the pot while my friends and I thought we were figuring out the secrets of the universe.

"I was thinking that later we might go for a hike out at Yellow Springs, if you wanted." I grip my coffee mug in both hands, practicing nonchalance.

Long gone are the days when Eli ran to me, clung to me, or even looked to me for solace. Now I'm the one who wants to cling. I know this is what happens. I understand about kids growing up and away from their parents. I did it with my own, who let me go, even when I was making mistakes they could have stopped me from. I don't begrudge my son his widening distance from me, his dad, this house, but I do envy it. He will grow up and go away. I . . . will not.

"Sure, okay." He forks bite after bite of sodden pancake into his mouth. He chews. Swallows. Doesn't meet my eyes.

"Yeah?"

Warily, Eli looks at me. "I said sure."

"Great. Good. We'll pack a lunch. Go around one, one thirty?"

A shrug. He pushes the plate away from him with a sigh and wipes his mouth with a cloth napkin. He looks at me again, this time with a smile.

"That was great, Mom. Thanks."

It's nothing close to the way it was when he was younger, but it's better than it's been lately. The pinch in my heart is of relief and gratitude. I love this kid more than anything in this world. More than I will ever love anything. He makes it worth giving up the chance to love anything else.

"I'll get that," I say when he stands up with his plate in his hand.

Eli pauses, forehead wrinkling. Clearing your own place at the table has always been our rule. Ken's rule, really.

Manners are very important to him. He never washes a dish, of course, but he clears his own place.

"You sure?"

"I'm sure."

"You want any help with the dishes?"

"I'll do them." I cast an eye toward the mess in the sink. "It's therapeutic."

He grins and laughs at our family's inside joke. I want to grab him for a hug, but I don't push my luck. My cuddly little boy grew into a standoffish child and an even more distant teen. You can't teach your child body autonomy and also insist on hugs.

"Okay. Thanks. I'll go get ready." Eli ducks out of the kitchen.

I listen for a heavy, thumping tread upon the stairs, the sort teenage boys are supposed to make, but Eli always moves quietly. I make quick work of the kitchen, and the joke about it being therapeutic is really more like truth. Loading the dishwasher, spraying and wiping the table and counters, filling the sink with hot water for the skillet, it's all mindless work that turns chaos into cleanliness. I hum under my breath as I finish up and run the garbage disposal to clear out the scraps of pancake and whatever else got washed down the drain.

When I flick the switch, the disposal grinds, but water rises quickly to the top of the drain hole. It smells gross. Not like sewage, exactly, but still nasty. I turn off the disposal and watch the sink slowly empty. I run hot water from the faucet, adding some dish detergent, and try again. Cleaning the drains with baking soda and vinegar is on my list of monthly chores, but although I make prominent check marks on the list in case Ken looks at it, I haven't bothered to do this task in a while. Another waft of stink tickles my nostrils while I grimace, but this time, the water goes down as it should. I run it for a bit longer, the water as hot as it will get. This house is a year older than I am. We both need more maintenance than we used to.

I head upstairs to get ready for the hike. I'm not expecting any messages, so when I pick up my phone and see a text notification from an area code and number I don't recognize, I almost swipe it away without reading it, assuming it's spam. At the last second, I stop myself.

The message is from Christian.

CHAPTER

6

HEY, BEAUTIFUL. WOKE **up hard as a rock, thinking about you. Was that what you had in mind? If you want to finish what you started last night, text me.**

Two things happen when I see this message. One, my hands shake so much I almost drop the phone. Two, gleeful triumph rises up in me with a rush of heat so fierce I feel as though I'm glowing with it. All those years of playing the pushmi-pullyu game with him have come to this. I was once his dirty little secret . . . but now he's become mine.

The triumph doesn't last long. I'm not going to answer him. I'm not even sure how he got my number. My game ended last night when I left him high and dry. I have no intention of dragging it out any longer.

It would be easy enough to block his number, obviously, but if I do that, how will I know if he texts me again? Just because I don't plan to reply doesn't mean I don't want to know if he does it again. I hesitate before deleting the message. My finger hovers over the "I" for "info." A tap brings up choices. Block is one of them.

Before I can make a decision, my bedroom door opens. I slide my phone quickly into the pocket of my sweatshirt.

I'm surprised Eli would come in without knocking. More surprised to see that it's Ken.

He greets me with a grunt and goes immediately into the bathroom. The shower comes on. I am frozen for a moment before I gather my wits enough to peek in on him. His clothes have been tossed onto the floor and on, but not in, the hamper. This is not like him. Ken is meticulous about laundry. He'd been the one to show me how to do it, as a matter of fact, when we were first married, and I tried to throw all the wash into the same load. His standards for his laundry are still so high that I've never managed to meet them. Everything else around the house is my responsibility, but he always washes his own clothes.

He's scrubbing himself beneath water so hot it's already steaming the mirror.

"Everything okay?" I ask him from the doorway.

Another grunt.

"I wasn't expecting you home until Thursday." I don't approach the dirty clothes, or what I suspect is a filthy husband.

"We have tomorrow off," he says. "Labor Day? I came home early. I thought you'd be glad."

I bite the tip of my tongue in irritation, but I make sure to keep my tone dulcet sweet. "Of course I am."

He bends under the spray and scrubs at his scalp, sending foam flying onto the glass shower door. When he twists to look at me through that same door, his features are distorted. "It's important to spend holidays together."

The water shuts off. Ken steps out, reaching for his towel. He dries his face first, giving me a full view of his naked body. In clothes, he looks soft and rounded, not fat but "Dad-bod." He's muscled, though. Deceptively strong.

I can't stop myself from comparing him to Christian, whose tailored suit gave him a trim waist and hard chest, but whose nakedness revealed softness and lack of attention.

"Jewel." Ken snaps his fingers. "I asked you to grab me another towel. This one stinks."

My cheeks tingle, and I'm glad for the excuse to turn away so I can grab a fresh towel from the linen closet. I hand it to him as he tosses the other one over the pile of his clothes with an odd deliberateness. He wraps the new one around his waist.

"I've told you so many times, Jewelann, even if I'm not here, you need to switch out my towel every three days. They start to stink like mildew."

I've never been able to smell it. I usually wait until the day I expect him to get home, assuming he will never know. Our marriage is a string of deceptions, one after the other, pearls on a necklace. Cut the string, and they'll all scatter.

He moves past me to the sink, and I study his body surreptitiously, looking for evidence of what I've been suspecting for a long time. Love bites? Strange bruises? Stripes of passion from a long-nailed hand? He's come home from trips marked that way before, but this time I can't see anything that shouldn't be there.

Oh, wait. There. A glimpse of something on his inner thigh as he bends over the sink to spit out his toothpaste. A small half-ring of red marks. Mosquito bites or love bites, I'm too far away to tell.

In the mirror, his reflection catches my gaze. He's got a froth of toothpaste in the corners of his mouth. He spits again. Wipes his mouth clean. Puts his toothbrush back in the holder.

"How was the reunion?" Ken asks, holding my gaze.

"Good. A lot of fun." Does he know I've spotted the marks? Does he care? I'm suddenly self-conscious there might be something on me that he can see, something I didn't notice when I looked myself over this morning.

We stare at each other in the glass.

"I'm glad you had fun," Ken says finally, looking away.

"Eli and I were going out to Yellow Springs for a hike, grab something from Ha Ha Pizza. Do you . . . want to come with us?" I wince internally at the way my voice skips on the invitation.

"Nah. I've got stuff to do."

"Do you want us to bring you anything back for dinner?"

He looks at me again in the reflection. "I'll manage here. You two go have fun."

This is also not like him. Dinner is to be on the table every night when he's home. Meat, potatoes, a side, a salad. Cloth napkins. Matching plates. Hands are to be washed and phones absent.

Regret scrapes at me for a single, fleeting moment. We used to be a family. We used to spend time together, all three of us, and although I always had that empty space inside me, it had not yet grown so gaping and vast, and Ken had not yet started spending more time away from us than with us, and our son had been a chubby-cheeked little boy who loved to laugh.

There'd been no secrets.

Now look what we have become. Three people living together beneath the same roof, but does that make us a family? It doesn't feel very much like it, not anymore.

I try once more. "You sure you don't want to come along? It would be a great day. You love hiking at Glen Helen, and pizza . . ."

"I've been on the road for a week, Jewelann. I've had more junk food than any one man should ever have to tolerate."

"But not from Ha Ha." I sound too desperate.

His eyes narrow, and he turns to face me. "I told you, I've got paperwork to catch up on."

"Okay, sure. No problem."

I nod and back out of the bathroom, fighting tears I don't understand. I want to spend the afternoon with Eli; him and me, not with Ken who hikes too fast and gets impatient if he has to wait for us to catch up. I want to come home later and take a shower, have some ice cream, watch a movie I'll forget the plot of halfway through, and climb into my bed alone. I want to do all the things I normally do while Ken is out of town so that I can forget about last night, when I'd been precariously close to cheating on him.

No matter how he got those marks on his thigh, two wrongs don't make a right. Ken can be unfaithful to me every time he goes out of town, with dozens of other women. It doesn't matter. I'll put up with it. I'm never going to leave my husband, and I cannot afford to have him leave me.

My phone vibrates softly against my belly in the pocket of my sweatshirt, and I pull it out, holding my breath, eyes going to the bathroom doorway to make sure Ken's not watching me.

**JEWELANN!** the text reads. **Great seeing you last night. We should grab a coffee sometime soon.**

This message is also from someone not in my contacts, but it has to be either Lisa or Beth. Before I can figure out a non-awkward way to ask, another message pings through.

**It's Lisa, btw. LOL. For real, let's get together.**

A string of emojis follow: a red high heel, two dancing ladies, a wineglass, a doughnut, a face with hearts for eyes.

"Who's that?" Ken asks from the bathroom doorway, a fresh towel wrapped around his waist. His wheaten hair, slicked back, is dark with wet, but I can see glints of silver here and there.

He's so handsome it hurts my heart, because I used to love him, or at least I thought I did. Now all I can do is wait for him to tell me he's in love with someone else. That he's going to leave and tear my life apart.

I hold up the phone, relieved I can show him the message. "Lisa Weaver. From high school. We hung out last night at the reunion. I think we might try to get together sometime soon."

Ken grunts and heads for the closet to grab some clothes. He grew up in Indiana, and before I met him, he'd lived all over the country. He often said how "weird" it was to randomly run into someone you went to school with at the hardware store, or to have your kid in class with the child of one of your old teachers.

My husband never has any trouble making friends, though. People seem to like and trust him automatically— the way I did when we first met. Ken doesn't have Christian's effortless charm, but his is more genuine.

I'm comparing them again.

Dressed in sweats and a T-shirt, Ken pauses to kiss me on the top of my head. I turn in his embrace to offer my mouth. The kiss is dry. When I part my lips, he pulls away.

"Not now," he says. "Not when the kid's still awake."

It used to be that when Ken returned from a trip, he'd be ready to tear off my clothes the first moment we could get behind a closed door. Now I can't remember how long it's been since we had sex. I think of the marks on his leg. All those nights in hotel rooms when he's supposed to be alone.

After he leaves the bedroom, I go into the bathroom. I gather up his discarded khakis, the polo shirt, the white briefs and socks. I lift the pile to my face. What do I expect to smell? Perfume? I breathe deep. A familiar scent drifts into my nostrils . . . fresh cut grass? No. Gas station burritos? No . . . It's—

"What are you doing?"

With my back still toward the doorway, I drop the clothes into the hamper. "Just cleaning up in here."

"I told you I'd take care of it." Ken pulls the hamper away from me.

I don't follow him out of the room. I need a few minutes to compose myself, which I do by washing my face. I swirl mouthwash to rid myself of what I smelled on my husband's clothes.

Sex.

# 7

THE SCREAMING WAKES me, but I have to fight through a dream of grabbing hands and sinking into quicksand before I can get myself out of bed. Ken stirs beside me, but I'm the one out the door and down the hall to Eli's room. He's sitting up in bed, no longer screaming, but his eyes are wide open, and his face contorts in the shifting screensaver light from his laptop, open on the desk.

"I'm okay," he says at once, already curling into himself. Blocking me off.

I sit on the edge of his bed but don't touch him. "Same dream?"

After a moment, he nods.

All kids fear the boogeyman. My son fears the candyman. I could blame a late-night movie he saw when he was far too young, but there's more to it than that. When Eli was six years old, a little boy who lived a few streets over went missing. Billy Peak had been playing at our house that day, but he left to walk home by himself. There were stories about a man in a white van who'd offered candy, but that had never been proven. They'd found one of his shoes in Riverscape Park, on the shore of the Great Miami River in downtown Dayton.

The boy himself had never been found, and nobody had ever been able to explain how he might have wandered so far all on his own. After that, Eli's nightmares had taken the shape of a man trying to steal him away. My happy little boy became sullen, quiet, and afraid of everything.

"He was trying to get me to go with him," Eli whispers with a hitch in his voice.

"The . . ." I cough to clear my voice. "Candyman?"

"Not him. Billy. He kept trying to get me to go with him . . ." His voice shakes.

"You haven't had that one in a long time." I let my hand rest on the covers, close to his leg but still not touching. My heart aches for him.

Eli sighs and puts the heels of his hands into his eye sockets. He shakes his head. "No. Not like that."

"Do you want to talk about it?"

"No."

The dreams come when Eli is stressed, but they also happen when everything seems fine. I wait a second before I ask, "Is there something going on at school you want to talk about?"

"Nothing is going on at school. It was just a stupid dream." He sits up and leans back against the headboard. His shoulders rise and fall with his breathing, still too fast.

We say nothing for a minute.

"I was looking at something on a forum," Eli begins.

Ken's voice interrupts him from the doorway. "Hey, Champ."

His hair is sleep-rumpled. His pajamas match, top and bottom. The shirt is, as always, fully buttoned.

Eli rolls his eyes at the nickname he hates. "I'm fine. You can both go back to bed."

Ken raps on the doorframe with his knuckles. "All good?"

It's not all good, of course. Our son has nightmares that wake him, screaming. Eli scoots down onto his pillows, already turning to face the wall. Ken leaves, and I remain, not sure of what to say.

"What were you looking at?" I ask.

"Never mind. It's stupid. It's nothing."

"You know you can always talk to me, Eli. About anything. If something's bothering you—"

"Nothing is bothering me. I need to sleep. That's all. I'm sorry I woke you up."

I put a hand on his shoulder and make sure he's looking at me when I say, "You never need to be sorry about needing me. Okay?"

I've probably embarrassed him, but Eli ducks his head in a nod of acceptance. "Okay."

This is the longest conversation we've had with each other in weeks. There's more to be said, but neither of us says it. I close his laptop, darkening the room.

My bedroom is already dark when I enter and slip between the sheets. I tense when Ken rolls to face me. His hand on my belly is heavy and warm.

"You should really wear a robe when you go in there," he says. "I could see your nipples through your tank top."

"He's my son. He was screaming. I didn't stop to think about a robe."

Ken's fingers move upward to cup my breast. "Well, you should. A teen boy can't help the things he thinks. You want him to get even more messed up than he already is?"

"He wouldn't think about anything like that, Ken."

"All teenage boys think like that about their mothers, Jewelann. They can't help it."

My lip curls. I'm repulsed and irritated at the chastisement, but I swallow both emotions. I push his hand away and turn on my side. He spoons me. His hand returns. His breath tickles the back of my neck.

I expect him to pull down my boxer shorts, to enter me, but he only thrusts against the fabric. I can't tell if he's erect or not. A vision of Christian's naked penis, hard and ready for me, fills my mind. I let out a small cry. Ken covers my mouth with his hand. Like his fingers on my nipple, his grip is too hard.

I writhe.

He retreats.

"Just be a little more appropriate," Ken says.

Thin and helpless fury rises in me. I am appropriate every second of my life. My hair, my clothes, my house, everything I am is designed to please this man and keep him contented. My opinions, the ones I voice aloud, anyway, belong to Ken. I vote the way he wants me to vote. I serve the meals he wants to eat. My body, even though he no longer seems to want it, is his. I have made myself everything he has ever said he wanted, and why?

To keep this family together.

Ten years ago, I'd been on the verge of leaving him. The emptiness that had haunted me since before we'd even met had only grown deeper the longer we were married. Motherhood didn't sustain me. The pills couldn't fill me up. Being the kind of wife Ken wanted definitely did not.

Then my traumatized son had started waking up every night with screaming nightmares. We were both catatonic with exhaustion. My doctor began making noises about not refilling my prescriptions because of "dependence." To make it all worse, after almost two weeks on the road, my husband had come home and fallen to his knees, weeping, with a confession that he had "strayed." He'd begged me to forgive him, crying that *he* knew *I* knew what he'd done, when the truth was that I would never have suspected him of cheating if he'd kept his mouth shut. I'd have preferred it that way. He'd sworn he would never succumb to temptation again, if only I would promise to be there for him.

Faced with losing everything I had, I discovered I could not afford to give it up.

I'd cut the pills, cold turkey. I'd focused my attentions on Eli, helping him with his trauma. I'd tried even harder to become the wife Ken wanted—June Cleaver in the kitchen, Jessica Rabbit in the bedroom. It had worked for a while, sort of. Mostly.

Then Ken took a new job and started traveling more often. His trips got longer. He started spending more time in the office he'd converted from my father's basement workshop. He secured his phone and laptop with passwords I couldn't guess. Our sex life fizzled. I started shopping. It was not a bad life. It was a *nothing* life, but I lived it for the sake of my son, who'd already undergone too much distress. I've done everything I can to make sure Eli feels safe, that Ken is happy.

And Ken dares to lecture me about being appropriate?

I close my burning eyes. I swallow bitterness. I wait until his breathing steadies, and then I creep out of bed and downstairs.

In the basement laundry room, I search the small pile of stuff Ken took from his pockets and left on top of the dryer. Spare change. A five dollar bill. A receipt for a fast-food burger joint with more than one meal on it, which tells me everything or means nothing at all. An empty, creased, and crumpled envelope, no sign of what it had once contained. I make sure to put everything back the way I found it.

Kneeling in front of the sink, I reach back, back, into the cabinet beneath it. My fingers fumble around the pipes. I feel paper, worn and creased, an envelope much like the one

I found in Ken's pocket trash. This one isn't empty. I press it, feeling the small lumps of something hard, like beads.

It would be easy, so easy, to pull out this envelope and open it. To take out the contents and let them slip past my lips, down my throat, into my belly. Then, at least for a little while, nothing could bother me.

The envelope rattles. I hold my breath as I open the flap to look inside. There should be twenty pills in it. There are only twelve.

I bend, looking deep into the recesses of the cabinet. On the bottom of it, I see one pill. It's perilously close to the hole for the pipe. I feel that open space, but my fingers come out with only rust and dirt. The other pills are gone, fallen into that hole from out of the envelope's open flap, or, who knows, maybe they dissolved over time. I could've miscounted them the last time I checked them, except of course I know I didn't, because I've known exactly how many pills were in that envelope since the day I put them there a decade ago.

Twelve is enough, though. More than. But I'm not going to take even a single one. I push them back into the envelope. I lick the glue on it, grimacing at the sour taste. I press it shut. It's so old that it doesn't stick, so I fold it over and over again, making sure to keep the opening upward as I tuck it away again.

Strength would be more than putting the envelope back in its hiding place. It would be flushing the contents down the toilet. I'm not that strong. I don't need to take the pills, but I do need to know that I could if I wanted to. Just like I needed to know I could sleep with Christian if I wanted to.

In bed again, I lie awake next to my husband. My eyes are wide open into the darkness. Yearning. The empty space inside me yawns wider. It is nowhere close to the abyss it had once been . . . but it's getting there.

# CHAPTER

# 8

"**I**S THAT NEW?"

I look up from the bowl of macaroni salad I'm mixing and pretend I don't know what Ken's talking about. "Hmmm?"

"That dress," he says. "Is it new?"

The spoon scrapes the side of the bowl. Mayonnaise and mustard mix together, covering the elbow noodles in creamy yellow. I concentrate on the bits of hard-boiled egg. I don't look at him.

"I've had it forever. I wear it all the time." My voice is light and lilting. Unconcerned. I've never worn the dress before. I bought it last week, along with the designer sandals I'm also wearing. Along with a lot of other things. Buying it felt better than having it. Having it feels better than wearing it.

Ken snags a carrot stick from the platter on the table. He's been pacing around the kitchen all morning while I get ready for the Labor Day barbecue I hadn't expected to prepare. "Looks good on you. Hey, did you invite the neighbors over?"

"I did not. It's very last minute. I didn't think you'd be home. But I guess you could if you want to?"

"Maybe I want to show off my beautiful wife." Crunch, crunch, crunch.

Finally, I look at him. "Do you *want* to invite them over?"

Ken's always been Mr. Congeniality, the one who waves over the fence, asks about the grandkids, the new puppy, the Christmas decorations. He shrugs. "Not if you don't want to. Hey, instead of burgers, how about we grill up some steaks? Asparagus? Corn on the cob! Really make a feast out of it?"

"I don't have any steaks. I only have burger patties." I pause, trying to figure out why he's being so . . . manic.

His phone buzzes from the pocket of his jeans. Ken pulls it out. Swipes the screen. Frowns. His eyes scan the text. He doesn't tap out a reply, but instead shoves the phone back into his pocket.

I think of the mark on his thigh and wonder if the person who made it is the one who messaged him.

"I'll go get some," he says as though we hadn't been interrupted.

"I don't know if the store will be open—"

"I'll be back in a bit. Can you make your tomato salad? You know how much I love your tomato salad." Ken kisses me quickly, before I have time to make another protest, and leaves the house.

Once he's gone, I check my own phone. Nothing new from Christian. I'm disappointed but also relieved. I tap out a quick message to Lisa, whose message I still hadn't answered from yesterday.

**Hey, girl.** I cringe at myself. **Getting together sounds great. Quick question. Did you give C.C. my phone number?**

She has her read receipts on. A few seconds later, the little bouncing dots tell me she's replying. **Nope. But maybe he**

**got it from the directory they gave out at the reunion? That's where I got it.**

Right, the directory. It was probably still in the goody bag I'd left on the floor of my car. My fingers tap the screen. **Mystery solved. When do you want to get together?**

**Did he text you?**

I don't reply.

**Gurrrrrrl.** More emojis, this time of a kissy face.

**How about Thursday?** I add her contact information to my phone and delete the previous texts.

Lisa might be easy to get into trouble with, but she's not stupid. She doesn't mention Christian again, but we work out a time and place to meet up. I get the goody bag from my car and pull out the directory, scanning it for information about Christian.

Unmarried. Lives in California. Undergrad at Kent State, then a med school I've never heard of, somewhere in the Caribbean. There's nothing about him that I don't already know. The photo of him is from our senior yearbook. He's laughing, covered in shaving cream from a pep rally. The photo's been cropped, but I remember the original one. I'd been in the background, wearing all black in stark contrast to the pastels all around me.

A low groan worms out of me. I put a hand on my stomach. Close my eyes. Why does the past have so much power to slaughter us, over and over?

My laptop used to be Eli's, and compared to the much newer and faster one I bought him in an online estate auction, this one seems to take forever to pull up the internet browser. I type in Christian's name. Dozens of results pop up, but none of them are *my* C.C.

I type in another quick search. "Buy prescriptions online." Results link me to a popular internet forum site I know Eli reads. I click on the link to a post about how to go

about buying pills illegally and skim it before my guilt stops
me from clicking more links.

I don't need this.

I want this, but I don't need it.

A small alert pops up in the upper corner of the forum's
header. Next to it is a username I don't recognize, but I figure
out quickly enough belongs to my son. Eli must not have
logged out of his account before giving me the laptop. Curious, I click on the name and bring up the list of forums he
follows.

You know how they say never listen at a door because you
might hear something you don't like? I'd say the same goes
for looking at your teen son's forum subscriptions. I'm sure
Eli would be mortified to know I've seen what he spends so
much time looking at. Anime, trending memes, true crime,
porn. Quickly, I close out of the tab.

Because I'm already online, I check in with my own ver-
sion of porn. The estate sale page has plenty of new listings,
and I look at the online sales quickly, but, mindful that Ken
will be back soon and of how deep down that rabbit hole I
tend to go, I shut everything down and put it away. My itch
has not been scratched, but there's a smug sense of satisfaction inside me too. I resisted temptation.

The tomato salad Ken loves so much takes time to mari-
nate. I have only a couple of tomatoes in the kitchen, but I
can see the plethora of red amongst the green vines in my
garden out back. I slip on the fancy harvesting apron he
bought me for last Hanukkah and head out.

The first year I planted this garden, it had bloomed so lush
and verdant I'd had to put tomatoes and peppers out by the
street for free. Since then, I've spent hours upon hours composting, weeding, tending. Nurturing. I've never matched the
output of that first summer, but I still manage to get enough
veggies to last the entire late summer and into the fall.

The sun beats hot on the back of my neck as I kneel in the dirt, pulling out the weeds and pushing the thick, heavy tomato vines back into their cages. The peppers are finally turning orange. A few of my jalapeños have bloomed crimson. I even find a fat, short cucumber, probably one of the last ones for the season. In another couple of months it'll be time to pull out all of these plants and plant some garlic bulbs before putting the garden to sleep for the winter. But not yet.

A shadow falls over me. I look up, shading my eyes. "Hey."

Eli takes the hand I put out to help me to my feet. "Where's Dad?"

"He went to get some steaks. What's up?"

"I came downstairs and nobody was around. I just wondered what was going on." He looks into the bowl and makes a face. "Tomato salad, huh?"

"You know he loves it."

Eli, on the other hand, won't touch a vegetable from my garden. Carrots, potatoes, onions, green beans from the store, sure. But tomatoes, peppers, or cucumbers grown by Mom? Never.

My phone buzzes from the pocket of my dress. "C'mon. I have to get going on this so it's ready when your dad wants to eat."

*Buzz.*

Eli follows me across the lawn, the grass soft and thick and getting too long.

*Buzz.*

I trip a little on a loose deck step, and he catches me by the elbow. A tomato flips out of my apron's pocket and onto the deck. It doesn't splatter, but it cracks open. Juice leaks out onto my hand when I pick it up.

*Buzz.*

"Aren't you going to answer that?"

"In a minute." I wave the broken tomato at him. "Go get the french fries out of the freezer downstairs, please."

*Buzz.*

Eli doesn't move. He stares. I frown.

"Eli," I say.

"Right. Okay." He looks over his shoulder at me as he goes through the sliders into the kitchen, and I stay on the deck with a split-open tomato in my hand.

*Buzz.*

Ken's car pulls through the horseshoe driveway and parks. Without checking my phone, I go into the kitchen, my fingers slick with tomato guts. I busy myself at the sink as my husband comes in.

Does he look more tousled than when he left? A little frazzled? Definitely distracted. He sets the plastic bags on the kitchen table with a thump and pulls out his phone to read something on it. The tip of his tongue presses his top lip the way it always does when he's concentrating hard. His brow crinkles, and he puts the phone away. He looks at me.

"They were out of steaks."

"It's okay. I told you, I have burger patties in the freezer."

"It's not the same," Ken says. "I wanted us to have a real feast. Something special."

"Well, we'll make the best of what we have. Okay?" I study him.

*Buzz. Buzz. Buzz. Buzzzzzz.*

"Someone's calling you," Ken says.

Smoothly, I pull out my phone and swipe to decline without even looking at the screen. I return it to my pocket. "Spam risk. Why don't you go fire up the grill while I finish the tomato salad?"

Again, my phone hums with a buzz like an angry hornet. It vibrates against my thigh with only the thin fabric of my dress between it and my bare skin. I put a hand over it, trapping it there, and use my thumb to discreetly slide it to silent.

"That dress looks good on you," Ken says again. "Are you sure you've worn it before?"

I shrug, never taking my eyes from his. "Yes. It's one of my favorites. I wear it all the time."

"Well, shame on me for not paying better attention. You know if you answer those spam calls and tell them to take you off their list, they have to do it, right?"

Of course I knew that. My smile is vacant and grateful and dumb. "I'll have to do that next time."

He nods, having reminded me that he knows better than me. As though speaking to a robot will prevent being called in the future. As though ignoring it and blocking the number later isn't easier and more efficient.

I pull out a cutting board and a knife from the block on the counter. I can feel him looking at me. I slice the tomatoes into thick chunks and toss them in a bowl. My fingers are slick with juice and seeds, some of which I set aside on a paper towel to plant next year. I put the scraps in my composting bucket. He's still watching me, the back of my neck prickling until I look over my shoulder.

"You're so beautiful," my husband tells me. "Like something right out of a dream. But you're real, aren't you? Tell me you're real."

This is not the first time Ken has asked me this. In the beginning, before a ring and a baby, we'd face each other in bed as he'd touch my skin, and he'd ask me the same question. I liked it then.

"I'm real. All of me is real."

He nods and leaves the kitchen through the sliding glass doors. My answer seemed to satisfy him. At least, it was the answer he was asking for.

But it's a lie.

I am not real. I am a doll, a puppet dancing ferociously from the pull of its strings. I am an empty space contained within the shape of a woman, sealed up with an ever-present smile.

## 9

"AND YOU DIDN'T answer? Not even to say screw off?" Lisa leans across the coffee shop table to say this in a hissing whisper.

She'd been fifteen minutes late. Not a surprise. She's disheveled, as though she got ready in a hurry, but she's overdressed for a midmorning coffee date with a friend from high school. Heavy makeup. Elaborately styled hair. Jewelry. I feel dowdy in comparison, although I'd dressed as carefully for this coffee date as I had for the reunion. I haven't met a friend for coffee since Eli was in kindergarten.

"No. I blocked him."

This is a lie. I'd hovered between blocking and not, back and forth, but I want to know if he's still trying. I finally simply silenced all notifications from his number and deleted the texts. He hadn't left a voice mail.

"Nothing happened after me and Beth left?"

"Nothing," I tell her.

She grins. "Well, that's why he's trying so hard now."

I'd ordered a mug of plain black coffee, endlessly refillable, and now I spin the mug around and around. "I shouldn't have gone up there with him in the first place."

"Probably not, but . . . I mean . . ." She trails off with a frown. She shrugs. "Everyone does stupid shit sometimes, Jewelann. I totally get it."

She can only think she does.

Lisa looks at my hand. My wedding band is of plain gold, but my engagement ring is a solitaire diamond big enough to weigh down my hand. It had been Ken's mother's ring, one of the few things salvaged from the fire. Selling it could pay off quite a bit of my credit card debt, but of course I can't sell it. Next, she tilts herself to look at my feet. My kitten-heel slides are Prada. My bag is a cute Kate Spade with some damage inside you can't see without looking for it.

"Does your husband buy you all those pretty things?"

Technically, yes, since I spend the money he earns. "Sometimes."

"My boyfriend likes to give me presents." She waves a hand in front of me to show off her bangle bracelets. I recognize the style of the charms. Each is worth about forty dollars. I have a few, but I don't like the way they clink against my arm, so I never wear them.

"Oh, you have a boyfriend?"

"Ex," she amends after a second's pause. "For now. We have an on-again, off-again sort of thing going on. I blame the fact he's married."

"Oh, I . . ."

"You can judge me. I know I'm being terrible."

"I'm not going to judge you, Lisa. Like you said, everyone does stupid stuff sometimes."

I think she might say more, but I guess it's too soon in this renewing friendship for confessionals. She changes the subject smoothly, clearly a pro. Her smile is sad, her tone is chipper. "We didn't have a chance to get caught up at the reunion. You have a son. How old?"

"Eli's sixteen."

"My Braydon's twenty, can you believe it? My daughter Brianna is eighteen. They both go to Bowling Green. I'm an empty nester. I just hope neither of them follows in my footsteps and makes me a grandma until I'm good and ready. You have just the one?"

"Yes."

"He and Beth's oldest are in the same class, aren't they?"

Warily, I nod. "I think so. Yes."

"And he was friends with . . . ?" She sits back.

She remembers. I see half-forgotten knowledge fill up her expression like water rising around the rocks in a vase, slowly but inevitably. Now I remember why it's been so long since I went out for coffee with a girlfriend, went out with any friends at all. I let everyone fall away because they all had the same curious look every time I saw them. Next will come the questions, and Lisa is not subtle enough even to pretend she's not morbidly interested in what happened.

Suddenly, I am desperate for her to ask me about it. I want to talk about it. I want to tell her how it felt when the police showed up, asking questions about the little boy I barely knew. How it has affected my son and me, how his nightmares are worse than mine, but at least he can scream his out loud. How the guilt over not protecting my son from the proximity of tragedy tattered my marriage and shredded my life. I don't even care if she'll gobble up all of that as greasy gossip, I want to unburden myself of it. Get it out, like squeezing a blister until it pops.

I say nothing.

Lisa says nothing.

If she asks me, I think wildly, I will tell her everything, all of it, even the parts I have never shared with anyone. I'll tell her every shameful secret about the drugs and the debt and everything else, and I won't have to carry it all alone anymore. The idea of this swells up, up, up, and up, and my lips part, ready to spill out the truth.

She doesn't ask.

Lisa says, "I think I'll grab a mocha latté. You want something? My treat."

Lisa says, "You sit, I'll get it."

Lisa says, "The chocolate croissants here are to die for. Let's get some."

And I say, "Yum, that sounds great. But you don't have to treat me."

She brushes me off and leaves me at the table. I stare out through the big plate-glass windows to the sidewalk beyond. Downtown Dayton is abustle today. Golden, early September sunshine slants through some slender trees poking up through metal grates in the sidewalk. It's still warm enough to go without a jacket. Beyond the buildings, out of my sight, is the river that weaves its way through the city. Somewhere close to here is where they say that little boy drowned. I've heard that his parents leave flowers there, but I've never gone to see them.

Lisa returns to the table with two chocolate croissants on plates. The server follows with our drinks, setting them down and leaving without a word. I take the plate Lisa slides toward me. I break my croissant into pieces. She bites directly into hers with a totally unself-conscious "ooh" of pure pleasure that I envy and admire. Our conversation turns to gossip about our classmates. Lisa has a lot of stories to tell.

"You've really kept in touch with a lot of people." My mug is warm against my palms as I wrap my fingers around it. The air conditioning is too high, giving me chilly tickles.

"I served at a lot of the local hangouts when my kids were little. Their dad and I split up when he went into the service, so my parents would take them for the weekends. I'd work doubles so I could have time off with them during the week. I got to see everyone who came in, you know, the ones who drank too much. The ones who were sleeping around. I always thought I'd move away, but here I still am."

"Yeah," I say. "Me too."

"You know who never kept in touch with, though?" Lisa winks. "*You* know."

I smile despite myself. "C.C."

"Nobody has," she says. "Beth was on the reunion committee, and she told me she about fell over when she saw his RSVP come in. Before that, I don't think anyone had heard a peep from him in years. Anyway, isn't he still hot as hell? But then, he always was. He said he's looking to get some step-kids. Think I should send him some pictures of mine?"

"He doesn't seem the paternal type," I tell her, and the words almost don't hurt. "But what do I know?"

"And I'm no sugar mama," Lisa says with a put-upon sigh. "Not like you, that's for sure."

She cackles laughter, brash and bold, and I can't help but admire her obvious comfort in who she is. She's authentic. I'm the shallow one, all surface, all shine, reflecting every gaze away from what's underneath.

"*Me?*" I laugh and shake my head, feeling heat creep into my cheeks. "No way."

"Oh, c'mon, Jewelann. You live in that gorgeous, enormous house in one of the most expensive neighborhoods in Kettering. You have a rock on your finger big enough to blind a gal, and . . . yep." She tilts herself again to take in my entire outfit. "Designer from top to toe. You could *totally* be Christian's sugar mama. Except I bet you're super happy with your hottie husband who buys you anything you want."

"Yeah . . . Ken's . . . great. I'm a kept woman. Not a care in the world." My laugh is half embarrassed, half ashamed.

"You're happy, but you went upstairs to C.C.'s hotel room," Lisa says as though her words don't matter, even though we both know they do. When I don't reply, she shakes her head. "I get it, though. He's hard to resist. Beth wanted him soooo bad, I had to be the good friend and wrestle her out of there. Her husband would shit a brick if he ever found out she was in that hotel room with him."

As would mine. "Did she and Christian ever . . . it seemed like they might have had something . . . ?"

"She wishes," Lisa says. "She got caught having a hot and heavy text conversation with him while she was supposed to be planning the reunion. I'm not sure exactly what they were saying, but it wasn't just about whether he wanted chicken or pasta, you know what I mean? Her husband was suuuper pissed off about it."

"Yikes. That's no good."

"Yeah," Lisa says. "They've been having some trouble for a while. I keep telling her to work it out with Steve, though. He's got a really good job. They have a nice house. She hasn't worked since before her kids were born. I keep telling her she's got it too good to give up."

"Like me," I say.

For the first time since she got here, Lisa's casual demeanor hardens. "She makes noise about leaving him, but I told her, look, you can be unhappy in a big house with vacations three times a year and your retirement fully funded, or you can be unhappy in a shitty condo struggling to pay for your pedicures and bitching about who your kids decided to spend the holidays with. Or you can hope your husband pops off unexpectedly," she adds, "but make sure you have a good life insurance policy on him, one that covers any contingency. I mean, I'd rather have my husband than the money, but at least the money has helped."

"I'm sorry." I'm alarmed at the sheen of tears in her eyes. The way she acted at the reunion when she said it was just her makes sense, now. I'm chagrined at how I'd dismissed her then. "I didn't know. I guess I've really been out of touch."

Lisa pats beneath her eyes with a napkin, getting herself under control before she looks at me again. "Don't worry about it. It's not like I posted a lot about it when it happened, so you could have missed it. Gary and I were only married for a few years. He fell off a ladder. I'd gone away for the weekend and found him when I got home."

"Oh. I'm so sorry."

She nods, accepting my condolences with a sniff. She dabs her nostrils daintily with the paper napkin. "I've offered to help Beth's husband up on a ladder, but so far, he's been totally resistant to any kind of household repairs."

I have no idea what to say to this, but her laughter pushes a stunned giggle out of me.

"Your face," Lisa says through a flurry of chuckles. "God, Jewelann. Your face. I'm sorry, that was really dark humor and nothing to joke about, right? If her husband does end up falling off a ladder, I guess I could be implicated in that, huh? I shouldn't make jokes like that. I guess it's just my way of dealing with a shit situation. I loved my husband, but Beth *hates* hers."

"That's too bad."

"What about you?" Lisa asks.

I'm not sure how to answer, but my hesitation seems reply enough. She laughs, again tossing back her head and drawing attention to the two of us. She knocks her knuckles on the tabletop and wags her finger at me.

"I don't hate him," I say. "At least not enough to get him up on a ladder."

Then we both laugh, long and hard and loudly, and I don't care who turns to stare at us.

I barely make it home before Eli gets back from school. I'm in a good mood. Lisa made me promise to get together with her and Beth for "something stronger than a latté," and although I don't think Beth and I will ever be friends, I had agreed.

To have a *best* friend, you need to have *a* friend. And to have a friend, you need to have someone who will look at the worst parts of you and not turn away. Someone who understands you even when you're not sure you understand yourself. Someone you trust with your secrets.

Someone you trust to keep them.

My smile disappears when I spot Ken's car in the driveway. It's the middle of the afternoon. He should be at the office. Parked at the far end of the horseshoe is another car, one I don't recognize.

He would not have brought *her* here, would he? To fuck in our house, *my* house, our bed? Unless, I think, he's finally leaving me for her. Unless he's going to show her off, this nameless, faceless woman who has taken his affections over the past few years, the one who so distracts him when he's with me that it's like I'm the one who's a stranger.

For a full minute, I consider driving away and not coming back until I'm sure Eli's home. I have errands to run, or at least to manufacture, but no money to spend until next week when Ken's paycheck hits the direct deposit. My fingers curl around my steering wheel, and when they start to ache I finally release it and sit back. I *have* to go inside.

A greeting rises to my lips, something cheerful and insincere, but the words die on my tongue the moment I step into the kitchen. Ken sits at the table, a mug in front of him, the coffee pot on a hot pad next to it. He is not with his mistress.

"Hey there, Jewelann," Christian says from his place at the table. "Good to see you again."

# 10

CHRISTIAN MOVES IN for a hug. I back away a few quick steps but then force myself to submit to the embrace, too aware that my husband is watching the exchange with interest. Ken does not know about me and Christian in high school.

But does he know about last Saturday night?

The warmth of Christian's lips on my cheek sends a perverse thrill up and down my spine. Not arousal, not quite, but my heart does beat faster. I disengage from his grip and make a show of getting a mug from the kitchen cabinet so I can pour myself a mug of coffee I don't want to drink. I've had too much caffeine today already. It will keep me up late tonight. Maybe I need to be up late tonight. Maybe I need to be prepared. If my husband is not confronting me with his mistress, he might be getting ready to do it with my mistake.

"Christian's going to rent the carriage house," Ken says.

I drop the mug but catch it before it can hit the counter, or worse, the floor. I turn with it gripped in both hands. "What?"

"Nice catch," Christian says. "Good hands."

I put the mug on the counter and my hands on my hips. "I'm sorry, what about the carriage house?"

"He's going to rent it." Ken says this slowly, enunciating not as though I didn't hear the words, but that I am not comprehending them.

With the weight of Christian's gaze on me, I make the effort of keeping my expression neutral. I shouldn't care what he thinks about me, my marriage, or anything else, but I'm trying to be careful. I don't trust him. I know better than to do that.

I swallow a rush of bitterness. "The carriage house . . . we aren't renting it . . . I mean, it's not in good enough shape to rent it."

The carriage house in the backyard was never meant for horses. My parents had converted it from a detached garage in the late seventies with the idea that my mother's mom, Gramma Nancy, would live there instead of a nursing home. She'd stayed there for only a few months before it had become obvious that she wasn't going to be able to take care of herself, even with the one-floor living plan that included a small kitchen, bathroom, living room, and bedroom. After she'd been moved into the care home, the carriage house had become a space for visiting relatives from out of town, off limits to me and Jonathan, and, of course, intensely attractive for just that reason. I'd given away my virginity in that carriage house to the man sitting across from my husband.

"He's going to take care of updating it for us," Ken says smoothly.

Christian gives us both a modest look. "I need a place to stay during my surgical residency. I'm hardly going to be there, really, what with all the stuff I'll have to do at the hospital. But I am something of a hobbyist when it comes to home improvement, so in my spare time, I told Ken I'd be happy to tackle some of the repairs in exchange for part of the rent."

"You always said you were going to fix it up, but you haven't . . ." Ken shrugs and gives me a thin-lipped smile.

He has managed to make me feel both guilty and defiant. I'm not handy, and I can't afford to hire anyone to fix up a building that, until today, had no real use other than to store more of the things I bought that I don't want him to know about. My fingers are clenching, and at the sting of my nails digging into my palm I force them to relax. Instead, I contort my lips into a smile.

"You didn't tell me you were going to put it up for rent, that's all." I flick a glance at Christian, not daring to allow my eyes to catch his.

Ken shrugs. "I put an ad online. Had a lot of people calling about it, but I hadn't gotten around to getting any background checks or anything. When Chris here called, told me about the two of you—"

"That we went to school together," Christian interrupts, smooth as cream, his smile never drooping so much as a fraction.

My husband stares at me, his expression unreadable. I used to be able to tell what he was thinking just by looking at his face. When did he become stone? Or when did I stop trying to know him?

"I figured you could vouch for him," Ken says. "Plus, he's willing to take the place as-is."

"Just a place to eat," Christian says. "And sleep."

"Have you even seen it yet? It's really a mess. I'm sure you could find something a lot nicer."

"I don't need something fancy. And you're so close to the hospital, I could walk, if I wanted to." Christian's smile widens. "But if you want to show it to me before I commit, I guess I could always change my mind. If it doesn't suit."

Ken stands. "Hon, I've got a pile of paperwork to do before I leave tomorrow. Could you take him over?"

Christian smiles. I do not. "Sure. Of course."

"Great."

Christian and Ken shake hands, pumping them up and down. Ken claps Christian on one shoulder. I'm surprised they don't chest bump, based on the enthusiasm of this parting.

Leaving my husband behind in the kitchen, I take Christian out the sliding glass doors, across the deck and the backyard, and into the carriage house.

"Like I said, it's a mess." I turn on the lights in the square living room that opens into the galley kitchen. It's furnished exactly as it was the last time he'd been here, although boxes in stacks fill most of the open space. "You really should find a much better place to live."

Christian stands too close behind me. The heat from his body sends a shudder rippling through me. I take a couple of steps toward the kitchen to turn on the next set of lights. These are amber glass, globed lamps shaped like pineapples. They hang on chains over the small breakfast bar dividing the space. Those lamps used to hang in my grandmother's living room but got added to the carriage house when they built it. So much history in this space . . . and not just the furnishings.

"It's not so bad. Same couch, I see." He takes a test bounce on the cushions, covered with a sheet he flips back to show off the brown plaid. "Ken said I could take the place furnished or, if I agreed to get rid of it all, I could bring in my own stuff. It's all in storage right now."

My back stiffens and my shoulders tense. I guess since we're married, everything I own belongs to Ken as much as it does to me, but none of it's from *his* childhood. It's not his history. Not his stuff. His name isn't even on the title to this house. He has no right to offer anything away.

"Did he?"

Christian shrugs and smiles, patting the couch again. He slides me a sly grin. "I don't know, though. I have fond memories of this couch."

"What are you doing here?" I pitch my voice low and look over my shoulder, although I know Ken hasn't followed. Again, my hands turn into fists.

"I told you—"

"No. What are you doing *here*," I say again. "*Why* are you here, Christian? And don't give me some bullshit excuse about needing a place to stay."

He stands. I tense again and take a step away from him. I imagine his hands on me, gripping. His mouth on mine.

Christian moves past me and into the kitchen, where he tugs open the harvest gold refrigerator. It hasn't been plugged in for years. He finds the switch for the under-cabinet fluorescents.

"Your parents used to store beer and liquor out here, remember? I told you it was because this was where they came to swing with their friends, and you bit me on the shoulder. Left a mark. I bet I was right, though, wasn't I?"

"Don't be disgusting."

"What's disgusting about Doris and Sidney getting it on with the neighbors down the street on a Saturday night out here in the carriage house while the kids are fast asleep—"

"Shut up," I snap.

He holds out his hands in a gesture of fake apology. "Nobody likes to think about their parents getting it on, but guess what? They all do. Or else nobody would ever become a parent in the first place."

"You're back in your hometown. Why don't you move in with *your* parents?"

His eyes narrow. "Why would you assume my parents are still alive?"

"I'm sorry," I say, chastened. "I lost my parents too."

"I know," Christian says. "You told me that the last time we slept together."

I don't want to remember the last time we slept together. I don't want to think about how I'd mourned the loss of my parents within a month of each other. So many bad decisions that haunt me every day.

"Are you going to tell me you just happened to find an ad for this place, when I didn't even know Ken had listed it?"

"Coincidence."

"I don't believe in coincidence, Christian."

He presses his lips together for a second or so before letting them curve again. That particular smile has haunted me for years, because this one is not sly or mocking or arrogant or even charming. This one is genuine.

"You said you were still living in your old house. I remembered the address. I looked you up online."

Something sharp twists inside me. Something cuts my soft and secret places. He sees it on my face.

"When the ad came up for the carriage house, I thought it must be a sign," Christian says.

I swallow hard. "A sign for what?"

"That you and me," he gestures back and forth between us, "aren't finished with each other yet."

"There is no you and me, Christian. There never was."

"No? You sure about that?"

"One hundred percent." My answer comes out in a whisper. Not convincing either one of us.

He laughs and turns in an unhurried circle to face me, his hands on his hips. His fingers make a V toward his crotch. His voice is bland. Neutral. But his eyes are cold.

"You tried to ghost me," he says.

My vindication is almost incandescent. He took me into his hotel room because he wanted *me*, and I was the one who walked away. I hurt him. I left a mark. Maybe this one won't fade.

"So you're going to get back at me by moving into my carriage house?"

"I need a place to live during my residency," he says. "And this way, you can't ignore me again."

"Find another place to live, Christian."

He laughs and shakes his head. He looks around the room, then fixes his gaze on mine. "No."

Hot and cold, suddenly feverish, I clench my jaw to keep my teeth from chattering. "If you're planning to tell my husband—"

His laugh cuts off my words. He waves a hand. "Why would I do that?"

"Revenge?"

Now he moves toward me, now he takes me by the upper arms, his fingers pinching deep into my flesh, now he slants his mouth over mine . . . but he does not kiss me. I should fight this, but I'm incapable of moving. I imagine biting his lips the way I once bit his shoulder.

Christian's eyes hold mine for a moment before he lets me go and steps back. "This might come as a shock to you, but med school is expensive. I've got loans. And I'm not making surgeon money yet. So a cheap place to live is exactly what I need right now, and this is a very, very cheap place to live."

I pivot on my heel to leave. He says my name. I hesitate.

"We both know you wanted to. We both know you *still* want to. C'mon, Jewelann. You remember how good it was with us."

I turn around.

"I already told you, there *was* no us," I hiss. "You're the one who always made that clear. Remember?"

His gaze sharpens, then softens, becoming a caress all over me. "I remember how you taste and smell, and how your body feels when I touch it. I remember the sound you make when you come. Tell me something, Jewelann, how long has it been since you made that sound?"

My tongue cleaves to the roof of my mouth, lips parting to let a small noise slip out against my will. My fingers curl against my palm, my nails too blunt to cut my skin, but still stinging the harder I make a fist. I shake my head.

Christian moves toward me. He touches the pendant nestled in the hollow of my throat. "Nobody would ever know."

"I would know." I've worn this necklace every day since he gave it to me. With a yank, I tug the chain, breaking it. I hold it out to him, and when he doesn't take it, I throw it on the floor.

Christian looks at it, then at me, his expression blank. He takes a step back from me. "Well. If you change your mind, you know where I'll be."

"I won't."

"If I text you now, you'll have to answer me. Since you're my new landlady and all. Right? You can't just ignore me anymore. Can you?" Christian says with a slide of his tongue over his teeth. He looks around the room and nods firmly. "Leave the keys."

I toss them on the end table and let myself out. Inside my kitchen, I listen for the sound of my husband. He's in his office, the closed door sacrosanct, but I can hear his agitated voice talking on the phone even from the top of the stairs. Another closed door greets me in the upstairs hall. When this was my brother's room, Jonathan played his music loud enough to drive my mother to distraction, but my son's headphones are a permanent fixture. I press my fingertips to the door for a moment, thinking of knocking, but what's the point? He won't hear me. I'd have to pound on it to get his attention, and then what will I say to him? It's not yet time for dinner. He no longer wants to spend his afternoons playing cards with me or building pillow forts he can jump on and destroy. I'd only earn his scorn.

In my bathroom, I pull out my phone. There was no noise to alert me, but my message app shows a number. I swipe to read the message. I take the number off mute and add the information to my contacts. It's from Christian, because of course it is, because of course the one time I walk away from Christian Campbell is the time he decides he can't let me go.

# 11

**L**OOKING FORWARD TO **getting reacquainted.**

That's all the text says.

I seek my solace in a shower hot enough to scald. My skin goes pink, then red, beneath the spray. And still I tremble, and I shake, and my teeth clatter together now that I'm no longer clipping the tip of my tongue between them. Laughter, frantic and desperate and without humor, bubbles up and out of me, and I choke it off with a mouthful of water.

The shower runs cold too soon. The water heater is ancient, like the rest of the appliances. They all should be replaced, but the money that spends so easily a dollar at a time, here or there, running like a silk scarf through my fingers, goes to other things.

I stand under the chilly stream, letting myself be punished. My face is numb. My body. I curl my fingers against my palm and feel the dents my nails made earlier. It's time to get out of the shower, but I can't quite make myself. It's the only place I can weep without anyone hearing me. Why am I crying? Why laughing? Why is my heart pounding so fiercely I swear I can see the pulse of it in the swell of my bare breast?

Love is what we tell ourselves will hold back the pain, but isn't it love that brings us the agony in the first place?

I'd always told myself I married Ken because I loved him, and I did, at least in some small way. The truth was that he'd charmed me, and I'd always been susceptible to a man who could do that. We met at a gas station. I was trying to buy cigarettes, but I didn't have enough cash. Ken was fixing the cash register. He covered the cost of my bill in exchange for my number. I had no direction in life, and he gave me one. He rescued me, and, as they say, it became a happily ever after.

Christian, on the other hand, has never saved me. He has never loved me. He will never love me. But if he thinks he can ruin me, he's the one who will regret it.

I turn off the water. Both the shower head and the tub faucet leak. The curtain catches on the rod as I push it back. Dripping, I step out onto the bathmat and reach for my towel. Both are scratchy and faded, and I close my eyes as I press the fabric to my face. I want softness under my feet and against my body. I want unlimited hot water. I want a new life.

The choices we make stay with us long after we make them. My son will grow up and move away. My husband will lock himself in his office when he's here and travel for weeks on end, and one day I suspect he will leave me for one of the women I'm convinced he has in other towns. But me? I will stay here until I literally die.

"What are you doing?"

Ken's voice startles me into a squeak of a response. I pull the towel from my face, grateful he didn't find me weep-laughing in the shower. I wrap the towel around my breasts, tucking in the ends to keep it up. There was a time when my husband would've tried playfully to tug it off me and see me naked, but he barely glances at me now as he goes to the toilet and urinates in a long, hard stream. His back is to me.

He's asked me a question he doesn't even seem to care if I answer.

"Taking a shower," is my reply. *Duh.*

He looks over his shoulder with a frown at my tone. "It's the middle of the afternoon."

"I have a chill."

Ken finishes, shakes, zips, and steps away from me as his expression warps. He's a germophobe, terrified of getting sick. During flu season our house smells constantly of bleach. He wipes down his phone. His wallet, his credit cards. I've seen him wipe his steering wheel, dashboard, and the interior of his car doors. Even the trunk. During the early pandemic, we were some of the few people I know who didn't have to fight to find antiseptic wipes and hand sanitizer, because he always had that stuff stocked up three rows deep.

"Are you coming down with something?" He washes his hands vigorously at the sink and keeps his distance. "I have a really important meeting tomorrow, Jewelann. I can't afford to get sick."

I wasn't trying to get him to stay away from me, but this will do it anyway. "Could just be something I ate."

I don't know why I'm saying this instead of going into the bedroom to dress. I clutch at the towel and shiver. I really do have a chill, but I'm sure it has nothing to do with any kind of illness.

"If I get sick, I won't be able to travel," Ken says.

I push a smile through reluctant lips. "I thought you were going to be home for a bit?"

"No," he says. "I've got trips planned. Important trips, I can't miss them. It'll throw off my entire schedule."

Right. Of course. Nothing like a sick wife to fuck up your plans.

"How long will you be gone?" I ask him sweetly.

He hesitates. "Ten days."

"Ten—" I cut myself off. These trips last longer and longer. How much longer before he decides not to come home at all? "I'm sure that if you're sick, you could reschedule, Ken. People have to understand if you're sick."

Unless those people are lovers who only get to see you when you're out of town and away from your wife.

Ken shakes his head. "Not worth the risk. I guess I'll sleep on the couch in the basement tonight."

Suddenly, violently, unnecessarily, I cough into my fist. The sound is rough and rasping and totally fake, but it sends him recoiling even farther away from me. I would laugh at the look of horror on his face, if it didn't make me want to weep.

During the first months of the pandemic, Ken slept exclusively on the basement couch. Even during lockdown, he still traveled, because he serviced gas stations and convenience stores that did not close. He'd come home, sanitize everything he owned, and isolate himself from us. None of us ever got sick, and he prides himself as the reason why.

Now it feels as though he's been itching for a reason to sleep apart from me, and I just gave him one. With him snoring on the pillow beside me I could pretend we are okay, that I have nothing to worry about. In the basement, he can spend hours sending messages on his laptop. He can use his phone to send dick pics. He can move another step closer to being happier somewhere else.

My stomach mutters in dismay.

He leaves the bathroom. I follow. I pull on my robe from the back of the door. It's heavy and fluffy, and in seconds I'm sweating.

"You should have asked me about renting the carriage house," I say to his back.

Ken pauses in the doorway. Turns. His expression is faintly surprised. When's the last time we had an argument? I can't even recall. I'm so very, very careful never to contradict him or let him down or be anything other than an opinionless, agreeable automaton.

"We've talked about this, Jewelann. We have a perfectly good apartment in that carriage house, sitting empty, doing nothing for us but adding to our school taxes."

"It's a dump."

"He's going to fix it up, and we'll end up with something better than we started with."

I clutch at the neck of the robe, even though I'm overheating. I taste salt when I lick my lips, and also the coppery undertone of blood, as though I've bitten the tip of my tongue. "I don't like the idea of a stranger living on the property."

"But he's not a stranger," Ken says. "He's your old school buddy."

He knows.

He can't know.

He *knows*, I think, watching him study me with a flat, inscrutable gaze.

"I haven't seen him since we graduated." My protest is weak. My husband has made his decision, and there's nothing I can do about it.

"Well, that's a lie, isn't it?"

My lips part, but no words come out. Ken laughs, wagging his head. Then his finger.

"You saw him last Saturday at the reunion, didn't you?"

Relief weakens my knees. "Right. Of course."

Ken puts his hands on his hips, fingers angling toward his crotch. One knee bends a little, cocking his body toward mine. "We talked about this several times. It doesn't make any sense to keep the place empty. It's just a place to fill up with more junk. In a few more years, Eli will be off to school, and we'll be thinking about downsizing. Best to get the place in order before then."

He's talking about the normal accumulation of belong-
ings that happens over time, but he doesn't have to say more
than that. Once again, I'm reminded of how I've trapped
myself here. In this house. In this marriage. This life.

A rat will chew off its own leg to get free.

What will I do?

# 12

THE HANDBAG HAS some scuff marks on it, but it's Etienne Aigner, and I have a soft spot for it because my mother used to love that designer. I don't have a bag like this, not exactly like this, and there's a matching belt and a wallet that is almost identical to one I have already, but this one is in the original box with soft tissue paper surrounding it and a receipt from 1986. I buy all of it. The woman at the table in the garage charges me twenty dollars and reminds me that if I come back tomorrow, the last day of the estate sale, everything will be fifty percent off or more.

I might come back tomorrow, but it's not worth waiting to see if someone else will have snapped up the bargains that now belong to me. Sliding into the front seat, I'm sweating. The September sun is hot today through the leaves that have begun drifting down from the trees, even though they're mostly still green.

The A/C puffs coolish air into my face as I tap out a search on my phone to bring up one of the resale sites I belong to. A purse similar to the one I just bought sold last week for eighty dollars. A handbag and wallet set in worse shape than the ones I now own sold two weeks ago for close to a hundred. If I buff out the scratches and put these up as a set, sell the belt separately, I'll make back what I spent, plus a possible hundred or so more.

I'm going to do it. I'm going to flip this stuff, which will justify having bought it in the first place. I don't need another handbag, no matter how nice it is. The belt isn't even my size. And what good is a wallet if you don't have any money for it to hold?

The cardboard box is soft with age as I take off the lid and pull out the wallet. I admire the reddish leather. The craftsmanship. Vintage items are so much better-made than new things. I peek inside, imagining my license in the clear plastic slot. A small crow of laughter slips out of me.

Inside the wallet is a hundred dollar bill.

My grandma once told me that you never gift someone a purse or a wallet without putting some money inside it. To do so would be bad luck. Well, someone had clearly felt the same way, but the bad luck was for whoever received this wallet and didn't bother to look inside it.

I spent twenty and got back a hundred. It's a sign, isn't it? Okay, so I'll sell the purse and the belt, but this wallet was meant to be mine.

I make a quick stop at my storage unit to tuck away the purse and belt. I nestle them in a bin next to the other Etienne Aigner pieces I've collected, each wrapped carefully in tissue paper. I take my cards and the photo of Eli out of my current wallet, a nice enough Coach piece that doesn't make my heart as happy as this new one. I put the cards in the one I just bought and the Coach wallet away in its own bin.

The key to keeping Ken from finding out how much money I spend is to never let him see more or new items in my closet. He has brand-name blindness; designers mean nothing to him. So long as there are only ever four or five pairs of shoes, a couple of purses, half a closet rack full of hangers, he never notices if I'm switching out one piece for another.

Except he did notice, didn't he? The dress I wore last week. He'd asked if it was new. He'd actually paid attention to me. But he has no idea about this storage unit, I'm sure of it. I'm good at diverting money from the budget for "miscellaneous household expenses" or "groceries" or "school supplies" to pay for my habits.

I'm careful to lock the unit when I leave. A few years ago, someone broke into one of the other units and cleaned it out. They added security cameras since then, and it turned out the thief was an ex who'd been trying to take back what they considered their own property. Still, I'm always sure to secure my unit. I have literally thousands of dollars' worth of goods in there, and none of it's insured.

The new wallet is making me giddy. I can't stop thinking about it on the drive home. As soon as I pull into my driveway, I take it out of my bag and admire it again. I smooth my fingers over the leather. I smell it. I open it to peek inside again. Everything sends a rush of warmth through me.

It won't last long.

In a day or so, it'll just be another wallet I picked up at an estate sale. The hundred dollar bill will be spent and gone, and then, I think, yes, then, I will list the wallet and purse and belt online and sell them for a profit. I totally will.

Movement from the far end of the horseshoe driveway catches my attention. Through my windshield, I can see the open door of the carriage house. Christian appears in it a second or so later. He's carrying two large black plastic contractor garbage bags toward the street.

I'm out of my car at once, wallet still clutched in one hand. I meet him as he's halfway back up the drive. His grin fades at the sight of my face.

"What are you doing?" I demand.

"Getting rid of a bunch of trash." He peers around me. "What are *you* doing?"

"What kind of trash?" I take a step toward the carriage house.

He takes a counter step, blocking me. "I mean trash. Garbage. Junk."

"You don't get to decide if it's junk."

"Ken told me I had free rein in there. I have to make it livable." He frowns. "You were right, it's a dump."

I shake my head and scowl. "Ken is not in charge of whatever's in there. You can't just start tossing stuff. It's *mine*."

"Where is Kenny boy, anyway? I haven't seen his car."

"He's at work." I don't mention that he's been on the road and isn't due home for another few days.

"So, you're alone. Nice." Christian's smirk rolls across his face, tipping the corners of his eyes. "Are you going to invite me in for coffee? Tea? You?"

"You know I'm not. Don't you have to be at the hospital?" I cross my arms. The wallet presses my side. My designer sweater that looked so cute when I put it on this morning is far too warm for the afternoon sunshine. Maybe it's a hot flash. Maybe it's the way he stares at me.

"Not today. I have all the time in the world, today. Especially for you." He puts his hands on his hips, arching his back a little. Squints up at the sky. Sunlight glints in his dark golden hair, picking up the hints of silver. He looks at me again. "What time does Ken get home?"

I won't tell Christian that I'm not sure. "Listen, don't you dare throw anything else away without asking me first. Do you understand?"

Christian looks perplexed. "But . . . it's literal garbage, Jewelann."

"And I told you, that's not for you to decide."

"Fine." He eyes me. "Is it valuable?"

"It's . . . sentimental. Not that it's any of your business," I add.

"Maybe I'm a little sentimental about it too. Especially that couch. Did you ever think of that?"

I shift from foot to foot. "Don't do that."

"Do what?" He sounds innocent and affronted.

"Don't pretend I ever meant anything to you."

He gives me a black look. "Is that what you think?"

"I don't have to *think* anything, Christian. I know it. I was that sure thing, the one you could always come back to, but not what you ever really wanted. So don't try to convince me that somehow, after all this time, it's different."

Christian moves closer again. "Yeah, you were what I always came back to. Didn't you ever think about why?"

"Not because . . . never because . . ."

His kiss lands on the corner of my mouth because I've turned my face away. He tries again, more insistent this time, but I push at his chest to get him to step back. He grabs my upper arm, resisting, and I think, *He won't let me go this time*, but he does.

"Stop it. The neighbors will see—"

"Nobody can see us back here."

"I'm *married*."

"You're miserable," he says.

I push him again, unsteady on my own feet. "Sleeping with you won't change that, Christian."

"It might change a lot of things, if you'd let it." He steps back but remains close enough to grab me again, if he wants.

"The only thing that would change is that my husband would leave me, and if Ken decides to leave me, I can't afford to keep the house."

"So, you'll get another one."

As if it were that easy.

"I love this house."

"I meant another husband." Christian winks.

"I love him too," I say. "And I love my son. I'm not going to disrupt his life by tearing apart his family or making him move from his childhood home or change schools. I won't do anything to risk messing up his life, and that certainly includes losing the only home he's ever known."

Christian laughs. "You think Kenny boy has a statute of limitations on fucking around? You were married back then, too. You think he'll really care that it was a long time ago?"

I've been doing nothing but grabbing at the rapidly unraveling threads of my marriage for years. It's as fragile and delicate as old lace. It would take very little to shred it completely.

Ken would absolutely care.

"Why are you doing this to me?" I have a lot of practice not screaming even when I want to.

"Because I can. Because nobody walks away from me. Because you've got great tits and a fuckable ass, and I want it. Because," Christian says in a flat voice, devoid of emotion, "I get what I want."

"And you want . . . me?"

His fingers snag my wrist, tugging, but I yank it free. I drop my new wallet on the driveway's pitted blacktop. The hundred dollar bill falls out and almost flutters away in an errant breeze before Christian steps on it to stop its flight. He bends to pick it up. He offers it to me, and I snatch it from his grip.

"I want what you have," he says.

Laughter grinds out of me. "I don't *have* anything."

"Bullshit," he says. "Look at you. Running errands in a Gucci fucking watch and matching shoes. Tossing hundreds out of your wallet like they're scrap paper. How do you even manage to lift that wallet with that rock on your finger?"

I almost can't speak because of how ludicrous this all is. I try to explain, but what can I say, what can I tell him without spilling the entirety of my truth and the years of lies I've been weaving to cover it all up?

"The ring belonged to Ken's mother, and my parents gave me this house instead of a cash inheritance. We've remortgaged it twice since then. And the clothes, all of that, it's . . . nothing, Christian, it's all smoke and mirrors. If you really meant it when you said you wanted a sugar mama, you're looking at the wrong woman. I promise you, I can't keep you in any kind of style."

"How's that lie taste, Jewelann? Because I bet I have something you can keep in your mouth that has a much better flavor."

"You're crude."

He laughs. "Yeah. And you love it. Bet Kenny doesn't talk to you that way, does he? Mr. All-American? Mr. Goody Two-Shoes?"

"You don't even know him, Christian." But he's right. Ken would never. Women who sleep around are whores, according to him, and although I never told him he was my first, I've also never told him how many others had been there before him.

"I know he keeps you in hundred dollar bills, and I know you'll do anything not to lose him. You just said so." Christian makes a tutting noise and wags a finger back and forth. "You were never good at hiding your hand, Jewelann. But hey, you don't want to let me back inside? Whatever. I don't need it."

Sweat trickles down my spine. My armpits are dank with it. I need to get inside the house, out of the sun. Away from him.

"What do you need? I really don't have money—"

"Money," he says, "is not the only thing I might need from you."

"If you want me to sleep with you," I begin in a low voice, but his laughter cuts me off.

"Please. Like I need to beg for trim. No, baby, right now I need a place to live. And after that . . ." His smile is bright. "I'll let you know."

"What if it's something I don't have?"

He shrugs, unconcerned, his gaze sharp as a razor. "If there's one thing I know about you, Jewelann, it's that you'll find a way to get it."

# 13

THERE HAS NEVER been a single time when I haven't been here when Eli gets home from school. Even though I want to run, run, run, I can't. So I turn my attentions to something else, something normal. Dinner prep. I sort ingredients. Pull out a cookbook. Sift and measure, crack an egg, compost the shell.

*Make a plan, Jewelann. Be ready.* I wasn't always good at keeping myself together, but I'm a master of it now. By the time Eli walks through the front door, I'm . . . not calm, but I am collected.

"Mom, I'm home!"

I greet him with a smile from my place at the counter, where I'm stuffing a roasting chicken with oranges and raw garlic. "Hey, you. How was school?"

He slings his backpack over a kitchen chair and heads for the fridge to pull out the pitcher of iced tea. "Fine. What's up with the guy in the extra garage? Says his name's Christian?"

"You talked to him?" I rub the chicken with sage and thyme and rosemary. Salt and pepper. I cover it with foil and slide it into the oven, then wash my hands.

He takes a glass from the cupboard. "Yeah. He was throwing stuff away when I got home."

I'm furious at the thought of Christian getting rid of stuff after I told him not to, but I keep my voice light. "He's fixing up the carriage house."

"Why?" Eli frowns as he pours tea.

"Well, it needs a lot of work, and I guess Dad thought it would be good to renovate it. Christian's going to do some of that work for us in exchange for rent."

Eli grunts. So much like his father. "But why does Dad want to rent it?"

*Why. Why. Why.* As a little boy, Eli's favorite word had been why. There are times I'd give anything to go back to those days, no matter how frustrated I'd been. I clutch at the memory.

"You're going to college in a few years, right?" I force a laugh. "We'll need the income."

It's the wrong thing to say. Eli fixes me with a look far too intense for my comfort. "Are you having money problems?"

"You," not "you and Dad." My little shopping buddy. That's what I used to call him on those endless trips through thrift shops and yard sales. *Don't tell Daddy, and Mama will buy you a toy, whatever toy you want.* I haven't taken Eli with me in a long, long time, but I'm sure he remembers.

*Don't tell.*

Of course he remembers.

"No. But college is expensive." I hear the front door open. Ken is home early again, no warning. "Don't worry about it. Me and Dad will take care of it."

"Maybe I don't even want to go to college," Eli mumbles.

We have approximately three minutes before Ken will finish hanging up his keys and taking off his shoes by the front door. I give Eli a stern look. He rolls his eyes.

Ken appears in the kitchen doorway. "What's this about college?"

"Maybe I don't want to go," Eli says. "Maybe I want to do something else. Get into cybersecurity. I don't need to go to school for four years for that. And then I can get a good job, start making money right away—"

"Of course you'll go to college." Ken dismisses him with a wave of his hand. "Who's been filling your head with this stuff? Just because your friends have some crazy ideas, that doesn't mean you have to follow along with them."

Eli's laugh is not as happy as the one he gave me earlier. "Right. My friends are influencing me. Sure."

Ken has to be joking, right? Eli is not popular. He doesn't *have* friends. It's like his father has simply glossed over that knowledge. I'm not the only doll Ken wants in this family.

"We'll discuss this later, Champ," Ken says. To me, he asks, "Dinner?"

I'm taken aback. "It's only three thirty."

"I'm starving," Ken declares in a booming voice, exuberant. Enthusiastic. "I've looked forward to your cooking all week. Rearranged my schedule to make sure I got home sooner than planned. It's Friday, right? Are you doing Shabbat?"

Shabbat is not something I "do" or "don't do." It is an integral part of my week. I've always celebrated the Friday night sabbath, but Ken's gone so often that maybe it has never occurred to him that the special meal I make every week happens whether or not he's there to share it. And why would he? There's nothing in my life that's not supposed to be meant, somehow, for him.

"Yes. It's Shabbat. Dinner should be ready in a couple of hours."

"You're the best. You know that? What a rockstar. Isn't your mother amazing, Eli? You should tell her how much you appreciate everything she does for us." Ken turns to him. "Go on."

"Thanks, Mom."

This effusive praise makes me uncomfortable—not because it's bad to be appreciated, but because of how exaggerated Ken is making it seem. Eli shoots me a look, but I can only shrug. When Ken pulls me close for a kiss, Eli flees so he doesn't have to see his parents being affectionate.

"What's gotten into you?" I ask. He's always been so cautious about exposing Eli to anything "inappropriate." Now he's practically shoving his tongue down my throat in front of him.

"Can't a man show how much he loves his wife?"

"Of course you can. I'm just surprised."

He hugs me close, pressing his lips to my hair. "You shouldn't be. Without you, Jewelann, I don't know what I'd do."

Then he's stepping back, already distant, dusting off his hands as though he finished a chore he'd been putting off and finally managed to complete. Paperwork, he says, in his office. He'll be up in time for dinner.

With Ken home, our little family bustles with domestic . . . okay, it's not bliss. But it's something, and it's ours. I call Eli down to set the table that's been in this dining room since before I was born. We use my grandmother's china. I set out the food, pour myself a glass of grape juice for the blessing, light the candles, and say the prayer.

"Don't you usually have wine?" Ken asks me when I lift the grape juice.

I'm surprised enough to splash a little juice on the white tablecloth. I do have wine when he's not here. "Sometimes, but—"

"Why don't you have a glass? You worked hard on this delicious meal for us. You should have a little treat. And I wouldn't mind a glass, myself. For tradition, right?"

I rarely drink around him, and Ken never drinks at all. Not a beer when he's grilling, not a cocktail in front of the

TV, no champagne at New Year's, and certainly no wine for Shabbat. In the worst times, when I struggled to get through a single day without obliterating myself, he always knew when I was stoned but never said a word. When I got myself off the pills, he knew that, too, and also never said a word. So here we are now, never saying a word to the other about much of anything, because if you can't talk to each other about something as vast and important as addiction, how can you really talk about anything that matters?

"Go get it," he encourages.

Eli and I share a look at Ken's joviality. I get a bottle from the built-in rack over the fridge. They're waiting for me to return before we eat, because that's good manners. I pour myself a scant glass of ruby liquid. When Ken lifts his glass, I pour some wine into it. I stumble over the blessings I should know by heart, and the peace I usually feel at the Shabbat table eludes me. Ken keeps his held high even after the prayer, waiting for the two of us to join. I lift mine again, and Eli follows with his after a second.

"To family."

Eli and I echo his words. My husband reaches for my hand. He squeezes it. He smiles at me. I say the prayer over the braided challah. The first piece I tear off and dip in salt usually goes to Eli. Tonight, I hand it to Ken.

"Amazing," Ken says. "Delicious."

He digs into the chicken and mashed potatoes and eats with enthusiasm. He's vibrating with good humor, effusive and chatty. He doesn't actually touch the wine beyond that initial sip, but I might otherwise think he's drunk. I've seen my husband be funny before, and charming, but this is . . . a lot.

The doorbell rings.

"Who could that be?" Ken says in a tone that clearly says he knows exactly who it is.

The delivery men struggle with the enormous television set, but Ken directs them downstairs into the basement rec room. They set it up in record time and are gone in about half an hour. Eli's excited. I am confused.

"Popcorn?" Ken says. "Movie?"

Eli's entranced, already using the new remote to program in all the streaming channels I keep trying to convince Ken we should cancel without telling him why I want the money for other things. He looks over his shoulder at us with the biggest smile I've seen on him in a long time. "Can we?"

"Only after you've cleared off the table." Ken says this with a broad generosity in his tone. He's pleased with himself, with this gift.

Eli nods eagerly and heads upstairs. Ken stands in front of the new television, his hands on his hips. For a second or so, his expression is blank, mouth a little slack. When he faces me, though, he's smiling from ear to ear again.

"Well? What do you think?"

"It's . . . very big. Why?"

"The company got bought out. There's been some restructuring. New management."

Panic strikes me like a bell. "Your job—?"

"Don't you worry a thing about it. They're giving me a big bonus. Huge. Because I'm such a valued employee. I thought we deserved something nice."

I think of the failing water heater. The dishwasher that doesn't get anything clean. The mortgage. The credit card. The credit card he doesn't know about. My storage unit. There are so many other things we need that are not an expensive television set, but I can scarcely chide him about spending money on something we don't need. I have my multitude of flaws, but being a hypocrite is not one of them.

"I need to make this family my priority." Ken says this with determination, as though he's trying to convince me.

"How much of a bonus?"

He waves a hand, dismissing the question. "You don't need to worry about that. Let's just say it's enough to keep you in candy canes and curlers for a while."

Neither one of those things is something I use, but I'm supposed to chuckle fondly at the down-home folksy saying, so I do. "Seriously, hon. How much?"

"Greedy girl." There's a gleam in his eyes as he pulls me close.

His hands are on me, and he's kissing me, too much tongue, his lips too dry. His grip squeezes hard, pinching. The stairs creak as Eli returns, and Ken pushes me away to turn to his son with a huge grin.

"You pick the movie. Anything you want. Even one of those shoot-em-ups you're always begging to go see."

"You boys have fun. I'm going to go read."

Eli is already scrolling through the movie selections. Ken settles onto the couch. He gives me a glance.

"Can you make the popcorn for us first, hon?"

"Of course. I'll bring it down." Because that's my job, to make the popcorn, to clean the kitchen, to run the household. To keep my husband happy.

Later, while they're both still downstairs, I take my laptop to my bedroom so I can log in to our bank account. It shows a deposit in an amount large enough to fill my eyes with stars. A big chunk of it will be eaten up by that new TV, but the rest of it will go a long way toward everything else. For the first time in years, we'll have a little breathing room.

And I swear to myself, I swear it, I will not spend this money on anything other than what we absolutely need. Yes, I'll pay down the balance on my secret credit card. Of course I'll use some to pay for my storage unit in advance, that's just smart financial planning. But the rest of it will be used for practical things. Necessary things.

My heart races and I'm flushed as I shut down the laptop. I'm already imagining my endless hot showers, courtesy of a new hot water heater, when Ken comes upstairs. He tries to tell me about the movie they watched, but I don't care. He lets out a muffled noise of surprise when I pull him down onto the bed.

After it's over, beside me on the pillow, Ken lets out a light snore. I'm about to get up to use the bathroom when he turns to face me. His hand pins my hip.

"That was different," he says. "Where'd you learn that?"

I roll to face him. His features are a blur of shadow and line in the dim light. I could touch his nose, his lips, his cheeks and eyes, and I would know him, but right now he might as well be someone I've never met.

He pulls me closer. Finds my mouth with his. The kiss is hard, open mouth, probing tongue. When he pulls away, he's breathing hard.

"This is good, with us. Isn't it, Jewelann? We have a good life together."

I cup his cheek. "We do. Yes."

"Good. You're happy?"

"I'm . . . yes, of course I'm happy. Are you?"

The silence beats on for one breath too many before he answers.

"Of course I am," Ken says. "How could you think anything else?"

"Just checking."

We are quiet.

He says, "It would be terrible if one of us did something to mess this up. Wouldn't it? Tell me nothing's going to mess this up."

"Nothing," I tell him, "will mess this up. I promise, I won't let it."

# 14

"THE FAUCET IS dripping." Ken looms over me, hands bracketing his hips. Inspecting. Judging.

I look up from my place on the kitchen floor, where I've been on my hands and knees scrubbing at stubborn stains I'm sure are decades old. I look at the kitchen sink, then at him. "Yeah. It has been for a while."

"Why haven't you had someone come to fix it?"

"I've been meaning to," I tell him.

This is the longest stretch of time my husband has been here since . . . well, since I can't remember when. For two weeks, I've been making a grand show of housewifing while Ken "works from home." Every day he spends a few hours in his office with the door closed, doing whatever he does on his laptop. The rest of the time, he hovers.

"I wanted to spend more time with you and Eli," he'd said when he told me about the restructuring, how he'll be able to do more consulting from home. Less time on the road. "More like a nine-to-five sort of thing. This'll be great."

It has not been great.

I've always known my husband has expectations about how a household should be run. I've never had him watching over me all day long to see how I run it. If I leave the house, he wants to go with me, or he grills me about where I went and what I did. If I get a phone call or even a text, he's peering over my shoulder, trying to find out who I'm talking to. It's frustrating and exhausting. I wanted him to pay attention to me, but not like this.

Up to my elbows in sudsy water, my knees and back aching, all I want is for him to be out of the house so I can stop pretending I spend all my time cleaning or cooking. I want to go shopping, but with him here, I don't dare.

"What's going on with the holidays?" Ken asks abruptly.

Rosh Hashanah starts next Sunday night, but honestly, I've barely thought that far ahead. My parents belonged to the synagogue back when it had a thriving congregation with lots of kids the same age as me and Jonathan. We'd spent a lot of time there for services and events. I used to love going to the long High Holiday services. The melodies of the prayers, the feeling of belonging to a community, the food served after services in the social hall. Friends. Family. When you're not part of a majority, the times you can connect with other people like you are the ones that make memories. I'm nostalgic for that time, but I know it wouldn't be the same now, even if I did go back. Anyway, shul dues are expensive. So are High Holiday seats. I spend my money on other things.

"The usual. Dinner. They're having online services again this year, so I thought I'd do that on Monday. Jonathan and Eve are going to her mother's, so they won't be coming over."

I get to my feet with a small groan and empty the bucket into the sink, half filling it. My back throbs, so I stretch. The dirty water drains slowly. Too slowly. I swirl it with my hand until it starts to go down a little faster.

"Online services. Sounds great," Ken says from behind me. "Maybe I'll sit in."

I face him. "You won't be working on Monday?"

He shrugs. "I should take the day off. Eli should too."

"I told him he could stay home if he wanted to, but he's got a big test."

Ken's brow knits. "That's not right, having a test on a religious holiday. I mean, what's the point of putting him through all that rigmarole to have a bar mitzvah, if he's not going to observe the holidays?"

Ken grew up with Santa and a Christmas tree, but he's never been religious. He's always said that losing his entire family put him off the idea God being real. He's never prevented me from observing my own holidays, or raising Eli as Jewish, but he's never shown any interest in being an active participant. Most of the time he's not even around for the High Holidays.

"Schools around here don't make adjustments for the High Holidays."

"Well, that's just dumb. They're listed right there on the calendar," he says with the indignation of a person granted the privilege of belonging to a majority.

"You've never worried about this before—"

His expression grim, he cuts me off. "Maybe I never really thought about how important it was before. We should really make more of an effort, Jewelann. Maybe even start going to synagogue more often. Really become part of the community."

"If that's what you want," I say carefully, taken aback by this sudden, almost frenzied, interest.

I'd spent years taking Eli to Hebrew school, attending the required services, making sure he got his tutoring from the rabbi. Yet I'd never truly felt like we belonged there. Not the way I had when I was a kid. I hadn't let myself feel connected to the community, the same way I'd slowly isolated myself from friends over the years. I didn't even see my brother and his family as often as we should, considering they lived only an hour away, and that, too, was my doing. Invitations not extended, invitations not accepted, until finally, my sister-in-law had stopped sending them. We spoke a few times a year but rarely got together. No wonder my kid's a social mess. Look at the example I've made for him.

Ken's body is tense and stiff when I take hold of his biceps. I search his face. "I never thought it was important to you, that's all."

"It's important to me to have something solid. You couldn't understand. You have your brother. I don't have anyone. I don't even have any family photos. Everything was lost in that fire, Jewelann. You have no idea what it's like to lose everything."

I don't want to ever find out.

"You have someone, Ken. You have me. You have Eli," I tell him.

He shrugs out of my grasp and stalks to the sliding glass doors to stare out. His hands rest on his hips, that same familiar stance. "You have friends in this town. People you've known for years and years. I don't have anyone like that. I envy you, Jewelann. I really do."

This is news to me, since he's always been more than a little condescending about the fact he's lived all over the country, but I've never moved away from home.

"Why don't you invite your buddy over for the holiday?" Ken asks suddenly.

I'm confused. "Lisa?"

"No. Christian."

"He's not my friend," I say after a second.

Ken's lips pull back from his teeth. Not a grin, more like a grimace. "He said you two had been tight back in school. Lab partners."

"Oh. Yeah, well. That was a long time ago, hon." I force out a chuckle even as my cheeks burn.

"I wouldn't have rented the place to him if I didn't think you'd vouch for him, Jewelann. It was my impression that you'd been *good* friends. Am I missing something?" Ken's voice is gravelly. Concerned. There's some other tone, too, underneath the rest, but is it curious or sly or confrontational? I can't tell. I could be imagining it.

"High school was a long time ago, Ken."

He turns and crosses the few steps to me with long strides that take me by surprise. His arms go around me too tight, his hands moving down to squeeze my butt. He presses me against his crotch, grinding against me. His mouth finds mine. He pries open my lips.

"Ken—"

He pushes me back onto the kitchen table before I have a chance to say another word. Ken looks into my eyes, but whatever he's seeing is not my face. His gaze is hot, but distant. He's between my legs in a minute, fumbling with the drawstring of my lounge pants, stripping them down to my thighs. My calves. My ankles. He yanks off one leg, leaving the other dangling on my foot.

I gasp. He covers my mouth, even though we're alone in the house. He likes that, I think. Forcing me to be quiet. And this, too, is new and strange and it could be, should be exciting. Maybe it would be, with someone else.

Over Ken's shoulder, I see a figure moving on the deck. It stands in front of the sliding glass doors. Watching.

Christian's eyes meet mine as my husband thrusts inside me. Ken mutters words of lust or love, passionate sounds I don't want to decipher in case they're another woman's name. The table rocks. He moves faster. He's lost in this. I'm not.

Christian is still standing there.

It's not the first time I've ever pretended to be turned on when I wasn't. Not my first faked orgasm. I give this one my all, a performance worthy of an award, and all the while I'm watching Christian watch us. His expression is blank. His hands hang at his sides, but the fingers curl into fists.

Then, to my astonishment, what I was faking becomes real. In the last few moments before Ken finishes, so do I. The pleasure forces a cry out of my mouth. My eyes close as my body tenses and releases. I open them when Ken collapses on top of me, but I'm not looking at him.

Christian is gone, not even a shadow falling on the deck to show me he's still near the door. As Ken gets off me and I take the few steps to the sink to grab a paper towel, I look out through the window to see Christian crossing the yard. It takes a few minutes for him to get to the carriage house. That means it took him a few minutes to get from there to the deck.

And that, I think with a sudden shiver that is half revulsion and half something I can't name, means that Ken saw him coming before he pushed me onto the table.

He did it on purpose, to make sure Christian would see.

# 15

K EN HAS TAKEN Eli hiking for the day so that I can be free to cook and clean in preparation for erev Rosh Hashanah, which starts tonight. They won't be back until this afternoon. Plenty of time for me to make the rounds of estate sales this morning . . . but I'm proud of myself, because although I got the email listings for at least four, I haven't left the house.

I paid some bills, instead. I researched hot water heaters and dishwashers. I stuffed a turkey, now roasting. My sweet potato tzimmes is baking and the matzah balls are simmering. I even made a special round honey challah from scratch. Now, in my clean and quiet kitchen, I stand at my sink with my coffee in my hand and stare out the window, across the yard, at the carriage house.

I can't stop thinking about the way Ken made love to me on the table a few days ago—no. Not made love. There hadn't been much love in that at all. The memory of Christian watching us is what fills my mind.

I could be over to the carriage house in three minutes, fewer if I run.

Here's the thing about addiction. You can tell yourself you have it under control, and maybe you can even keep yourself from giving in to it, but there is no stopping the craving. There is only the struggle to resist. Sometimes that struggle is day by day. Sometimes, it's second by second, breath by breath, it's that free-fall space between one heartbeat and the next, when you hope you're strong enough to stop yourself, but you're not . . . quite . . . sure you'll be able to.

If I'd been what Christian always came back to, he was what I'd always run toward. I had abased myself for him. I'd willingly accepted the scraps of his attention and affection, knowing he was using me and not caring because being with him had always been a rush and a high that nothing else could replicate. I'd wanted to make him desire me again so I could turn him down, so I could wound him. I wasn't arrogant enough to think I could break him, but sting him? Yes. Make him doubt himself, even just a little? Oh, yes.

I'd walked away from him. I'd controlled my addiction. But the craving . . . that I can't stop.

A woman comes out of the carriage house. Her heels are high. Her dress, short. She carries a clutch bag under her arm, and she's scanning her phone, looking down the horseshoe driveway toward the street, where a car is pulling up. She waves and heads for it while I watch until my sneer becomes an open-mouthed circle of surprise.

It's Beth.

Christian comes out of the house a minute later. He wears scrubs and a lanyard around his neck with an ID badge. I wait until I see his car leave the driveway. Then, running, I cross the yard and let myself into the carriage house.

The rust-colored shag carpet in all the spaces is gone, leaving bare concrete beneath. The carpet is in rolls leaning against the spackle-dotted walls in one corner. Two small squares of slightly different shades of pale blue are painted on one wall. Two of light green on the other. The furniture has been pushed all to one end of the living room. The boxes are all stacked together at the other.

He's rearranged the furniture in the bedroom, too. His clothes fill the closet, no sign of the garment bags and shoe boxes I'd stored in there. Was that what he'd taken out to the curb in the trash bags? I'm enraged. I can't even remember what was in this closet before he emptied it, but that doesn't matter. Whatever it was, it was *mine*.

Just like he's supposed to be mine. Not Beth's. My fists clench, so I force myself to uncurl my fingers. I take a deep breath. It's none of my business who Christian sleeps with, and it's not my business if Beth cheats on her husband. I can hate it all I want, but I have no right to worry about it. If anything, I should thank her. If he wants a sugar mama, let her be the one, make him leave me alone.

An open suitcase on the bed tempts me to snoop. A few more items of clothing. Some toiletries. Nothing interesting or revealing, but what had I been expecting? A big sign that said "Hi, I'm Christian's Real Motivation for Fucking with Your Life?"

Working quickly, I start with the boxes in the living room. None of them are labeled, and many of them date back to before my parents had moved to Florida. Some are even older than that. I should carry them right out to the curb for trash pickup, but instead, one by one, rushing in case he comes back, I carry them over to my house. I don't have time to drive them all to my storage unit.

When Christian returns and sees the boxes have been cleared out, he will know I've been in the carriage house, but I don't care. He'll know I avoided him on purpose. Maybe he'll get the hint and back off.

My attic is narrow and low-ceilinged, accessed by a pull-down ladder. I have a few boxes stored up there. Some of Eli's baby clothes and toys. Bins full of old tax folders. That sort of thing. I need to move it all to one side to make room for what I'm putting up there now.

The box containing my old high school stuff is shoved toward the rafters, just out of reach of my grasping fingers as I stand on the ladder. I strain and manage to snag it enough to drag it closer. Moisture beads at my hairline and trickles down my spine. It stinks up here, dust and mouse turds and ancient insulation that's probably going to give me lung cancer.

Inside the box, photos and old notes and a couple of hardbound yearbooks mingle with other mementos from my youth. I flip open the yearbook from my senior year and a laugh bursts out of me at the sight of my black eyeliner, dyed black hair, black lips, black nails. I wore fishnet arm stockings. I touch the small face in the photo. No smile. Despite the getup, I don't remember being sad, not about life in general, anyway. Only and ever about *him*.

Turning back a few pages, I study Christian's picture. Under Future Ambitions, he'd listed "surgeon." His smile in the photo is shiny. Plastic.

Licking away the taste of salt on my upper lip, I look at the other pictures. Beth. Lisa. Toward the end of our senior section, Jen Tillis smiles into the camera. No hints that she would take her own life a year or so later.

There are a few pictures of her and Christian together. Homecoming Court. Prom. There aren't any pictures of me and him together, but I'd been with him on prom night too. After he'd dropped off Jen, he'd come to my house. We'd gotten high in the carriage house, and he'd buried his face against my neck, whispering words that sounded a lot like love if you were young and stupid enough to believe a guy with an erection could ever tell you the truth about anything.

The book closes with a snap in my two hands, and I shove it back in the bin. One day I'll sort through all of it and toss it out, but not today. As I'm shoving it back to its place beneath the rafters, I nudge a padded mailing envelope free of its place among some other bins.

Inside is a sheaf of photos held together by crumbling rubber bands. The pictures look to be from the sixties or seventies. Lots of plaid pants and wide ties. The names scrawled on the back are familiar, aunts and uncles and grandparents, and a melancholy sweeps over me. My parents must have missed taking this envelope when they moved.

Grief never really goes away, does it? It might hide for a while, like an envelope of pictures shoved out of sight in an attic, but it's still always there, ready to be discovered. Ready to hurt you all over again.

It takes me almost two hours to put all the boxes away. I'm filthy, and my clothes are rank and damp. I shower so quickly I don't even run out of hot water.

Noise from downstairs alerts me to the return of my husband and son. By the time I get to the hallway, Eli has already gone into his room and closed his door. Ken's in the kitchen, peeking into the pot of matzah ball soup.

"He didn't want to keep going," he explains. "The kid's soft."

I glance at the clock. "You were gone since eight this morning, Ken. How far were you planning on hiking?"

"Whatever, it doesn't matter, because he started complaining about it before we even got an hour in." He shakes his head. Hands on hips. Brow furrowed. "What's he going to do with his life, Jewelann?"

"He's not going to be a professional hiker." My retort is sharp.

Ken scowls. "He's not going to be a professional anything if he doesn't learn how to commit to something. You can't keep coddling him forever. He's got to toughen up."

"You talk about him like he's stupid. He's not." I've worried about Eli's life skills, but I've never once believed he lacked intelligence. "You're his father. You should be . . . kinder."

"My father made me the man I am," Ken says after a beat of silence, without turning around. "He didn't allow me to be soft. He made sure I knew exactly how to get along in life. He could be hard to please, but it was only because he loved me."

This is the most I have ever heard Ken say about his father, and although I think he means what he said to be positive, I'm hearing a hard undertone. When he finally faces me, his expression is aloof and cold.

"Do you want me to go talk to him?" I gesture at the ceiling.

"Will it make a difference?" Ken sounds snide. Derisive. He runs a hand through his hair, cutting his gaze from mine. He shakes his head. "Never mind, Jewelann. Forget about it. I'm going out for a run. I'll be back in time for dinner."

\*   \*   \*

I wait until he leaves before I knock on Eli's door. Of course I have to knock again, harder. When he opens it, his headphones are around his neck. From the doorway, I can see his laptop open on the desk. I recognize the header of the forum site I saw before that he's been browsing.

"Can I come in?"

He steps aside with a sweeping gesture that's not an actual welcome. More like an acquiescence. When I sit on the side of his bed, he slips back into his chair and closes his laptop.

"Dad says you didn't want to keep hiking with him."

He sighs, shoulders hunching, before spinning to face me. "He wanted to hike for like, miles. I mean, *miles*, Mom. He doesn't get it. I don't want to spend all day walking."

"You like it when we go out," I begin, but his expression stops me.

Eli's scowl reminds me of Ken. Nature, nurture, or neither? "He talks about himself all the time. He never listens to what I have to say about anything. He makes fun of anything I tell him I like. He has this entire picture of me that's not anything close to who I am. *You* know what I mean. He does it to you, too."

I do know what he means, but it's upsetting to hear that Eli does. "Your dad . . ."

"If you're going to say he means well, just don't." Eli shoves his hands into his hoodie pockets.

"He has a different idea of how things work. That's all."

"Yeah, an unreal idea."

"I'm sorry you didn't have a good time." It's the best I can think of to say.

"I wish he was more like Christian," Eli says, and I freeze.

". . . What?"

"Dad. He's not like Christian. When I'm hanging out with Christian—"

"Hold on," I say. "Since when did you start 'hanging out' with Christian?"

He shrugs. "He was heading into his place when I was getting home from school, and he asked me to help him with some stuff. So I did. And then we hung out a little bit. Sometimes I go over there after you go up to bed."

"What stuff? What do you mean, you go over there after I go to bed?" My mind races, trying to think of how this might have happened without me noticing.

Another shrug. "Moving some furniture. Ripping up the carpet. Stuff like that. Since Dad's been home so much, you've been going to bed early, and he hangs out in his office. I went out one night to check out the meteor shower, and

Christian was checking it out too. So we hung out a little bit. He knows a lot about constellations and shi—stuff."

I have been putting myself to bed earlier than usual, but learning my son has been leaving the house after dark without my knowing about it is unsettling. Guilt slashes through me. Mom being unconscious while he does whatever he does is probably quite familiar to Eli, even if it hasn't been like that in years.

"I don't want you leaving the house at night without letting me know, Eli. What if something happened to you?"

"Nothing's going to happen to me in the carriage house," he scoffs. "It's right in our backyard. And Christian's cool. He said he'll teach me how to lay flooring and stuff like that. He's really fixing it up. You should see it."

"I'll have to go check it out," I say lightly, although I've already seen it. His enthusiasm is so fresh, how can I dampen it? "Hey, are you sure you don't want to stay home from school tomorrow? I can write you a note. They'll have to let you make up the test."

He shakes his hair out of his eyes. "Are you going to services?"

"Only online."

"Are they doing Tashlich at the river?"

I pause. "I think so. They usually do."

When Eli was a toddler, I'd taken him to the service every year. The tradition of casting away sins by tossing bread into a body of moving water had been meaningful and kid-friendly. We hadn't gone since he was six.

"Could we go to that? It would be after school, so I wouldn't have to miss my test."

"We could," I say cautiously. "Are you sure you want to? It's . . ."

I can't bring myself to say aloud what it is. We both know. Eli nods.

"Christian says that if you want to get anywhere in life, you have to face the things that scare you."

A sudden rush of tears blurs my vision. I blink them away rapidly, hoping they don't spill out. I sit up straight and take a breath to keep my voice from shaking.

"That sounds like good advice. Why were you talking about things that scare you?"

Eli's smile is small, his expression thoughtful. "He asked me about who I hang out with at school and stuff. What kind of kids I knew, what they're into. What I'm into. I told him the truth. I don't really have any friends. And he asked me why."

"What did you tell him?"

Eli shrugs. "I said because nobody wants to hang out with the kid who wakes up screaming at sleepovers. So he asked me why I did that. And then we talked about stuff that scares us, and how to get over it."

"What did he say scared him?"

"Moooom," Eli says, drawing out the word. "I can't tell you something the dude shared with me in confidence. C'mon."

"Fair enough," I say, although it doesn't feel fair at all. "I'll take you to Tashlich. If that's what you want."

"Yeah. I do. It's a good thing, right? Getting rid of the bad stuff so you're not hanging onto it for the next year?" He grins.

"Yes," I tell him. "It's a good thing."

I am suspicious, though. For the first time, I text Christian. **Eli says he's been spending time over there at night. I don't think that's appropriate. In the future, please don't allow him to come over there after it's dark.**

The response comes in a minute later. **What are you worried will happen, Mama? I promise you the sorts of**

**things you and I did over here after dark are not going to happen with your kid.**

My jaw clenches. So does my fist, fingers gripping the phone. I force my entire body to relax before swiping away the text so there's no chance Ken can see it. Another text comes in before I can put away my phone.

**You need to give me notice before coming in my apartment, by the way.**

**It's my apartment.**

Three dots, bouncing. Then nothing. Dots.

**I'd have helped you move all that stuff out of here. All you had to do was ask.**

My fingers fly over the phone screen. **I will never ask you for anything. Ever.**

There's no hesitation in his response this time. No emojis or LOL or even any punctuation to give it a tone. Just three simple words.

**Yes you will.**

# 16

THERE'S A GROUP already gathered in Riverscape Park when Eli and I get there. We each have our small baggies of breadcrumbs. The rabbi is greeting people, but some are already tossing their crumbs into the water.

"Do you want to stand over there? Or down farther?" I point discreetly away from the group.

Performing Tashlich can be done without a rabbi's guidance. I downloaded the prayers onto an app for my phone. I don't read Hebrew, but I made sure to get an English transliteration.

Eli shrugs. "We can go down a little bit. We don't need to be part of the crowd."

A voice comes from behind me. "Jewelann Kahan? Is that you?"

The man behind us looks familiar. Older, grayer, a bigger belly. The same smile in his eyes, though. I bet he's got Werther's butterscotch candies in his pocket along with the crumbs.

"Mr. Stein?"

We don't hug, but he nods at me with another smile. "I haven't seen you in a long time. And this is your son. Elijah, yes?"

"Eli," he says with a nod. "We're here to do Tashlich."

"Well, now. Isn't that nice? It's good to see young faces here. Your mother and dad, Jewelann, they were so active in the shul. Now it seems like the congregation has become so small." Mr. Stein shakes his head with a small frown and a sigh. He looks past us to a woman standing with a younger woman carrying an infant and a man holding the hand of a little boy. "Excuse me, the kids are in from out of town with my grandbabies. So nice to see you, Jewelann. Maybe you'll stop by the shul again sometime soon. *L'shanah tovah.*"

When Mr. Stein is out of earshot, Eli says, "I remember him. He always had those candies in his pocket."

"Yes. The butterscotch." I watch the family greeting each other. People are moving down toward the water. The rabbi looks as though she's getting ready to lead the service.

Eli and I stand apart from the rest but still close enough that we can hear her. It's a short service, but I find myself moved by it. She guides us through the concepts of casting away our deceptions, arrogance, selfishness, indifference.

I add my own, silently. *I cast off indulgence. Greed. I cast off not letting go of that which does not serve me.*

"Aid us to stop carrying the baggage of our poor choices," the rabbi says, and I am weeping, still silent but not trying to hold back the tears.

The gathered people take their places along the edge of the water. Eli and I move even farther away. He holds the open baggie of crumbling bread in one hand, but he doesn't throw any yet.

"This isn't where they found his clothes," he says.

"No." But it's the same river.

Together, in silence, we stare at the water. To me it seems to move slowly, but I'm sure that's an illusion. If we fell into it, we could easily be swept away. We could drown.

Eli takes my hand. The last time I can recall us holding hands, his was so much smaller. It fit neatly inside the curve of my fingers, protected by mine. Now his hand dwarfs mine, and I'm the one who feels engulfed.

I hold it tight.

We stand there, watching the river take what everyone else has cast away, but it's not until most of that other group has dispersed that Eli and I let go of each other's hands. He steps closer to the concrete edge keeping the river in its place, and I stop myself from physically holding him back. He tosses his crumbs into the river, whispering under his breath.

I do the same, standing at his side. I empty my plastic baggie and tuck it into my pocket. He finishes about the same time and shoves his baggie into his hoodie pocket, along with his hands.

"Mom," he says, but nothing else.

I want to hold his hand again, but that moment has passed, maybe for truly the last time. He's so tall now, like his father. Eli hasn't been my little boy in a long time, but it's so suddenly clear how close he is to becoming a man.

"Mom," he says again. "When's Dad going back to work? I mean, going on the road."

I shake my head. "I don't know."

Eli keeps his eyes on the water. "It's just weird having him home all the time. I like it better when it's just us."

I lean closer. Lower my voice. I know I shouldn't say this, but I do anyway. "Don't tell your dad, but so do I."

"If I don't go to college, you wouldn't need so much money, right?"

"I told you not to worry about that. If you don't want to go to college because you don't want to go, we can talk about that, but I don't want you to think you *can't* go. Okay? I will always make sure you get what you need, Eli."

"I don't need you to stay with him," Eli says. "If you're not happy."

I don't know how to answer that.

He bends to find a few rocks and tries to skip them. One skips three times before vanishing beneath the water, and he turns to me with a grin so beautiful I want to cry. I let myself drink in the sight of him.

I was never one of those women who yearned for a child. I didn't babysit for extra money in high school. I didn't offer to take care of younger cousins at family parties. The idea of growing something inside my body, like a literal parasite, always repulsed me.

Ken was the one who wanted a child. I'd told him from the start I wasn't interested in parenthood. I didn't tell him about the abortion I'd had my senior year of high school, or the fact I'd asked my doctor every year since if I could finally get a hysterectomy. If I had cancer, they'd take out everything, but merely deciding for myself how I wanted to use my own body? Forget about it. Some vague shape of a potential father to my unborn children might want me to bear them, and I was told I had to honor that.

While sitting shiva for my mother, I stepped with a bare foot on some broken glass from a dropped casserole plate in her Florida kitchen. The wound got infected, and I was on antibiotics. I was grieving and careless and not surprised when my period was late.

I peed on a stick. Nine-ish months later, Eli was born. Ken had his son, and due to some birthing complications, I had my hysterectomy.

Oh, you hear those stories all the time, about how you look into your newborn's eyes and everything centers around that child for the rest of your life. It wasn't like that for me. I held the squalling, writhing bundle of him in my arms in that hospital bed and could think only, *Put it back. Or put it anywhere but back. Anywhere but here.*

We went home. Ken returned to work within days of our return, traveling for days on end. He'd wanted to be a father, but not to change diapers or do the midnight feedings or comfort a screaming child who can't be soothed. Eli and I were alone.

I could not sleep. I was in pain, torn apart and stitched back together. I mourned my mother, who surely would've flown in to help me, but who'd never had the chance to hold her first grandson.

The baby woke every three hours whether or not he was wet or soiled or hungry; I walked the floor for hours with him. Singing, soothing, praying my milk would come in. When it did, my nipples blistered, but he was fed, which meant that I wasn't totally failing as a mother.

Somehow during all of that, I turned from someone who'd never wanted a child into a mom.

Not a good one, though. Motherhood stressed me out. Reading the backs of food packaging, monitoring television time, dressing for the weather, eat your veggies, brush your teeth . . . it drained me. I never lived up to the image I had in my head of what a good mother should be and do. Maybe because I knew if it had been up to me, I'd never have had a kid at all. Maybe guilt for the child I'd chosen not to have. Maybe something deep-seated inside me that I would always lack.

I love my son, but I've always felt as though I was failing him. Now he's almost grown, and my heart breaks for the sunny little boy who'd say "Hi" to everyone as we walked through the neighborhood. The Mayor was what Mrs. Boonshoft called him, the elderly woman who'd lived across the street from my parents, and then us, until she'd passed away.

"A tragedy," she'd said. "Those poor parents, never knowing what happened. How's our little Mayor doing, then? It must be hard for him to understand. And for you, too, my dear. It's hard for a mother to watch her child suffer with grief. You'll want to protect him from it, of course. But if you don't mind an old lady's advice, I'll tell you not to hide the truth from him. Children always know when an adult is trying to hide something from them."

I'd never hidden the truth from him about his little friend Billy. I did the right thing, but the right thing and the worst thing turned out to be the same. That terror and sorrow had changed us both.

# 17

KEN'S PAYCHECK WAS supposed to hit the direct deposit yesterday, but because I was observing Yom Kippur, I didn't look for it until this morning. It wasn't there. Courtesy of the restructuring bonus he got, the balance in the account is higher than it's been in a long time, but it's been whittled away for the new hot water heater I had delivered and installed a few days ago. The new dishwasher is on back-order.

"Hon," I say when he comes upstairs from his office. "Is something changing with your paycheck?"

"I told you, I got that big bonus." He says this without concern, careless. "What's for lunch?"

Right. Lunch. Since he's been home during the day, that's one of the things he expects me to take care of.

"I think there's some lunch meat in the drawer. And yes, the bonus was in there from a couple of weeks ago, but aren't you supposed to also get your paycheck?"

He bends into the fridge to pull out the slender package of sliced turkey. He adds a bottle of mustard to the counter beside him. "Do we have any more tomatoes?"

A quick glance through the window over the sink tells me there are. "I can pick at least a couple more. Ken . . . hon . . . the paycheck?"

Ken grunts something that is not an answer and takes a plate from the cupboard. A knife from the drawer. He begins assembling his sandwich.

"You know, when I'm on the road all the time, sometimes all I really want is a simple sandwich. Do you know how hard it is to find a place that can do just a turkey on wheat, nothing fancy, none of this brioche buns and aioli crap? It's hard, Jewelann. Sometimes, almost impossible."

"Ken," I repeat, irritated.

"I'll call Marie at the office and find out about it, okay? Relax. They said there might be a glitch in the system while they restructure. That's one of the reasons why they gave such a big bonus. It's like an advance against the paychecks." He's facing away from me as he says this, and I'm glad, because I don't think I can hide the dismay writing itself in every line on my face.

"Like an advance . . . so, you have to pay it back?"

Ken laughs, scoffing. As though I'm an idiot for asking, although that's literally what an advance means. "No, of course not. But it might take a bit for it all to even out. That's all."

"It's just that I got the new hot water heater—"

"Yeah, I noticed. It's so much better than it was. I don't know why you waited so long," Ken says.

I test my words in my head before I dare say them aloud. "Any idea of when you'll get the paycheck? I need to know."

His voice changes a bit as he faces me. "There should be plenty of money in the account, Jewelann. Are you worried?"

Of course I'm worried.

Ken's always been the breadwinner. That's how he's always wanted it. Insisted on it, even, and it made sense when Eli was little for me to stay home and take care of things here, especially because Ken was on the road so much. He's always made a fine living, more than enough for what we should need. I'm the one who keeps us on this edge, the one who lives beyond her means, the one with the spending problem.

"The budget is supposed to be your job," he says. "But of course, now that I'm home more often, if it's too much for you to handle, I can take it over—"

"No. It's not too much for me to handle." And I can't lose control of it, either.

"Tomatoes?" he asks, holding up the single one from the counter.

"Right. I'll go get some."

"Great. You're the best. Have I ever told you how lucky I am to have you?"

"Never enough," I say.

I grab my harvesting apron and head out to the garden, where I spend a few minutes selecting the ripest tomatoes and peppers I can find. The plants have exploded with new fruit, but this late in the season it's a toss-up if they'll ripen on the vine before the frost comes.

The sound of a car pulling into the driveway turns me toward the carriage house. From this angle, I can't see the front door, but a car door slams and footsteps crunch along the walk. Christian is home. I've been waiting for two days for the chance to talk to him.

When he opens the door, his expression makes it clear I am not who he was expecting. He looks tired, hair rumpled, lines in the corners of his eyes. He wears a pair of sweatpants. No shirt. Bare feet. "Hey."

"Can I come in?"

I'm expecting a flirtatious grin or an innuendo, but he yawns and shrugs. "Sure. Fine. Whatever."

I inspect the space, noting the changes. Several black contractor bags sit by the front door. No new flooring has yet replaced the rust-colored shag carpet still rolled up in long tubes, but the bare concrete looks swept clean, at least. The walls are all painted pale blue, white trim.

"What do you think?" he asks.

"I'd like it much better without you in it."

"Ouch." He puts a hand over his heart, but his expression is sour. "That hurts."

"I hear you've been spending a lot of time with my son." In the kitchen, I open drawers and cupboards. He's stocked the fridge with beer and vodka but little else. A total bachelor pad.

"Help yourself," he says sarcastically.

I turn. "Eli says he's been helping you fix this place up. And that you've been giving him life advice."

"He's a great kid. A little weird, but we've been working on that."

Knowing something about your kid is different from hearing someone else say it out loud. "You're an asshole. You know that?"

"I believe someone might have told me that before, once or twice. Oh, yeah." He snaps his fingers. "It was you. Look, the kid comes by after school, he's clearly in need of a strong male influence. What am I going to do, tell him to get lost? That really *would* make me an asshole."

I think about Christian's advice to Eli, about facing what scares you. I hate that it makes sense. I hate that he's given my kid something I haven't been able to.

But I don't hate him.

Christian's gaze holds mine, that damned smile tipping up his lips in the corner as though he can read my mind. "You think really I'm going to do something to mess up your kid?"

"Don't you dare try."

Christian laughs and rakes both hands through his hair, standing it on end. He puts his hands on his hips, right above his waistband. His fingers dent his flesh.

"I like it when you get all Mama Lion. It's hot." He yawns, jaw stretching wide. The flirting falls so short I don't even feel like I can chide him about it.

I head for the front door. "Just so we're clear. Don't mess with him. I'll tolerate a lot from you, but not that."

That might have been the wrong thing to say, because his tired demeanor perks up. "You will, huh? Like what?"

"Like letting you live on my property, for one thing." My hand's on the doorknob.

His laughter tickles the back of my neck. "Hey, by the way, the toilet in here isn't flushing right."

"I thought you were supposed to be doing the handyman thing to get cheaper rent. Keep the receipts, and I'm sure Ken will take it off what you owe."

"I'm not a plumber, but okay. Sure. I'll take a look at it. I'm just letting you know. Hey. Jewelann," he says as I turn the doorknob. "Hang on. Look . . . can't we be . . . friends? Or at least, can't we be friend*ly*?"

"We were never friends." I feel like I keep denying it, over and over, but the only person who believes that is me.

"So what's stopping us from being friends now? High school was a long damned time ago, you know?" His voice lowers. I tense at the slap of his bare feet on the concrete as he comes closer, but he wisely doesn't try to touch me.

"High school isn't the only reason we can't be friends, Christian."

He has always been many things, but never stupid. Christian was never the clueless boy who hurt you because he just didn't get it. He always got it, and that cruelty always made the hurt so much worse.

"Tell me why," he murmurs.

"You were spying on us."

"So you did see me. I wondered if you were looking at me. I thought you were, but I couldn't be sure."

I press my lips together. "Did you like that?"

His low, soft laughter sends rivulets of ice up and down my spine. "Did I *like* watching you get railed by someone else?"

"You stayed for the whole show." I release a breath. "Did you get off on it?"

A shadow of something flickers over his expression. "Did *you*?"

When I don't answer him, Christian smiles. When he moves closer, I don't pull away. His fingers twist the errant strand of hair that had come out of my ponytail.

"What's going on with you and Beth?" I immediately regret asking, but it's worth the flicker of surprise that passes over Christian's expression.

"Who's been watching who, Jewelann?"

I shrug and fold my arms across my chest. There's a distance between us, but it could be crossed in a second. He frowns.

"Beth's just a friend. You don't need to worry about her. I've got plenty of room for you."

"I don't have any room for *you*." My sneer hurts my face.

Something at least masquerading as sincerity crosses his face. "You can't be happy with that guy. C'mon. He's—"

"He's my husband, Christian. The father of my son. Watch what you say about him."

He puts up his hands. "Fine. But he doesn't make you happy. He doesn't get you off. This happy little homemaker life? That's not you, Jewelann. Never was. Never will be."

"You don't know anything about me!"

He laughs. "I know everything about you that anyone could ever need to know. Kenny's the one who doesn't know who you are. Why do you put up with that? The way he talks about you—"

"How does he talk about me?"

"Like you're something he owns." Christian actually seems angry on my behalf. "Like you're stupid."

Icy fury floods me, but at who? Christian, or my husband? "Did it ever occur to you that I might love him?"

"But do you, though? *Do* you?" Christian makes a face.

"I'm not even going to dignify that with an answer," I tell him. "But I want you to leave me alone. Please."

"You won't even look me in the eye," he says in a low voice. "Did I really fuck you over that bad?"

I will admit nothing to him.

Christian's voice rises, rasping. "Why did you go upstairs to my hotel room? Why did you stay after they left, if you didn't want me? You know what? Never mind. It doesn't matter. You should have fucked me when you had the chance. You want me to leave you alone? No problem, Jewelann. Watch how alone I can leave you."

He takes me by the upper arm, his other hand turns the doorknob and neatly, easily, he sets me out on the driveway. He slams the door behind me. The lock clicks.

It's the promise from him that I wanted. Why, then, does it feel more like a threat?

# 18

"WHAT'S HE DOING in there?" Eli asks this in a low voice. Ken's been tinkering in the kitchen for the past hour, trying to fix the leaky faucet and figure out why the sink's been draining so slowly. Before that, he'd gone to the carriage house to check on the plumbing issues over there. Eli and I are in the living room, working on some homework he doesn't really need me to help him with.

"He's fixing the sink."

Eli's eyebrows raise. He looks toward the kitchen, where Ken is whistling. The sound is piercing, an out-of-tune warble I don't recognize. Every now and then it stops, and I hope he won't start it up again. He always does.

"Is he ever going to start traveling again? It's been almost a month. He's never home for this long." Eli turns his attention back to the papers in front of him on the coffee table.

We haven't spoken about our conversation by the river, but it hangs between us now.

"I'm sure it will be soon." I hope it will be soon.

From the kitchen, Ken shouts what sounds like a curse. Eli frowns as he looks that way. Clouds cover his expression. My heart twists at the sight.

Ken shouts louder. There's a horrific clatter. I get to my feet.

"Hon? You okay?"

"This fucking thing—!"

Eli and I look at each other. Ken never swears. He rarely even raises his voice. I've seen him angry, stern, disappointed. I've never heard him scream like this.

"Mom."

I should go see what Ken is doing, but I'm frozen in place as we both listen to him shout and break things. When I finally force myself to move, I find him in the kitchen with the faucet torn apart and a wrench in one hand. He's breathing hard.

"This fucking thing," he repeats with a gesture at the mess. His eyes are wild, lips wet with spittle. High color paints his cheeks.

The sight of me seems to put some sense back into him. He smooths his hair with the hand not holding the tool. He sets that on the counter, carefully, lightly. His hands go into that familiar pose on his hips as his back straightens. His smile is hard.

"I just want," he says, now calm, "things to be in order. Is that too much to ask? I want my house to be clean, my kid to behave like a normal goddamned person, and my wife to be home where she can take care of everything, and I want to work so I can take care of them both. Does that make me a bad man, Jewelann?"

"Of course not." I think, *he knows*. He went over there, and Christian told him about the hotel room. About everything else.

Ken draws in a breath, his shoulders rising and falling. "I just want to be *happy*. Don't *you* want that?"

"Yes, of course I do." My voice wavers, so I clear my throat.

"Everything's going to be okay, Jewelann. It's going to be fine. I'm taking care of everything. I even called Marie about the paycheck snafu. This new accounting system has it all bungled up. My next check should go in, no problem. Just try to go easy on the shopping sprees until next month. How many pairs of shoes do you really need?"

It is the first time, ever, that he's even acknowledged my shopping habit. I force a laugh, giddy and giggly, and wave a hand in his direction as though he's caught me out. "You know a gal can never have too many pairs of shoes."

"Well, hold yourself back a little bit."

Hold myself back a little bit, he says. I haven't hit an estate sale or thrift shop in weeks. I've only spent money on things we really need, which does not scratch the itch. I'm used to watching the money go out, but since that bonus hit, there hasn't been any coming in.

"I was thinking about maybe checking in with that temp agency I was with before I had Eli. You know, for a little 'me' money," I tell him casually.

His expression darkens. "You know how I feel about you working. I've been kind of a fuddy-duddy lately, and I'm sorry. But I always take care of you, don't I? Hmmm?" He puts a finger beneath my chin to tip up my face. His breath is sour.

"Eli's in school all day. In a few years he'll be out of the house. I don't need to be a stay-home mom forever, Ken. I need . . . more."

"So join a book club. Take up a hobby. I don't want you to need a *job*. That's never how it's been with us. My dad worked so my mom could stay home, and that's always what I wanted. That's been the routine. Bad things happen when you try to break out of the routine, Jewelann. A strong and happy home is based on a strong foundation. And we have to work on that together. Don't we? Can I count on you? Because you can count on me. I promise you." He moves closer but doesn't touch me. "Hey, I have an idea. What do you say we go out for dinner tonight? A date. You and me. Like a real married couple."

Somehow, we are swaying, dancing, with his hands on my waist. I laugh a little awkwardly. "Aren't we already a real married couple?"

"I haven't taken you out in a long time. You should get dressed up. Be treated to a night out. How about it?"

"What about Eli?"

"He's sixteen," Ken's tone is short. He looks annoyed. "He's not a baby, even though you insist on treating him like one. He can make himself dinner. He'll probably love having the house to himself for a few hours."

"Sure. Okay." I push up to kiss his lips. Anything to keep him happy. "I'll go get ready."

"Wear that black dress you wore to my company party," he calls after me as I climb the stairs.

I freeze, a hand on the railing. I turn to peek over it at him. "I was going to wear the blue—"

"I want to see you in the black. Heels. Those diamond earrings that were my mother's."

It's the same exact outfit I wore to the reunion. "That's really dressy, Ken."

"If you can't get dressed up for a date with your husband," he says, "who can you get dressed up for?"

Beneath my hand, the smooth wooden railing feels suddenly slippery. "Nobody?"

"That's my girl," my husband says.

He takes me for sushi, even though he doesn't like it and orders a noodle dish instead. He even orders wine and dessert, and he whisks the bill away before I have a chance to see it. He pays with cash, a small sheaf of bills that's depleted quite a bit by the time he tucks it back into his pocket.

"Courtesy of the rent from your buddy," he says. "Oh, sorry. I forgot. You barely know each other."

Ken's stare is intense. He rubs his thumb over the back of my hand, over and over. I want to pull it away, but I don't.

My bland, adoring smile sits on my face like a mask. "I guess it's a good idea to have a tenant, after all. You were right."

"I'll certainly feel better about having someone on the property once I'm back on the road," Ken says. "I'll be starting back tomorrow, by the way. Bright and early. Turns out they just can't trust any of the new hires to maintain the relationships with the clients. I'm the best they've got."

"I'm sure you are."

"Best to get home, though. Since I'm leaving in the morning."

At home, when we try to pull into the driveway, it's already full of cars. We have to park at the curb. The carriage house is ablaze with light. Shadows move behind the curtains, and even from the street I can hear a thump-thump-thump of music. I imagine Beth over there, dancing with her blonde hair tumbling all down her back, her face flushed and eyes gleaming. I imagine Christian kissing her. My sushi dinner isn't sitting steadily any longer.

"Someone's having a party," Ken says but otherwise seems unconcerned.

In our bedroom, he presses himself against me. The sex is fast, even frantic. He clutches at me with what almost seems like desperation. I want to enjoy it, but he's doing nothing to get me even close. For the first time in all the years we've been together, Ken doesn't finish.

He withdraws, breathing hard. I can smell the sour tang of body odor in the cool air between us. He sits on the edge of the bed, facing away from me. In the quiet, I can hear the party from the carriage house, faint but still going on.

I touch Ken's back. His skin twitches under my fingertips. He shifts, looking at me over his shoulder for a second before he gets out of bed.

"I've got some stuff I need to do. Paperwork stuff before I leave. I'll be up in a while. Don't wait for me."

I sit up after he's gone. I draw my knees to my chest, resting my face against them.

He knows, I think.

He can't know.

He *knows*, I tell myself and hold back a shuddering sigh that fights to become a sob. I'd made a valiant effort, but I had been a fool to think that just because I'd been able to keep some of my darkest secrets, that I'd be able to keep all of them.

CHAPTER

# 19

A SERIES OF TREMORS rips through my entire body as I think of Ken finding out about . . . everything. Quaking, I swing my feet over the edge of the bed. I stagger toward the bathroom. I think I might throw up, but even then, my feet won't move fast enough. The floor shifts beneath them, and I have to clutch the dresser to make sure I'm standing still. I'm outside of myself, drifting but tethered. If I suck in a breath, will I return to my body, or will I simply float away?

My eyes close tight. This feeling of being unmoored is awful now, but it's the same one I used to chase. I could take or leave alcohol, but I've always loved being high.

Skunky weed in a joint under the football field bleachers on a Friday night because that was what everyone did. After school before my parents got home. Eventually, I started to smoke up in the mornings before class. I would float, float, float, until the world crashed back in around me and I started thinking about the next time I could smoke. I wasn't depressed. I had friends and nice parents and teachers who mostly liked me. I just really, really liked being high.

The first time I ever got stoned on downers was with Christian. He stole his mother's "little helper" from her dresser. It was different from smoking. A tiny little bit of bitterness on the tongue, and after a while, bliss. Serenity. I liked living in a haze, moving from moment to moment with nothing being able to penetrate it. I didn't care about anything, because I couldn't care about anything.

Years later, finding a doctor to prescribe something similar had been easy enough, at least at first. Because that's what they do, don't they? Tell women we are supposed to be happy with our lives, and when we aren't, a pill will make it all better . . . only needing the pills means we are bad wives and mothers, which then makes us feel even more miserable, which means we want and crave the pills that take away the pain we aren't supposed to feel.

I have not been high since Eli was in kindergarten.

I have wanted to be high every single day since then, but it wasn't until Christian showed up back in my life that I actually felt like I might slip back into those old, bad habits. Right here in my bedroom I want to fall onto the cold floor with my face pressed to the worn carpet and never get up again.

I go into the basement, but not to knock on Ken's office door. I can hear a low murmur of voices, some music. He's watching a video. It doesn't sound like porn. I wouldn't care if it was.

In the powder room that's also the laundry room, I check the envelope tucked behind the drainpipe. It rattles as I ease it free. My mouth puckers with the remembered taste of the glue I licked to shut it. The flap gapes, now, and a single pill slips free. It bounces on the bottom of the cabinet, and I watch it disappear into the hole around the drainpipe. I try to feel for it, but my fingers come away stained with rust and cobwebs. I can't get them deep enough into the space to find a small pill.

And that's where I am. Willing to stick my fingers in a dark hole for the possibility of finding a pill amongst the dirt and bugs. And then what? Would I put that dirty pill on my tongue, let it dissolve, tasting of mouse shit and desiccated millipedes? I disgust myself.

I put the envelope in my pocket.

"Jewelann. What are you doing?"

Slowly, carefully, I turn around. I get to my feet and keep my voice calm although it wants to waver. "The kitchen sink is draining so slow. I was making sure this bathroom drain isn't stopped up or anything. You know we had the problem down here a couple of years back. I just wanted to make sure—"

Two years ago, on Christmas Eve afternoon, there'd been a major backup in this bathroom. I'd called a local plumber, totally forgetting about the holiday I didn't celebrate, but there wasn't anyone available to come out for a few days. Ken had managed to do something to it before then. I'd cleaned up the mess. We turned off the water to the toilet and canceled the plumber. The bathroom had become one of those things families deal with, the broken things you step over or work around or pretend are fine even though they periodically overflow.

Ken looks past me, at the open cabinet door. His gaze drops to the pocket of my robe. I don't know if the corner of the envelope is sticking out. I don't touch it to find out. I don't even look.

"What were you doing in the kitchen so late?"

"I got a little snackish. Sushi, you know." I pat my belly and give him a smile. "Doesn't stick."

Ken rakes a hand through his hair, standing it on end. His forehead glimmers. He swipes his fingertips across his mouth before putting his hands on his hips. "You scared the heck out of me."

I used to rave in underground, black-box clubs and wear platform boots that gave me an extra six inches of height. I pierced my own ears with a safety pin. I used to have a personality. Now, I'm married to a guy who says "heck" unironically.

I close the cabinet behind me and ease out of the bathroom, past him. The door to his office is open. From here I can see through it to the tool bench that had been my father's. A few of the tools have been missing for years, but the outlines for them are marked with permanent ink on the pegboard remain, a reminder of my father. A reminder of how quickly life can change.

Ken stares. "Is the drain in there okay?"

"Seems to be. When you went over to the carriage house, did you manage to fix the toilet?" I head for the basement stairs and say this over my shoulder. I want to put distance between myself and my old hiding place.

"Seemed to be fine. Call a plumber if you're worried about it. Jewelann," he says, and I pause.

Turn.

"Hmm?" Sleepy eyes, slack lips, I'm on the way to bed, nothing to worry about. Just a pretty little wife with nothing going on in her dumb-blonde head. Nothing to worry about.

Please, not a thing.

"Are you coming up?" I ask him, all soft and breathy. A caricature.

"Soon," he says. "Good night."

I force my feet to move. Up the stairs. Through the kitchen, the hall, up the other flight of stairs. Down another hall, with a pause at Eli's door to make sure I can't hear anything from inside. He's too old for me to go inside and tuck him in, to brush the hair off his slightly sweaty sleeping face, to kiss his cheek softly enough not to wake him up. But I want to with a fierceness that makes my heart ache. All I've ever wanted is to protect my boy; all I can do is keep trying.

In my bathroom, I lift the lid of the toilet and spill the contents of the envelope into it. I'm already flushing it as they spill into the swirling water. I don't know how many were in the envelope, but I shake and shake it until I'm certain they're all gone.

There's a small bit of powder on the inside of the worn and crumpled paper. I lick my finger and drag it through. I touch the tip of it to my tongue, closing my eyes, waiting for the bitter taste to fill my mouth. There's not enough powder in there to make a difference, or the pills are too old. I can taste only the sourness of my guilt, which does not wash away even when I brush my teeth hard enough to make my gums bleed. I flush the toilet again, making sure all the pills are gone.

The music from the carriage house surges louder, then fades. Furious, I go to the window. A dark figure skulks across the lawn, heading for the house. I'm livid. I told Eli I didn't want him going over there after dark, and especially not while there's an obvious party going on.

I expect to confront him sneaking into the kitchen, or maybe even on the staircase, but by the time I get down there, the kitchen light is still dark. I stare out through the sliders, but I can see no signs of anyone in the yard at all. The carriage house door opens, spilling out light and a few more figures onto the driveway.

A creak on the basement stairs has me whirling to face it. The door rattles in the frame, but lightly. Is that click of it closing, or an air current shaking it? This old house is full of creaks and groans. Another few creaks and the slide of a hand along the basement banister, then silence. Eli wasn't the one sneaking across the lawn.

It was my husband.

# 20

T HE PLUMBER FIXES the leaky kitchen faucet and makes sure the drainpipe is reattached correctly, but he says there's not much he can do about how slow the water drains. He suggests calling a company that will come in with a camera on a long tube that can check out the pipe, see if something's blocking it.

"You have some big trees back there along the back of the property," he says. "Could be roots. Most of the houses in this plat are hooked into the city sewer system. You still have septic? What about a well?"

"Yes, septic, but city water."

"You know you can get hooked up to the city sewer, too, right?"

I do know that. It costs about fifteen thousand dollars to do the work. The city sent a letter about it a few years ago.

"How much would it cost to get someone to do the camera thing?" I tuck my hands beneath the points of my elbows, arms crossed over my stomach.

"Couple hundred bucks, maybe? But they'd be able to rotor out anything that's in there, roots or whatever. That'll cost more, obviously." He spins a finger in the air. "You said you started having more issues after you got a tenant back there?"

I nod.

"He got a washer and a dryer over there? Dishwasher?"

"No dishwasher, but there is a washer and a dryer. Yes."

"Probably an old toilet, too? The old one takes about six gallons for each flush. You might oughtta invest in some new ones. Way more efficient. Anyway," the plumber says, "all that extra use could be putting more of a strain on the system. Honestly, I'd get someone out there to take a look at that old tank. They do fail after a time."

"Could he have been doing something to make it fail? On purpose, I mean."

The plumber looks bemused. "I guess so. He could be flushing stuff that's not meant to be flushed. If he really wanted to bork your system, yeah, he could do that. He could be running water, nonstop, something like that. Has your water bill been noticeably higher? More than normal extra use?"

"I haven't had the quarterly bill yet."

He taps the side of his temple. "Keep an eye on it. But it's probably just age. And if you think your tenant is deliberately trying to ruin it, you might oughtta consider booting him out."

I would if I could.

The plumber says the company can send a bill, and I take that option. Buy now, pay later. I'm used to that.

I busy myself with my usual Friday afternoon tasks but pause at setting the table. Two places, or three? Will Ken be home for dinner? He's been gone since the morning after I saw him sneaking across the yard; he never even came to bed that night and left before I got up. It's been four days.

Four days of seeing the lights on in the carriage house, late into the night. Strange cars in the driveway at all hours. Strange people leaving. Music thumping. Christian hasn't contacted me at all. Not once.

I *do* hate him.

My son doesn't, though.

I don't want to give Christian any credit for any of it, but I also can't deny that Eli's friendship with him has seemed to encourage a blossoming. A confidence Eli didn't used to have. He even has friends, or at least kids he's been hanging out with after school. People are texting and calling him.

"Mom, Christian says he's getting tickets to a Blizzrd show, and he's going to take me." Eli waits until after I've said the blessing over the challah to announce this, but his tone tells me he was just waiting for the chance.

I pause in tearing off a piece of bread. "Who? Where?"

"Blizzrd," my son repeats. Impatient. Derisive. "At the Downtown Stop."

"Is that an under-twenty-one venue?" I take my own seat.

"Dunno. I don't think so, except for the concert. Anyway, you can go with an adult." Eli dishes himself a full plate of gooey lasagna. The sauce and melted cheese spread out all over the plate, making a mess he doesn't seem to mind as he digs in.

"I'm not sure I like this idea."

Eli pauses mid-shovel. "Blizzrd haven't played around here since before COVID, and they announced they're breaking up after this tour. It's the last time they'll ever be playing together again. I'm going to that concert."

His flat tone sets me back. It's not an argument, if only because he's making it very clear he's not making any compromise. A thin fury fills me. Not at Eli, but at Christian.

I rejected him, so now he's going after my son. Maybe my husband too.

"I don't like you spending so much time with him, Eli." My silver kiddush cup was my father's, and it's heavy. I lift it, sipping, and set it down carefully so I don't spill.

Eli laughs. The sound of it is bright and genuine, and it's been so long since I heard anything like that from him that I am at first convinced it didn't come out of his mouth.

"Mom," he says, sounding too much like Ken. Indulgent. As though I'm an idiot, but one he's fond of.

"He's my age, Eli."

"Yeah, but *he's* cool," Eli says. "Did you know he's been like, all around the world?"

"I didn't."

"Well, he has. He says I should think about taking a gap year. Do something, like real-world experience, before I go to college." Eli drags his fork through the mess on his plate. Takes another bite.

"Somehow, I doubt your dad will be down with you taking a gap year." I push a napkin toward him for the sauce at the corners of his lips.

Eli wipes his mouth. "Just because you guys have never gone anywhere or done anything—"

"What are you talking about? He travels all the time."

"*You* never do," Eli replies in a low voice. "Christian's been to Bali, Mom. New Zealand. He even went to *Japan*. How cool would it be if I did a gap year in Japan?"

"Very cool," I admit. There's a glow in his eyes that used to be there all the time when he showed me the forts he built, the pictures he drew, the sparkly rock he found in the park. I haven't seen him look like that in so long.

"Christian says I have all the time in the world to go to school."

"Yes, well, Christian is not your parent."

Eli puts his fork down with a clank. "You're always nagging me about making friends, being more social. But now that I am—"

"Friends your own age," I interrupt.

"Christian said I could take a friend to the concert. I asked Ryan Lee, and he said he wants to go. And we can't go without an adult. Shit."

I rap the table with my knuckles. "Hey. Language. We can have a disagreement without you cursing."

"Sorry." He has the grace to look sheepish. His brow furrows, but he meets my gaze straight on. "I'm sorry, Mom. But I have to go to the show. If I back out, Ryan will think I'm a giant dick."

He must be able to tell that I'm still not happy about this, because he adds, "Christian actually talks to me. Dad never . . ."

He trails off. I serve myself a sloppy slice of falling-apart lasagna. I don't have much appetite for it now.

"What do you two talk about?" I don't contradict Eli about Ken. There'd be no point. What Eli said about him was true.

Still, I am wary of this relationship between my son and Christian Campbell, growing like a tumor. Malignant. I know too well how charming Christian can be. How he can make you feel like you're special. How quickly he can make you feel worthless, too.

"Everything," Eli says. "We talk about everything."

I wonder if this is true. It can't be. We might not speak of them, but surely there are still things my son could only talk about with me.

"He says you and him were tight in high school," Eli says now.

Nothing in his voice indicates that Christian told him exactly, in what way, we'd been close. I'm sure Christian never mentioned the times he cut me cold in front of other people only to show up at my door later, expecting me to let him in. I always let him in. I'm sure Christian cannot have told my son about the things we did in the carriage house where he now lives.

"Yes," I say. "We used to be close."

Eli looks at me. He chews slowly. Swallows. "So why don't you like him now?"

"He's arrogant, Eli. And he exaggerates about himself."

"You're saying he's a liar?"

"I'm saying," I reply gently, "that Christian Campbell is the sort of guy who tells a *good* story, but it might not be a *true* story. He makes promises he doesn't keep. So if it turns out that he doesn't get those tickets, or for some reason he cancels on you—"

"He's not going to do that," Eli protests.

"I don't want you to be disappointed, that's all." I cover up the tremble of my lips with my napkin.

"But you're going to let me go, right?" His earlier defiance is not quite gone, but it's subdued.

"I'll talk with him about it. Okay? I'm not giving you an answer until I get the details."

"Promise me you'll talk to him."

I sigh. "I promise. Okay?"

He's mollified. We finish the meal in relative silence. I give up on asking him questions about school when I get only one-word answers. Eli excuses himself, getting up from the table to take his plate to the kitchen.

"Don't use the dishwasher," I call after him. "I'm still trying to figure out what's going on with the drain. In fact, just leave the dishes in the sink. I'll wash them."

He peeks his head back into the dining room. "You sure?"

"I'm sure."

Eli knocks on the doorframe, a rapid one-two-three. "Okay. I'm going upstairs, then."

"Do you want to watch a movie in a little bit?" I'm sure he will decline.

"Like what?"

"Like whatever you want," I say, surprised and hopeful.

"Maybe." He shrugs.

It's better than a "no." I'll take it. In the kitchen, I wash each dish carefully, running the water on low and watching for any signs that the drain is backing up. The water goes down, but slowly. So long as I don't use too much at a time, it seems to be okay, but clearly something is wrong. I do a quick web search for places that will come out with the camera, like the plumber suggested.

Tomorrow, I think with a glance at the clock. It's after dinner, now. And it's Shabbat. I'll do it tomorrow.

To my delight, which I keep tamped down so I don't embarrass him, Eli consents to settling in for a movie with me. He picks some action flick with lots of guns and shooting and car chases, a sequel to a long-running franchise I haven't seen before. I'm not entirely sure what's supposed to be happening, but I don't think the plot really matters. I take surreptitious glances at my son's face, lit up in the glow from Ken's enormous TV and with glee as he gets into whatever's going on in the movie.

It's a good night.

He seems happy.

His phone is what eventually pulls him away. A series of texts he answers with a chuckle or two. He doesn't even look at me when he says, "I'm going up to bed. 'Night."

A good mother doesn't begrudge her child a social life, especially not after worrying for so many years that he'll always be on the outside. She encourages whatever helps him grow and succeed. I've always wanted Eli to fit in. I wish Christian wasn't the one offering my son all of this.

I wish he was offering it to me.

CHAPTER

21

"WOW, ARE THOSE tomatoes?" Lisa shades her eyes to look across the yard as she settles into the Adirondack chair on my back deck. "In October? It's almost Halloween."

When she found out Ken was out of town, she and Beth invited themselves over for what Lisa called an "adult playdate." I thought this meant coffee, but the two of them showed up with their own bottles—yes, multiple—of wine.

"It's been so warm," I say with a shrug. "They'll keep going until we get a frost."

Beth sets her bottle on the side table. "I can't grow a damn thing in my yard. The soil around here is so bad. What's your secret? Never mind, Jewelann, you're going to tell me you do something crunchy like compost, and I just don't have the time for that."

"I *do* compost," I say with a self-conscious laugh. I can barely stand to look at her face. Jealousy tastes like the smell of stagnant water. "Anyway, the grass is always greener over the septic tank, right? So's a garden, I guess."

"Erma Bombeck was *not* crunchy," Lisa says in an aside as she opens the first bottle.

Beth groans. We all know everything there is to know about Erma Bombeck, since she was raised and lived in Dayton, in a house not too far from mine, actually. "How can someone who wears Louboutins be crunchy?"

I stretch out my legs to point my toes, clad in Frye boots, not Louboutins. "I don't garden in them."

"Gawd," Beth says. "If I had a pair of Louboutins, I'd do everything in them."

"You wouldn't. You'd be too afraid of messing them up. That's what shoes like that do. Make you afraid to wear them," I say.

It's early to be drinking. Just past eleven. Somehow, I think Beth and Lisa have made this a habit. I accept the glass of white wine Lisa pours into a delicate Waterford crystal glass. Estate sale. The entire set had been under fifty bucks—champagne flutes, white and red wine goblets. This is the first time I've ever taken more than one out of the china cabinet.

"Burn the candle," Lisa says. "My grandma used to tell me that all the time. Why have pretty things, if you don't use them?"

She takes a pull off the vape pen she got out of her purse. She uses a sanitizing wipe to clean the tip and hands it to Beth, who offers the pen to me, but I decline. Beth shrugs. Takes a draw. Holds it. The smoke that puffs out of her open mouth is pale, translucent. I catch a hint of weed smell, but only that.

"No, thanks. I haven't done anything like that in years," I say.

Lisa settles back into her chair, letting her chin tip up toward the sky. She sighs happily and slants a glance my way. "You used to be a real stoner back in the day."

"Weren't we all?" I give an involuntary look across to the carriage house, where I used to get high with friends.

With Christian.

"*I* wasn't. I wasted my youth on being 'good.' I mean, I'm not judging you, Jewelann," Beth says, although she totally is. "But you also had a little . . . thing . . . didn't you? With pills?"

They both look at me. I set my jaw and sit up straight. I'm not ashamed, I remind myself. I have nothing to be embarrassed about. Beth does, though. She just doesn't know that *I* know.

"It's not like I had to go to rehab or anything like that. I just let it get out of hand."

Lisa nods sympathetically. "It could happen to anyone. After Gary died, I swear there were some days the only difference between me and the guy who stands in front of the Liquor Mart with the cardboard sign was that I had all my teeth."

"You're still a fucking lush," Beth says, but clearly the joke is an old one between them, because they both laugh.

I don't think it's funny, but I smile grimly. "Addiction is hard to overcome. Some people use drugs. Some drink wine in the middle of the morning. Some make themselves puke after eating."

Shots. Fired. Beth blinks rapidly, her mouth thinning, but not into a frown. Her grim smile is also grudgingly respectful.

"I haven't done that since high school," she says.

Lisa lifts her glass. "Well, I'm unabashedly a midmorning drunk, and I'm not ready to quit it yet. So cheers, bitches."

Beth leans forward to clink her glass against Lisa's, and after a second, so do I. They drink. I sip. The wine is too sweet for me.

Beth gives a low, throaty laugh. "When is your hubby supposed to be home?"

"Later today. Maybe tonight." Somehow, that glass of too-sweet wine is empty. I lift my face to the out-of-season sunshine and close my eyes. The weather this week is still supposed to be in the seventies, but fall is inevitable, and winter after that, and I'm looking forward to it. Long, dark nights, excuses not to leave the house. Frozen ground.

"Same," Beth says in a different tone this time. "Only mine's not traveling. He's just 'working late' with that bitch from accounting."

It's the first time since she got here that she sounds sincere about something. A little sad. Lisa leans over to squeeze her shoulder and gives me a look. I'm not sure what she expects me to say.

"You get married, you think it's supposed to last forever, right? And then your husband starts 'traveling.' Or 'staying late at the office.'" Beth draws in a long, deep sigh. "I'm like, living in a *Mad Men* episode, I swear. And maybe if I was married to Don Draper I could deal with it, but I'm married to Steve Richards, who works for a furniture warehouse and can't get his athlete's foot under control. I mean, he has it on his damned *balls* because he can't keep his hands off them."

She convulses with disgust, squirming in her chair. Lisa bursts out a small, strangled laugh and looks embarrassed. Beth glares at her, then dissolves into slightly sodden laughter herself, a mix of tears and hilarity. I join after a few seconds, not sure what the hell is going on. A flare of sympathy for Beth surprises me.

"It's disgusting," Beth says.

Lisa looks sympathetic. "Men are pigs."

"I know. But who else would have me?"

I share a look with Lisa. Hers says she's heard this all before, but I'm stunned. Beth had been a pretty girl, and she became a pretty woman. I doubt she has to work at it, either. Not as hard as I do.

Beth turns to me. "You don't have any clue. Look at you. You look better than you did in high school. I've got an ass the size of the *Titanic*. Crow's feet. And I've seen your husband around town, Jewelann. He's *hot*."

I blink. "You've got to be kidding me."

"You know he is," Lisa chastises.

"But you . . . you're . . ." I wave my hands, helpless to put into words exactly what I'm trying to say.

Beth rolls her eyes. "Three kids, stretch marks, saggy tits. I used to complain about how Steve was always on me, but now he doesn't even look at me. We haven't had sex in three months. Three. *Months*."

I reach for the bottle to pour some more wine. If there's a moment to let them in, it's this one. But I'm wary of these women. Cautious about sharing too much. I'd thought that renewing a friendship, or in Beth's case creating one, might be good for me, but it's clear that neither of them is going to be a positive influence. Still, is it wrong for me to want someone to talk to?

*Christian says that if you want to get anywhere in life, you have to face the things that scare you.*

The inside of my cheek is sore from where I've bitten it too many times. I probe the pain with my tongue before speaking. "I think Ken might have someone else that he sees when he's on the road."

My hesitant laugh scratches at my throat. I see by their expressions that both of them understand. Here the three of us sit, middle-aged women drinking wine before noon. None of us happy, but all for different reasons. Lisa's single, not by choice. Beth's needs aren't being met, at least not by her husband. And me . . . what, exactly, *is* my problem?

"I don't think he loves me," I whisper. I say it again, louder. "Ken doesn't *love* me."

Beth and Lisa both nod as though they aren't surprised.

"Do you love him?" Lisa asks.

I think of the promise I made to my son, that I would protect him and take care of him. Give him a stable home life. Provide for him. I think of the mortgage and the bills and the emptying bank account.

"I *need* him."

"I need something," Beth groans.

Lisa lifts her glass. "I need to get a little lit right now. How's that?"

Beth downs her glass and holds it out for more as she leans to look toward the carriage house. "Tell me what it was like. With Christian. Tell me he's great in bed."

Lisa and I both look at her. Beth's expression goes hard. She stares into her glass before setting it on the table between us.

"I just want to know," she says.

"You don't already?" I ask her.

She frowns. "No, I unfortunately do not."

"But you—" I start, then stop myself.

Self-doubt pokes a needle in my side for a second. *Beth's just a friend. You don't need to worry about her.* I hadn't told Christian I saw her coming out of the apartment, but he hadn't said she was there, either. Could I have mistaken someone else for her?

"I party with Christian sometimes," Beth says, "but we aren't fucking. If that's what you're getting at."

Her voice is cold, full of stung pride. She lifts her chin and stares me down with a sheen of tears in her eyes and lips that tremble until she presses them together.

"It was a long time ago. I hardly remember it," I tell her, trying to be kind. Or maybe because my lie will hurt her worse than the truth.

"I bet you remember it every time your husband comes to bed," Beth says.

"Huh?"

She and Lisa share a look. Lisa shakes her head. Beth sits back in her chair with a triumphant smile.

"Your husband and Christian could be brothers. You can't tell me you never noticed."

"Maybe more like cousins," Lisa puts in.

I blink rapidly, my breath clawing in my throat. "I don't . . . No. I mean, no, they don't look that much alike."

"Girl." Beth sounds more sympathetic than smug. "Please."

Lisa comes to my rescue. "So what, she has a type. So do you, Beth. So do I. There's nothing wrong with that."

"The night of the reunion. After we left," Beth asks, her gaze gleaming, holding mine tight. She leans closer. "You got some of that, didn't you?"

"No. I'm *married*."

"So am I, but I'd sleep with C.C. in a hot minute."

"And then your husband would find out, and he'd kick your ass to the curb," Lisa says.

"Christian's a *surgeon*. Steve's a freaking manager in a furniture warehouse. I'd leave Steve for Christian like *that*." She snaps her fingers.

"If he won't fuck you, then he wouldn't *marry* you," I tell her, remembering the vague look of disgust on his face when we'd all been together in his hotel.

Beth's lip curls. This shot hit her someplace soft. Lisa leans in between us to refill Beth's glass.

"I already told you, Beth, get yourself a tall ladder and a leaky roof," she says breezily, although underneath that light tone is a hard kernel of something that sounds like sincerity. "Then you and me can retire someplace together. Total *Golden Girls*. How about you, Jewelann? You in? We'll get a house in Florida. No boys allowed except our sons."

"Not me. I like dick," Beth says.

Lisa puffs out a breath through pursed lips. "Jesus, Beth. You know what? When you drink and vape at the same time, you're a real bitch."

"Being a real bitch is better than being a fake one," Beth says with a haughty lift of her chin.

The two of them crack up. They clink their glasses together. Once again, I'm left out.

Christian's SUV pulls into his half of the driveway. We can see him easily from the deck, but he doesn't seem to notice us as he goes inside. I watch Beth watching him. She looks at me with a small smile that does not match the look in her eyes.

"It's a good thing you have such a great marriage, Jewelann. I hate to think what would happen otherwise, with your old high school fling living right there. Not that I'd ever tell your husband I saw the two of you making out or anything."

I don't join her in laughter when she bursts into a string of delighted guffaws.

"Your face," she says. "Oh, my God, Jewelann. Girl, I might be a bitch, but I'm not that much of a bitch. I would *never* tell anyone about that night. Okay? Are we good?"

We are nothing close to good, but I nod. "Of course we are."

She lifts her hand in a wave. Christian has come out of the carriage house. He stands and stares for a second or so.

"Christian!" Beth calls, waving. "Hi!"

He looks and raises a hand in Beth's direction. "Hey, there."

"Come on over!" Beth says.

I'm never going to like Beth.

"Another time," he calls out in reply.

I hadn't realized how certain I was that he was going to insist on joining us until the tension in my shoulders eases. I watch until he goes inside the carriage house. Beth is pouring more wine into her glass. Lisa is puffing on the vape pen. She doesn't offer it to me this time, but my glass has been filled even higher.

"I'll tell you what, though, just between the three of us." Wine sloshes over Beth's fingers, holding that irreplaceable, hundred dollar crystal wine glass so loosely I'm afraid she'll drop and break it. "If you don't want him, Jewelann, I will happily take him."

"Beth," Lisa says reprovingly.

"I definitely don't want him," I tell them both.

But I'm lying.

# 22

"I WANT TO TALK to you about my son." My voice is steady. Nonconfrontational. Firm.

Christian leans in the carriage house doorway, arms crossed over his chest. "I figured you would. Where'd your day drunk booze buddies go?"

"Are you going to let me in?"

He steps aside with a smile and a wave of his hand. "And here I thought you didn't trust yourself around me alone."

I wait until he moves far enough for me to get past him without touching him. It's not that I don't trust myself, or even that I don't trust him. I just remember, that's all. How it used to be.

Inside the living area, I stop short. My teeth shut tight on a gasp. My fists clench until I put one over my heart. It doesn't stop the pounding there.

Everything is gone.

The brown floral couch with the wooden arms and legs, omnipresent in every single house I ever entered in the eighties. The matching wagon-wheel coffee table. The pineapple pendant lamps.

"You *asshole*." I think I say this aloud, but it must only be in my head, because Christian doesn't react.

"Looks much better, huh?" He takes a slow spin, arms out. "Next up is new flooring. There's still something going on with the plumbing, by the way. Ken and I had a nice little talk about it when he came over."

He sounds like he's taunting me, trying to get me to ask what else he and my husband discussed, or at least see if I knew about that nighttime rendezvous. I can't focus on that right now. My stuff is gone, and my heart thumps hard, and my throat closes in a panic.

"What did you do with everything you took out of here?"

His eyes slant away from mine as his lips thin. That look, oh, I know it. I've seen it. He's getting ready to lie. But about what?

"I had St. Francis thrift come and pick it up. I didn't think to grab a receipt for you, but I guess you could deduct it on your taxes anyway."

I shake my head. My skin feels clammy. I swallow hard, my mouth dry. The place is empty. All of my things, given away. *Taken* away. If I hadn't moved all my boxes out, he'd have gotten rid of those, too. And I know it's just stuff, only things I didn't even use, but it's always been about *having* them, and I'm ashamed that I know this and still can't stop myself from feeling the overwhelming rush of fury that they're gone.

"What about the bedroom? Did you clear that out, too?"

"Not yet. Gotta have a place to sleep until I get my stuff in here from my storage unit."

This is another lie, based on the way his expression twists. How do I still know him so well after all this time? I know he's not telling me the truth, but I don't know what, exactly, he's lying about.

"Relax, Jewelann. You're so tense."

I straighten up, squaring my shoulders. "I don't need any advice from you, okay? You know what, while I'm here, I do need the rent."

Christian looks apologetic, but this expression is also a lie. "I gave Ken the receipts for the stuff I've done. It all evened out. Didn't he tell you that?"

"That's not going to work for me. I need the money now."

A sigh. He shrugs. Runs a hand through his dark gold hair. He knows how he looks, so casual. So sexy. I am unmoved.

I wish I was unmoved.

"I've been so busy with the hospital, and then taking care of this place . . . I'm sorry, Jewelann. Most of my stuff's still in storage. I don't even know where my checkbook is. Can you come by tomorrow? Tell you what, I'll even make you dinner. How about it?"

"Too busy partying, you mean."

"You're always invited, you know."

"I thought you were going to leave me alone."

He smiles. "I thought you wanted me to. Yet here you are."

The tension that crackles between us is familiar, but it doesn't feel good.

"I came over to ask you about the concert Eli says you're taking him to. That's all."

"You could have texted me about that," Christian says.

Beth and Lisa were right. Ken and Christian share the same dark wheat-colored hair, and there's a similarity in the shapes of their jaws, but it's the way they move and stand, the way they talk, that's so much alike. I don't want to think that I might have married my husband because of how much he reminded me of Christian, but there's no denying that I definitely seem to have a type.

When he takes a step closer, I don't move away.

"The concert is general admission, but I got us tickets to the early entrance. They check IDs and wristband kids who are underage. It'll be over by eleven because it's an all-ages show, and I promise to have him and his buddy back home by midnight. Is there anything else you need to know?"

"Why are you taking him?"

"Because I dig the kid," Christian says, "and I like the band. It's a thank-you to him for all his help."

I look around. "It doesn't look like you've done anything except get rid of my family heirlooms."

"He's still been a help, and I've got plenty more for him to do for me. Look, if you really don't want me to take him to the show, I'll tell him something came up and I can't make it. You can make me the bad guy."

Eli would be so disappointed. It would prove what I told him about Christian being unreliable, but it also wouldn't be the truth. I sigh, aggravated.

"No. He can go."

Christian smiles. When he puts his hands on his hips, he reminds me too much of Ken. I can't unsee it, or how much Eli resembles him, because of how much the two men look alike. Our child would be almost a quarter of a century old by now. Is that why he's so fixated on mine?

"What was Ken doing over here the other night?"

"Came over to ask me to turn the music down," Christian lies smoothly. His eyes widen a bit in fake innocence. "You should've come over, too. Beth was here. You'd have had fun."

Turning on my heel, I leave before he can further work his wiles. I'm breathing hard as I cross the backyard. My boots squelch in a soft, wet spot in the grass. We haven't had rain in weeks.

*Shit.*

In the living room, I light a fire in the gas fireplace and cozy myself up on the couch under a blanket. The days have been unseasonably warm, but the nights are getting cold. I fire up my sluggish laptop and do some research. The charge just to have someone come out and scope, or whatever they call it, our pipes, is three hundred dollars. If they need to rotor out anything blocking them, a portion of the fee gets refunded, but the cost of the other procedure is unlisted. That means it could be a lot.

Ken's supposed to get paid every four weeks, but after the last mix-up, I'm not sure when the money will come in next. What will happen if it's late again? Or worse, doesn't come in at all? The bank account balance is just large enough to cover a couple of mortgage payments and some utility bills. The monthly fee for my storage unit goes onto my secret credit card, which always carries a balance. I try not to look at it very often, as though not seeing the monthly interest charges racking up will make them go away. I make the payments on it, but every month the charges keep coming back in.

I check it now. The balance is high enough to make small black and red spots dance in my vision. Years of stay-home toddler moms stuck in the carousel of home sale parties. "I'll go to yours if you come to mine." Years of "bargain hunting." Years of lying to myself that I was going to support myself by flipping this stuff, years of being unable to let any of it go.

Years of minimum payments. More interest. I'm never going to pay this off. The best I can hope for is to keep it from being overdue. It's been that way for a long time, but until the past month or so, I've never been worried about not being able to pay the *mortgage*.

Browsing the internet for "how many mortgage payments can you miss before you lose your house" fans my anxiety into an inferno. The lilt of laughter floats down the stairs from Eli's room. I can't tell if he's got a friend over that I didn't know about, or he's talking on the phone.

I get a wineglass from the cupboard. The wine doesn't do much but churn in my stomach and make my fingers clumsy. I think about the pills I flushed away. I'd kept that stash for a decade without taking a single pill, but the need, the craving, the yearning for oblivion rises up inside me now with such ferocity I almost start to cry.

I don't deserve to have my entire life ruined because I made stupid mistakes. And not only my life—Eli's life would be ruined, too, because of my bad choices.

Another burst of laughter, some words I can't make out, come from upstairs. I close out of all the browser tabs. I force myself to sit up straight. There is no way I'm going to lose this house and turn my son's life inside out. A few more taps of the keyboard take me to some local sale groups where you can list items. I can start, at least, with the home party stuff I have stashed all around the house.

I check out listings, my heart sinking with each one. Everyone's trying to unload this crap. Page after page of leggings, candles, food choppers. At least I'm not trying to sell anything with an expiration date like spices or beer bread mixes. Box lots seem to be the best way to go. I won't make back even half of what I spent, but it's better than nothing.

The warmth of the wine has finally kicked in, but having a solid plan is what really intoxicates me. Tomorrow, I will go to my storage unit, and I will spend the day sorting and boxing up all of that stuff. I will list it, I will sell it, and, no matter how much it pains my husband to not be the sole breadwinner, I will check in with the temp agency and see about getting something at least part-time. This living on the edge is bullshit. I am better than this. I can *be* better than this.

I scroll the listings. I've never been much of an online shopper, preferring the tangible sensation of lifting and holding items before I buy them, not to mention that it's harder to hide packages that could arrive at any time than it is to stash things I bought in person. Even so, I'm getting a little boost, just a little one, from imagining adding something to my shopping cart.

As I'm scrolling through the listings, one catches my eye. It's a set of pendant lamps. Amber glass pineapples. "Mid-Century Modern! Mint condition!" The price isn't the only thing that staggers me.

Those are my grandmother's lamps.

"Y**OU FUCKING LIAR**," I say to Christian before he can get a word out of his mouth. "You sold my stuff!"

"Hi, Jewelann," calls a familiar female voice from inside the carriage house.

I push past him. Beth sprawls on a new couch that wasn't there earlier this afternoon. Her eyes are bright but glazed. She's not quite slurring her words, but neither is she speaking with crystal clarity. She waves the tips of her fingers in my direction.

"You *sold* it," I repeat, not shouting this time.

Christian's expression is one I remember so well. The dishonest one, the one that shows how clever he thinks he is. Well, he's not.

"I *know*," I tell him. "I saw them listed online."

"I don't know what you're talking about, Jewelann."

"Want a drinky drink?" Beth sits up, then falls back against the cushions. "Ooooh. Mmmm. Christian, get Jewelann a drink."

I turn toward her. My question comes out the opposite of subtle. "Does your husband know you're here?"

"Does yours?" She sits up straight, or tries to. "C'mon. Have a drink."

She's stoned. I don't smell weed, but that doesn't mean anything. Could be edibles, could be pills. Whatever it is, Beth's deep in it. Her lipstick is smeared. Her hair is mussed. The top button of her blouse dangles by the thread. The longer I look at her, the more details stand out. The longer I look, the angrier I get.

"I don't want a drink."

He leans close enough to brush his nose against my neck. "Smells like you've already had one."

I step away, out of his reach. "I want the money you got for my stuff. Plus the rent."

"Nothing has actually sold yet, okay?"

The fact he's no longer denying it is no comfort. I close my eyes, tears burning behind the lids. I keep myself standing straight, facing away from Beth so I don't give her the satisfaction of seeing me cry.

"I want you to take down the listings. And get me the rent. No . . . no, keep them up," I say, hating it but thinking of the possible cash. "Give me the money when anything sells."

When I open my eyes, Christian is studying me closely. He nods and takes a step backward, toward the kitchen. He rummages in a drawer set into the island separating the kitchen from the living room, then holds up a checkbook in a blue vinyl cover. "Okay. Sure. The check doesn't have my address on it, I hope that's okay?"

More lies. He knew where his checkbook was all along. "It's fine."

"You know where he lives, right, Jewelann?" Beth's gravelly laugh grates in my ears.

Christian waves a paper rectangle at me, taking my attention. "The next part of my program hasn't officially started yet, so I hope it's all right that I postdated this. I won't get paid until next week."

My guts snarl into a knot. Who the hell postdates a check anymore? For that matter, who uses checks at all? I can't remember the last time I cashed one, much less wrote one.

"Where did all this furniture come from?"

"Mostly Ikea." He's bending over, scribbling something on the check.

"So you have money for new furniture, but not the rent? Not cool, Christian." I kick at the still-bare concrete, now partially covered by a colorful throw rug. "You're supposed to be renovating. You don't get rent credit for buying furniture."

His gaze goes hard. "Some of it was in storage. And I've done a lot around here. More than you know. If anything, based on everything I've done, you owe *me*."

"How . . . mmmuch do you need?" Beth hauls herself upright.

She is . . . wrecked. I'm surprised she can even get to her feet, but she does, and grabs her purse from the new chair angled next to the couch. She pulls out a leather wallet bearing a designer crest matching the handbag, and for a second, I think she's about to tumble over right onto her face. I remember how that felt, like the world moved in slow motion, and a sickness tangles at the base of my throat. That's what I used to look like, I think, and hot shame gurgles in my gut.

Beth rifles through the wallet and pulls out a fistful of bills. "Eight?"

Bitterness squirts into my mouth. Beth has eight hundred dollars in her hand. I'm actually salivating, Pavlovian, at the idea of what I could do with that cash.

"Ken said three," Christian says.

I swivel to face him. "Three hundred a month for rent? That's—"

"Crazy cheap," Beth says at the same time Christian interrupts with "fair."

"C'mon, Jewelann. I'm putting my sweat and labor into this place. Putting out for materials out of my own pocket. And I already told you—"

I hold up a hand to stop him. "Yeah. I know. Ken bartered."

Beth weaves her way toward me. "Here. I have three hundred for you. Take it."

"Bethy, you don't need to do that," Christian says.

*Bethy.* My lip curls. He calls her a pet name?

"I don't mind." She presses the crumpled bills into my palm, leaning much closer than is necessary. Her dangling earring tickles my cheek as she says into my ear, "Anything to help out a friend."

I wonder which one of us she means.

When she pulls away, her earring tangles in my hair for a few seconds. She laughs while she tries to free herself, but it takes my fingers to unknot the jewelry. She takes a few of my hairs with her.

"I'm going to use the ladies' room." Beth lists and rocks her way down the short hallway.

Christian waits until she closes the door before he pulls me closer by my upper arms. His voice goes low. "Look, you should really talk to your husband about the arrangements for this place. Okay? First of all, I've kept to our agreement. I already paid him whatever rent I owed him. And also, he's the one who had me list that stuff. He said I could take a seller's fee."

"I haven't seen a single cent," I tell him, but I think about the wad of bills Ken waved around the sushi place. Wine spins circles in my brain.

Christian's grip loosens, but I don't pull myself out of it. His support is kind of the only thing keeping me on my feet. His fingers stroke upward for a second, and I think he's going to kiss me. He does not. He stares into my eyes, though, his expression inscrutable.

The toilet flushes.

He gently pushes me away, one step. Another. There's not a lot of distance between us, but there's enough. He's putting it there because of *her*.

I look into his eyes. "Did you tell Ken about us?"

"No."

"Liar," I whisper.

He shakes his head.

Beth comes out of the bathroom, slamming open the door hard enough to rattle the hinges. "Oooopsie. Hey, so, this is embarrassing, but the paper won't go down. I flushed twice, but it kind of swirls around without going down."

"I thought you fixed that," I tell him.

He shrugs. "I tried. You want to stick around?"

I'm already backing up toward the door. "No. Thanks."

"I'll call you," Beth says after me.

There's no answer for that but a nod. I don't trust my voice. I shove the money into my pocket as I leave. The rise of Beth's laughter follows behind me. I imagine her tripping, falling on her face. Breaking her teeth.

My foot isn't even off the front step before I hear the lock click behind me. I keep going, across the yard and the squishy spot in the grass, and onto my back deck and into my kitchen, where I pull out the money and toss it on the counter. I scrub my hands at the skin, the water so hot it almost scalds. My hands feel dirty. So do I.

Listening for Eli, I head upstairs. The low murmur of his voice doesn't even give me pause outside his door. In my room, I tuck the cash into my wallet, which has not turned out to be so lucky for me after all. I put it in my purse.

Three hundred dollars won't go very far. Again, I pull out my laptop and look at the bank balance, hoping that somehow, miraculously, Ken's check has been deposited.

I check the household credit card next. It gives cash back, which I usually apply directly to the balance, but this time I might be able to get the money as a deposit into my bank account and use it toward other bills. The balance on that card is higher than I'm expecting. Ken has been making charges during his trip, some of which should be reimbursed by the company. Fast food restaurants. Gas. A . . . corn maze?

A few more taps on my keyboard take me to an internet search on the name listed in the recent charges. Apple Tree Farms is, in fact, a corn maze, pumpkin patch, apple-picking farm, and a stand that sells cider. Pictures of happy families fill the screen. It's the sort of place you go when your kids are little so they can do a hayride that isn't scary.

Ken and I had gone on one of our first dates to just such a place. His suggestion was not the sort of place I would have chosen, but it had been fun. Back then, flush with the possibility that this might turn into something permanent, something like love, I hadn't minded holding his hand as he guided me through the rows of corn. When we hit a dead end, he'd laughed. When we made it out on the other side, he'd said, "See? We make a good team."

And we had, hadn't we? At least for a time. Compared to the boys I'd dated, Ken had been a *man*. Trustworthy. Responsible. Reliable. That had been very appealing. So maybe I'd confused a desire for stability with actual desire. So what? We had a life together. Like I'd told Lisa and Beth, I needed Ken. But once, and not so long ago, I'd also wanted him.

Who has he been wanting?

What if there's not another woman in his life, but an entire other family? Again, I scroll through the credit card charges, trying to both convince myself it can't be true and looking for proof that it is.

There.

Not a big charge, one so small it would've completely slipped past me if I hadn't been searching so closely. It's for a toy store. There's another small charge for a candy store. A quick search shows me they're both at an entertainment complex that, according to the website, also features an indoor amusement park, waterslides, and a 3-D movie theater.

"He's in the fucking Dells," I whisper.

I've always wanted to vacation in the Wisconsin Dells, but Ken's always spent too much time on the road for us to have more than an annual trip up to Cedar Point for a few nights, or maybe to rent a cabin in Hocking Hills. Now he's in the Dells by himself . . . no, clearly not by himself.

Tears fill my eyes, burning, and slip down my cheeks. I lick them away from my lips, grimacing at the salty sting. My hands become fists, and I pound my knees, but in silence. Again, I hit myself. Pain throbs in my muscles. I slap away the tears on my cheeks. I smack at my mouth.

Ten years ago, our son was adjacent to a tragedy that continues to affect him to this day. Ten years ago, my husband begged me to forgive his infidelity. Ten years ago, I got myself clean and off drugs, and yes, I did it because I was scared into it, but I did it, and my darling husband never said a word about it.

I've been the good little housewife. I've taken care of every bill, every meal, every holiday, every car repair, every grocery store visit, every gift, every teacher meeting, every doctor and dentist and haircut appointment. I have fucked when I didn't want to. I have kissed him hello and goodbye and put a smile on my face when I didn't feel like smiling. I have laughed at every stupid joke. The only thing I haven't done for Ken is his laundry, and that only because he insists on doing it himself.

Ten.

Fucking.

Years.

I've done my best to make the kind of family Ken always said he wanted. I've kept this family together, here in this house. I've kept my son safe.

How do you lose a house? By getting underwater with the payments. How do you lose a home? Stay in a marriage with someone you no longer love or trust, clinging to memories of what had been, wishing for what might be. How do you lose a husband?

Get him up on a ladder.

# 24

"A ND HOW MUCH would that premium be?" I scribble the information on the notepad in front of me. The woman on the phone has been very helpful, considering I told her I'm only gathering information and not ready to commit to anything. I was surprised someone even answered the phone at this hour. "And he won't need any kind of physical or anything like that?"

She assures me that he won't, based on the information I've given her. "He will have to sign for it, of course."

"Of course," I say smoothly, even as my pen scratches so deep into the paper it rends a hole. "Does it need to be notarized or anything like that?"

"Nope. We'll have some proof of identity requirements, but it's a very easy process. We should be able to get you all set up in no time. You say your husband travels a lot?"

"On business. Yes. And, you know, all that time on the road . . ."

Her laughter is like the tinkle of wind chimes. "Better safe than sorry, as we say around here. So, can I get that paperwork squared away for you and sent out?"

I look at the numbers I wrote on the paper. I grip my phone tighter. "That would be great. Yes, thank you."

She has me answer a few more questions. I know the answers to them all. Ken's social. His birthday. Height, weight, health history. I even know his driver's license number, because when you've been doing everything for someone for almost two decades, you have that sort of stuff memorized. She promises to get me the forms ASAP. And then, she says with another of those wind chime laughs, it'll just be a few quick signatures and "safe sailing from there on out."

I had no idea that it would be nearly impossible to take out life insurance without Ken's knowledge or consent. Crime shows make it seem so easy. I'm not too worried, though. I've been forging his signature for years.

Sipping coffee while I stand at my kitchen sink, I look out at the backyard and see the first hints of orange and red in the trees there. No more ripe tomatoes in the garden. Fall might finally be here.

I'm not spying. I can stand at my own window and enjoy a cup of coffee, looking at my own property. I am absolutely not trying to catch a glimpse of Beth leaving the carriage house.

Nevertheless, I see Christian come out the door, alone. He first takes some long boxes from the back of his SUV, making several trips. I can't read the labels on them from this distance, but when one tilts in my direction I can see what looks like a picture of plank flooring. The next time he comes out, he's got one of the long rolls of carpet he tore out before. He goes back inside, returns with the other one, struggling and nearly falling as he shoves it into the back of his SUV. This time, he drives away. I watch a few minutes more, but there's no sign of Beth.

I used to make a big breakfast for Eli every morning before school. He'd eat while I'd read a chapter from a book we both picked out. He stopped eating breakfast when he started high school, so I know the eggs I'm beating now will be scrambled, cooked, and returned to the fridge without being eaten, but I need something to do with my hands so I don't break something worse than a couple of eggs.

The clock ticks through another few minutes. Eli should be downstairs by now, filling his insulated cup with coffee, at least, if he won't eat an actual meal. I call upstairs, but he doesn't answer. I don't think he slept through his alarm, but I head up anyway to make sure he's on time.

"Eli!" I knock on his door. He doesn't answer. I knock again, this time rattling the knob. When he still doesn't answer, I start to turn it.

The door is yanked out of my grip as he flings it open. "What?"

He's high.

I stare at him and take a step back into the hallway. "You're going to be late for school."

We stare at each other. I've never spoken to my son about my troubles with drugs. Never asked if he remembers the days when Mama napped a lot while he watched cartoons for hours on end.

While I study his face, Eli shrugs. "I'm almost ready."

I can't be positive he's using. He's not slurring or unsteady on his feet; his eyes aren't red. His pupils seem fine.

I look into his room, but of course there's no convenient evidence laid out for me to see. No prescription bottles, no envelopes bulging with pills. I don't smell weed.

Still, I know. I feel it. How many times did I greet my own mother in the morning before leaving for school with the same expression on my face, the one that said *I'm kinda fucked up right now, but I hope you don't notice*? She'd never confronted me, never once, and I'd always convinced myself she never knew.

Eli gives a long, jaw-cracking yawn. Rubs his eyes. What looked to me like intoxication becomes exhaustion.

"You okay? Dreams?"

Eli shakes his head. "Nah. I stayed up too late."

"Doing homework or reading internet forums?" His sheepish look tells me the answer he doesn't need to say aloud. I laugh, relieved. "Why do you do that to yourself?"

"I can't help it," he replies honestly. "I get sucked in and have to read all the updates."

If I ask him about the forums he's subscribed to, that will reveal the low-level stalking I did on his old laptop, so I pretend I don't know. "Anything interesting?"

"True crime stuff, mostly," he says.

"Too scary for me."

He shrugs again.

"You'd better get moving."

He looks over his shoulder at the clock on the wall. "Yeah, shoot. I'll be down in a few minutes."

"Hungry?" I ask him when he comes into the kitchen to fill his insulated cup.

He yawns again. "Nah. Thanks, though. Don't forget, the concert's tonight."

"Tonight?"

"You said I could go," he begins, but I wave him quiet.

He looks wary. He looks like me. He has his father's hair and eyes, but the set of his mouth is mine. So's the expression.

"I didn't remember it was tonight. That's all. Do you need money for anything? A T-shirt or something?"

"You don't have to give me any money, Mom."

I'm already looking in my purse for the cash I got from Beth. "I know I don't have to."

"Mom," he says sharply. "I don't need you to give me anything. I know . . ."

I look at him.

"I gotta go," Eli says.

And I am left behind with eggs that have gone cold in a pan on the stove.

My fingers tap in the code for my bank app. I hold my breath. The mortgage came out. Nothing else came in.

Three hundred dollars is not going to go far at all. I call my husband and get sent to voice mail. As I'm leaving him a message, a call from him comes in.

"Did you find out what's going on with your paycheck?" I ask without preamble.

"I told you I'd take care of it, okay? It's just a glitch in the system or something. I got that huge bonus. We should be fine for another month, at least."

Alarmed, I take a sudden breath. "You think it's going to take *another* month—"

"It's not going to take a month," he interrupts.

"Did you really tell Christian he only needed to pay three hundred dollars for rent?"

Silence.

"He's paying for the renovations out of pocket. Bartering," Ken says when I refuse to be the first to speak.

"Are you overseeing his choices at all? Is he running anything by you?" I demand. "Did you tell him he could sell my grandmother's furniture and take a cut?"

"We'll have to talk about this when I get home, Jewelann. I'm about to meet a customer." Ken's voice crackles and breaks up, static.

"Where are you?"

More electronic noise. ". . . Indianapolis . . . I told you . . ."

"Ken," I say, but before I can confront him about being in Wisconsin, the call boop-boop-boops into disconnecting.

I don't call him back.

The life insurance rep told me it would take three or four days to process the application. I have no idea when he'll be back. I text Lisa.

**GM. What's up with you today? Anything fun?**

I clean the kitchen while I wait for her reply. I throw in a load of laundry. I vacuum the living room. I unsubscribe from the estate sale email list without even looking at the current sales. I avoid looking at any bank or credit card balances, but I do take a peek at Eli's forum site to see what's been keeping him up late. He's following a couple of different threads, all about the same topics, but I don't read any of them. That stuff doesn't interest me and, in fact, gives me nightmares.

But maybe I should read up on the women who take out big life insurance policies on their husbands right before they happen to die by accident.

The buzz of the dryer sends me to the basement. A faint hint of sewage drifts from the bathroom down there. It tickles my nose, but it might be my imagination. When I check it, everything is bone dry. The toilet flushes slowly, but it doesn't overflow.

Ken's office door is locked, and nothing I try will get it open. The door won't budge. I want to know what he's hiding in there, in fact I am now desperate to know, so I take the door off the hinges.

There's nothing to find.

The space is tidy and mostly bare. My dad's old workbench is clear of all but the most basic tools and supplies. The big wooden desk toward the back of the space has nothing on it. Nothing in the drawers other than a few notepads, a few pens, some paper clips. Ken has his laptop with him, of course, and I'm not sure what, exactly, I was looking to find. A framed photo of this other family I keep imagining? Love notes? Stacks of cash?

The absurdity of it all hits me, a punch to the gut that has me doubling over with harsh, whistling laughter that sounds a lot like gasping sobs. I punch at my thighs. Grip my belly. I dash the tears from my eyes with fierce flicks of my fingertips.

I've been unhappy for a long time, but now it feels as though I am becoming a little . . . unhinged.

By the time I get back upstairs, Lisa has replied.

**Nothing much. Thinking of getting my nails done. HBU?**

Not getting my nails done, that's for sure.

I type, **Ken's still out of town, and Eli has plans tonight. Do you want to get together?**

Her answer is exactly what I was hoping for. **Sure. My place, this time? Eightish?**

**Sounds great,** I type. **I'll bring the wine.**

# 25

WALKING TO LISA'S condo takes about twenty minutes. The night air is crisp, and there's a hint of what promises to be snow infiltrating it. The wine bottles clink together in my shoulder bag as I pass by the Fraze Pavilion, its fountains dry now. A handful of workers are putting up Christmas lights. It's not even Thanksgiving yet.

Lisa takes the wine with a happy giggle as she lets me through the front door, but her laugh becomes boisterous when she peeks inside the brightly patterned gift bag I also hand her. "What the . . . ?"

WINE MOM is patterned all over the leggings, along with red and white wine bottles and glasses and grapes. They should be cute, but they're hideous. Still, the aesthetic is one I hope Lisa will appreciate. I picked them up from my storage unit earlier today. I have an entire bin of stretchy clothes in ugly patterns. Handing over the leggings isn't as hard as I'd thought it would be. In fact, it feels good. If only I could do that with the rest of the stuff in that storage unit.

"I got them from one of those home parties a few years ago." I shrug, no big deal. Super casual. She'll never know how long I sat clutching them to my chest, working to convince myself I didn't need to hang on to something I was never going to wear. "I thought you might get a kick out of them."

"Come into the living room." She leads me there and holds up the leggings in front of herself. "Am I that obvious? Never mind. Thanks. They're perfect."

Her hug surprises me, but I squeeze her in return as she gestures for me to settle into her soft beige couch. She lights the gas fireplace and clears the coffee table of the stack of vintage hardcover books and a wooden tray laden with carved bowls containing decorative balls. Her condo's decorated in shades of cream and brown and hints of gold, understated and minimalist, but there are hints of her personality here and there. A vintage Santa doll high on one bookshelf, legs dangling. A horse made from costume jewelry on the wall.

"I love your place."

"Thanks. You're sweet." Lisa puts two wineglasses on the coffee table. I'm glad she opens the bottle of white instead of the red. Now I won't have to be afraid I'll spill and stain her shaggy cream rug. "After Gary died and I had to put my house on the market, I vowed to myself I would never make it hard on myself to sell a place again. When I moved in here, I decorated it like it came out of a magazine. Ready at any moment to show up in a real estate listing. I look at those house sale websites every day. I thought I'd move out of here pretty fast, but I confess, I like that someone else handles the repairs and the landscaping and all of that. Owning a house is so much work. On the other hand, I have no emotional attachments to this place."

"I have a deep and abiding attachment to my house," I tell her honestly. "I'll never move out of it."

"You've lived in that house for practically your whole life. You must have so many good memories in it." She pours us both generous glasses and settles into her chair, putting up her feet on the table between us. "Some bad ones, too."

I sip carefully. "Sure. A few. You can't get through life without a few bad memories here and there."

"Maybe that's why I get rid of everything every few years and start from scratch. Can't hold on to bad memories if you don't have any reminders, right?" Lisa lifts her glass toward mine to clink them together. She takes another drink. "Oooh. Yummy."

The idea of getting rid of everything gives me a cold sweat. "You have a real knack for it. Have you ever thought about doing it for other people?"

"What, like staging houses to go on the market? Or decorating them?"

"Both. Either." I take in the rest of the room, noticing more cool details I envy because they're all clearly there to make Lisa happy.

"You really think I'd be good at it?"

"You are good at it, Lisa. From what I see here, I think you're really good at it."

"Hmm." She looks around the living room, her head tilted. "You know, there are services that will rent décor and furniture to people who are selling, to make the house look fresh but not too personal. I bet there's good money in that. You probably have to have some kind of storage space, though, for your inventory. And you'd have to market yourself. Work with realtors. Sounds like a lot of work."

"Fun work. Maybe even a dream job."

"My dream job is not having to work," she says with an acerbic laugh. "I'm living it."

I study the yellowy gold liquid shimmering in my glass. "Me too. It's not that great."

"So what's your dream job?" She refills her glass.

"Buying stuff and reselling it," I tell her honestly and also self-consciously. "You're the first person I have ever admitted that to."

Lisa beams. "Why don't you do it, then?"

There's so much to this story, where do I begin?

"My son. It's always been important to me that I'm there for him. After what happened, I wanted to make sure Eli felt safe. I wanted him to know I would always protect him. And Ken wanted me to stay home, take care of the house. He's old-fashioned like that."

It's only a tiny piece of the truth, but it's a start.

"Eli won't need you forever."

I feign shock, a hand over my chest, my head turned, but I'm laughing. "Bite your tongue. A boy will always need his mother."

"Sure, if he's Norman Bates." She laughs too.

"He struggled, you know? He still struggles." My laughter fades. "I'll do whatever I have to so he can be okay. Sacrifice . . . whatever."

"You're a good mom, Jewelann."

The wine is crisp on my tongue as I take a long swallow. "I try. I don't know that I'm doing such a great job."

"Who ever knows?" Lisa says. "But one thing I do know for sure. If mama ain't happy, nobody's happy. If starting a resale business would make you happy, Jewelann, you totally should do it."

"I'm going to. I will. I could open up an online shop. Ken would never know about it." I cough lightly, shifting on the couch. The wine warms me from the inside out. I can feel it in my chest, my throat, my cheeks.

"And if you had an online shop, you could still be home."

"And you," I say, "could share my storage space for your house staging inventory."

Lisa sighs. "I'm glad you texted me."

She lifts her glass. I lift mine. We clink them together.

"Cheers," she says. "Here's to possibilities."

We chat for a few minutes, this and that. I watch as she empties the last of the first bottle into her glass. "I thought you might be hanging out with Beth tonight."

Mid-sip, Lisa frowns and shakes her head. "I haven't heard from her in a few days. She didn't answer my last text. I can see if she wants to come over now?"

"You don't have to," I say.

She eyes me. Sips her wine. "She's changed a lot since high school. I know you don't like her much. She can be hard to deal with, but . . . we've been friends for a long time. I guess I'm willing to give her the benefit of the doubt."

"Beth was in the carriage house with Christian." The words blurt out of me, and once they're free of my lips, I wish I could take them back.

Lisa sits back, blinking, and sets down her glass. "Shit."

"Yeah."

"She's going through stuff at home. But I didn't think she'd like, actually . . . well, we don't *know* what she was doing. Do we?" Lisa's sigh rumbles into a groan. "She always had such a *thing* for C.C., and he just strung her along. You know, flirting, asking her if she had a date for the dances but then never asking her out. Talking to her on the phone but never calling her first. High school stuff. Stupid. She was so jealous of you."

A burbling chuckle forces itself up my throat. "She had nothing to be jealous about."

Lisa snorts lightly. "You had more of him than she ever did."

"Is that what everyone said back then?"

"Beth knew you two hooked up, which meant I did. But did everyone? I don't know," she says.

"Did Jen Tillis know?"

After a second, Lisa nods. "I'm sure she did. But I don't think that was why she . . . you know. Killed herself."

"I bet he had something to do with it," I say.

She looks surprised. "You think he killed her?"

"I'm not saying he did it physically," I say. "But I think he hurt her enough times that maybe, finally, she just couldn't get over it."

"And he did that to you, too."

"If someone hurts me so many times I can't get over it, I'd be more likely to kill them than myself," I tell her.

Lisa pours herself more wine and adds some to my half-full glass. Glug, glug, glug. She removes a small makeup bag from a drawer in the coffee table and unzips it to bring out a vaporizer pen and a prescription bottle.

"You want some?"

It's not bad, I tell myself. Wine is made from grapes. Marijuana comes from a plant. All natural.

It's not the same as pills.

I'll be sobered up by the time Eli gets home from the concert.

I deserve a little relief, don't I?

I swirl the wine in my glass. I could drink the whole bottle, and I'd get drunk, but it wouldn't make me want more. I want the weed, but that's one step onto a slippery set of stairs waiting for me to fall down them.

"No, thanks. I'm good," I tell her. "I'll have to get home before Eli gets home."

Her laugher is rueful. "I shouldn't either, but I will, because I don't have anyone coming home to me tonight."

We both fall silent.

"I'm sorry," I say after a couple of seconds.

Lisa waves a hand, drinks, tops off her glass. "My own fault. If you date a married man, you can't be surprised when he decides to go to his kid's birthday party with his wife."

"Why do you keep seeing him, then?"

"Because every time I tell him it's over, he comes back around and tells me he's sorry, that it'll be different. I never believe him. Honestly," Lisa says, "I don't even *want* to be with him all the time. I like the fact he's got someone else he needs to be responsible to, because it gives me a lot of freedom. I just want him to be honest about how he feels, and of course, asking a man to be honest about his feelings . . ."

"Or honest about *anything*." My laugh is harsh and choking, and I put my glass on the table so I can cover my eyes with both my hands. "I'm considering your advice about the ladder."

"Oh, honey." She's at my side in an instant, her arm around me. She smells of wine and weed and perfume, but I let her pull me close anyway. "That sucks. Did you find out for sure that he's been cheating?"

"He's been lying about where he's traveling. There are odd charges on the credit card. His pay isn't getting deposited, I'm worried about paying bills . . . Everything is falling apart all around me. I'm trying to hold onto it all, but it's slipping through my fingers. I'm taking out a life insurance policy on him, that's how messed up this is."

Sobs burst out of me. Lisa lets me cry for a minute or so, then hands me some tissues. She pats my back as I get myself under at least a little bit of control.

"Getting life insurance is being smart. You don't really want to kill him, though," she says finally.

"No. I guess I don't."

"You definitely don't," Lisa says and leans closer to whisper into my ear. "You want to get someone else to do it for you."

\* \* \*

It's an hour past when I was expecting Eli to get home from the concert. I think all mothers worry about their children not making it home safe and sound, but not all mothers actually know a child that disappeared. I've been watching the clock, but before I can text him or dissolve into a panic, the back slider from the deck opens.

"You know you're supposed to text me if you're going to be late." I study him, looking for signs that he's intoxicated or on something, but he seems fine.

Eli shrugs. "We got home a while ago, but I was hanging out with Christian."

"I was worried," I tell him.

"I'm sorry."

"How was the show?" My eyes are drooping. Now that he's finally home, my bed is calling to me.

He lights up. "Awesome. So, so cool. We had the best time."

"I'm glad," I say, and I am. "It's late. I'm heading up to bed now. You are not to leave the house after I go. Understood?"

There's a moment when I think he might argue with me, but it passes so fast I probably imagined it. He shakes his head. Dismisses me with a wave of one hand.

"It's all good."

He goes upstairs. I hear water running in the bathroom. The toilet flushes, water rushing through the pipes in the kitchen wall.

Eli shouts for me, and I run, taking the stairs two at a time. He's standing over the toilet with the plunger as water spills over the sides. A gurgle of stink comes out of the sink and the tub as brownish water backs up into them. The toilet tank finishes filling, but water's still splashing over the rim as he tries to use the plunger to get the toilet draining.

"Give it to me." I work the plunger quickly, grateful the water in the toilet, at least, seems mostly clean. The water swirls down, sending more gurgles up from the sink and tub. Everything quiets.

"Gross," Eli says.

Carefully, I run the taps to see if the water goes down. It does, draining slowly, rinsing away the dark streaks. I sit on the edge of the tub and let my head hang for a moment as I laugh, because what else can I really do?

"I guess I'll have to call the plumber again," I say and mutter a curse.

It's almost two in the morning, and I'm exhausted from the wine I had at Lisa's house and my emotional breakdown, from the low-grade and ever-present tension I've been unable to shake for the past couple of months.

"Are you okay, Mom?"

"Tired. Annoyed. It'll be fine," I reassure him. "Go on to bed. Just try not to use too much water, okay? Only flush if necessary. But wash your hands before you go to bed."

We both make faces and laugh at the same time. He washes his hands carefully as I make sure nothing else happens with the drains. I do the same.

Eli hugs me in the hallway. When did he get taller than me? Only by about an inch, but he's definitely grown. I squeeze him, patting his back. Long ago, before he was born, my mother gave me the best advice I ever had about parenting. When hugging your children, never be the one who lets go first.

I hug my son. He smells a little of sweat, a faint hint of cigarette smoke, perhaps a splash or two of beer. I don't let him go.

Eli's the one who steps back first. "'Night, Mom."

In my own room, I look across the backyard. The carriage house is dark. I can't see if Christian's SUV is there, or any other vehicles.

**Thanks for taking Eli to the concert**, I text.

No immediate answer. None after I'm done brushing my teeth with a dry toothbrush and not flushing after I use the toilet. No answer as I'm slipping into bed.

**Goodnight**, I text, and this time the tiny message beneath turns from Delivered to Read.

I turn my phone face down on the nightstand so I don't see anything lighting up in reply. Love or money, Lisa had said. People will do anything for love or money.

She was drunk by then, expansive, not quite morose but heading in that direction. She wasn't serious. She certainly wasn't offering to help me.

But she had a point.

I understand what it's like to do bad things for the sake of love, and I know how it feels to be willing to do bad things for money, too. I don't have anyone in my life right now who'd do something for me out of love, but do I know someone who could be motivated to do it for money?

I think I might.

# CHAPTER

# 26

CHRISTIAN LOUNGES IN the carriage house doorway. He yawns. I've woken him, even though it's two o'clock in the afternoon. He wears only a pair of dark denim jeans hanging low on his hips, no shoes, no shirt. Gooseflesh ripples his chest and arms. His hair is rumpled, maybe damp.

"To what do I owe this dubious pleasure?" He's quoting *Fright Night*, a movie we fooled around to more than once.

I hate the way these little hints make me think he remembers everything about me, the same way I do about him.

"I need more money for rent, Christian. Or you need to get out, and I need to get another tenant in here who'll pay. Promises don't cover my bills."

"Good luck finding someone willing to put up with a backed-up toilet every other week," he shoots back and follows my gaze over his shoulder, then returns it to my face. "I'm alone, by the way. In case you were wondering."

"I wasn't." I was.

"Do you want to come in? We can talk about it." Without waiting for me to answer, Christian pivots and leaves me standing on the doorstep.

I could turn around and go back to my own house, but my bank account is bare as a fairytale cupboard. I'm reaching desperation levels.

I need him.

"Red or white?" Standing at the bar between the kitchen and living room, he holds up two bottles of wine.

The smell of fresh paint tickles my nostrils. Underneath it I can still smell the faintest sewer stink, or maybe it's my imagination. My skin crawls.

I give a grudging look around the place. A shining stainless steel fridge has replaced the harvest gold one, but the oven is the same old one. The kitchen cabinets are missing, nothing but wooden studs nailed into the wall. The drywall has some patches and some paint splotches. The floor is still bare concrete.

"Where are the dishes supposed to go?"

"It's open concept. I'm going to put up some shelves." Christian pulls the cork from the half-empty bottle of red and divides the contents between the two glasses. "Hey, at least there's no shit sludge coming up out of the sink."

"What about the bathroom?"

"What about it?" Christian tosses the now empty wine bottle into the recycle bin at the end of the counter. I wince at the crash. He slides one of the glasses toward me. I don't take it.

Without waiting for permission, I move past him and down the short hallway leading to both the bedroom and the small bath. The smell is slightly worse in here, but I can't see any evidence of dirty water in the sink, tub, or toilet. The faded linoleum is clean. The medicine cabinet has been replaced with a square of plywood screwed into the wall beams, not yet painted. The fixtures have been removed and not replaced. A bare bulb with a pull chain hangs from a hole in the ceiling.

I bend to look under the sink. There's evidence of an old leak, with corrosion on the drainpipe and warped wood, and more of that lingering stench overlaid with the smell of bleach. Nothing dripping now, though.

On the floor next to the toilet, gold glints and catches my attention. I pick it up, an earring, the hook bent and broken. Blonde hairs tangle around the rest of it. Beth's earring. I put it on the edge of the sink and wash my hands. The water drains without a problem. I wait, but there's no rising tide of brown water.

"Told you," Christian says when I return to the main living area.

"Whatever you did is making it back up to the main house now," I complain. "Last night after Eli got home, we had a little trouble."

"We had a great time at the concert, by the way. His buddy seemed to dig it, too. You're welcome. I made your kid cool." Christian nudges the glass another inch closer to me. "I could go over there and take a look, if you want."

"You are surprisingly good at fixing things," I tell him. Again, I do not take the glass.

His eyebrows raise. "Surprisingly? Why should you be surprised?"

"Because I've only ever known you to be good at breaking them."

He frowns. "Oh, c'mon, Jewelann. That's harsh."

I fix him with a look but say nothing.

Christian's frown deepens into a scowl. "Surgeons have to be good at fixing shit. That's kind of the point."

"They're also supposed to have a God complex," I point out.

"It's not a complex. It's a necessary self-confidence. You can't cut into someone without being absolutely convinced of your own invincibility."

"And you've always been very good at that," I say. "Cutting into someone, absolutely convinced of your own invincibility."

Christian lifts his glass in a one-sided toast. He sips with a small grimace that could indicate pain or pleasure; I can't tell which. He swirls the liquid in the glass and holds it up to the light. Sips again.

"Look, I know we've had our issues in the past. I don't blame you for being angry with me. I used to be a real dick."

"Oh, you think?" Humorless laughter huffs out of me. The sincerity in his words stings me. Once upon a time, I'd have done anything for an apology from the man across from me.

"I think," Christian says. "Yes. And I'm asking you to forgive me."

He sounds as though he means it. I can't trust him, of course, but everything inside me that I've been holding back yearns now toward him. I take the glass. Sip. The wine is thick and rich and laden with notes of cherry, chocolate, vanilla. It's good, but of course it is. Christian wouldn't drink anything but the best.

"You think I don't know how bad I fucked up?" His voice goes low and rasping. His gaze cuts from mine for a second before returning. "Back then, but also now? I look around this room and think about how it was with us . . ."

"Stop."

Christian moves around the counter toward me. Wine swirls in his glass as he taps it on mine. I can smell his cologne. He tips the glass to his lips and, fascinated, my eyes lock on the up-and-down pulse of his throat as he swallows. He looks me in the eyes again.

"You always tasted so good," he murmurs.

I take a step back, turning away from him. I'm already shaking inside. My mouth dries.

"And your body . . . damn, Jewelann. You know how they say wine gets better with age? So did you."

When he moves up behind me to push aside the fall of my hair, to brush the back of my neck with his fingertip, I have to put a hand on the counter to keep myself steady. He puts his arms around me. His chin on my shoulder, his cheek pressing mine. My body curves into his.

"I'm not one of your desperate fuck buddies, Christian."

"No," he says. "You're definitely not."

Red wine always makes me melancholy, and it's hitting my empty stomach with ferocity. I'm too dizzy, too soon. How could I have thought I'd be the one in control here?

When I don't speak, Christian says, "You don't like the wine? How about a little something else?"

When he pulls out a small cloth pouch from the kitchen drawer, I hold back a gasp. I recognize that little bag, pattered with vivid orange and yellow flowers. It had been his mother's. It's where she kept her "happy pills."

"Where'd you get those?" I ask when he holds out his hand, palm open, to show off the loose pills.

"What? Mommy's special candy?"

I freeze. "How did you—"

"Eli told me all about it. You think that kid doesn't remember, but he does."

"I never thought he didn't remember," I tell him.

Christian closes his fingers over the drugs and acts like he's going to tip them back into the pouch. "Going once? Going twice . . ."

"Put them away."

My fingertips press my forehead. I close my eyes. Am I swaying? It's hard to tell. When I open them, the room isn't spinning. Only I am.

Then he is kissing me, and my mouth is open for him, and his tongue is on mine, stealing away all my protests.

He's breathing fast when we pull apart from each other. His lips are wet. He pushes hair away from my face to cup me on both sides of my jaw, holding me in place as though I'm trying to get away, even though I'm not.

"Do you still want what I have?" I murmur.

I know it's not love. It's never been love, at least not for him. But I still have a chance at getting him to do what I want.

"Maybe. Why?"

I smile. "Because I know a way we can both get a lot of money."

\*     \*     \*

"You'd never get away with it." Christian has not said yes . . . but he hasn't said no, either.

"This couch is not comfortable." I shift on it, firm blue foam, and wish for the squishy brown plaid cushions on the couch he sold.

Next to me, Christian leans back and drains his glass. "Maybe not, but it's clean and doesn't have a nest of mice living in it. Did you hear what I said?"

"I heard you."

"I can't even believe you're talking about this," he says with a shake of his head but a gleam in his gaze. "So much for you never asking me for anything. I just never thought it would be this."

I ignore that last statement. "You've already wrecked this place. What's a little hole in the roof going to set you back? Only some time and a little physical effort. It's a lot of money. I could pay off all my debts, including the mortgage. You could pay off your school loans."

"But why go through all of that?" Christian asks me. "Just leave him, Jewelann. Get alimony. A couple years of child support. I get that you want to keep the house for Eli's sake, I mean, the kid's got a complex about it."

I sit up straight. "What do you mean?"

"He's worried about your money problems. He's worried about having to move. He says he knows how important that house is to you. It's like the idea of living anywhere else never occurred to him as a possibility. He's not worried about you dumping Ken's ass, I'll tell you that." Christian's low, throaty chuckle brims with smug satisfaction.

"Divorce is expensive."

"But it won't send you to prison," Christian says, and then, gently, "Life isn't like the movies. Killing someone isn't *easy*, Jewelann."

Curling up next to him, my feet tucked beneath me, my head on his shoulder, I feel something I never expected to feel with him. Content. Calm.

"And you'd get caught," he continues. "*I'd* get caught. Don't you ever listen to those true crime podcasts? It's always the boyfriend. Especially if there's a fresh insurance policy."

"You're not my boyfriend."

He hesitates. "I think you should consider all your options before you do something like that. That's all. C'mon, Jewelann. You're smarter than that."

It's still not a "no."

I twist to look at his face. "You think I'm smart?"

"Smartest girl I've ever known," Christian says.

The kiss is sweet, but with a hint of heat. He looks surprised when I pull away. He touches his mouth, briefly, with his fingertips.

"You should go," he says. "Before my lack of morals takes over."

"I don't want to go."

My knees dent the couch cushions as I straddle him. My hands find his face, cupping it the way he did mine earlier. I tip his head back. Find his mouth with mine.

His low groan sends a thrill all through me. Christian's hands move up over my hips to cup my breasts. He pushes himself against me. He's hard.

"Does this mean you forgive me?" he says around the tangle of our tongues.

"No."

His laugh is rough. His hands, rougher. His grip moves me, rocking our bodies together. Skin on skin, we're naked, we're touching, writhing, groaning, moaning, sweating, coming. It's the same as it's always been, but different, too. For the first time in all the times Christian and I have had sex, I don't worry, after, what it "meant." As I collect my scattered clothes and freshen up in the bathroom, I'm not trying to figure out how he feels, because it doesn't matter.

I don't trust Christian.

But I can use him.

# 27

I'M DRUNK, BUT not on wine. High, but not from drugs. I'm boneless with satisfaction. I'm glowing with it, my cheeks hot, my neck hot, my chest burning. My coat is open to the cold November air as I cross the backyard. The soggy patch in the yard crunches with frost.

*This isn't love, it isn't love, it's never been love and will never be love . . .*

It's potential. A plan. Possibilities. My mind whirls with thoughts of the freedom within my grasp.

In my kitchen, I fill a glass with ice and then water, and I gulp it greedily. Splashing. My hands shake. More water spills. I'm no longer calm.

I put the glass on the counter, then both my hands. I lean against it, head down, drawing in breath after breath to hold my hysterical, sobbing laughter at bay.

The sound of footsteps behind me straightens me up. I turn to see Eli and another boy about the same age standing in the hallway outside the kitchen. Eli looks aghast. The other boy smirks.

"That's your mom?" He makes a gesture I can't interpret, but Eli can.

My son scowls. "Yeah."

It's the first time he's brought home a friend. I can't do anything to hide the rising heat in my cheeks, but I clear my throat. I put on a smile.

"Are you boys hungry? I can make some snacks."

The other kid looks at Eli, then back at me with another smug grin. "No thanks. I have to get home."

"Are you sure? It's no trouble—"

"No, Mom," Eli interrupts. "Jesus."

Minutes later, I can't be sure how many, he returns to the kitchen alone. I haven't managed to move away from the sink. I'm running cool water over my wrists and trying to get my shit together.

"You're drunk," he accuses.

I turn off the water and dry my hands with a dish towel without looking at him. "I'm not *drunk*, Eli."

"It's the middle of the afternoon, and you're shit-faced. Where were you?"

"I don't have to explain myself to you," I say. "But I was in the carriage house talking with Christian about the renovations over there."

He glowers. "Great. That's just fucking great."

"Hey. Language."

Eli ignores me and leaves the kitchen. His footsteps thud, heavy, on the stairs. His door slams. I give myself another minute or two to compose myself.

He doesn't answer when I knock on his door. I try again, harder this time. "Eli. Open up."

The door opens a crack. He looks out. "What do you want?"

"Can I come in and talk to you?"

Reluctantly, he pulls open the door. His room is a mess. I sit on the edge of his unmade bed. He sits in his desk chair, pushing it back and forth, not looking at me.

"I'm sorry if I embarrassed you in front of your friend."

He snorts. "Scotty's not my *friend*. He just came over to get something from me."

"Something like what?" A headache has begun throbbing behind my eyes.

"Just something for school."

"Well," I say, "I'm sorry that I embarrassed you. Do you want to talk about it?"

"No, Mom. I don't want to talk about anything with you. Stop asking. Okay? I'm fine." He spins around to face his closed laptop on the desk.

I press my fingertips between my eyes, trying to pinch away the growing pain. "Clearly, you're not fine."

"Oh, and that matters *now*?"

His words push me to sit up straight. "What's that supposed to mean?"

"You're just worried I'm going to tell Dad about you and Christian. Well, don't be. I'm not going to tell him anything." He fiddles with the laptop but doesn't open it.

"There's nothing you need to tell your father about me and Christian." I'm running hot and cold, my cheeks blazing but my fingers numb.

Eli spins his chair to face me. His expression is hard. His lip curls. "I mean, look, I don't blame you for cheating on Dad. He's gone all the time, and he doesn't seem to make you happy. But you don't have to jump on the first dick that'll have you—"

'That's enough!"

"Christian's supposed to be *my* friend!" Eli leaps to his feet. "Mine!"

"He's not," I begin, but Eli shouts again.

"It's *your* fault I don't have any friends. That I'm a fucking mess. I'm the weird kid. It's all your fault! And you know it!"

He fights off my attempt at an embrace, and panting, falls back. Both of his hands go up. I retreat.

"I thought you were making new friends at school," I whisper.

Eli shrugs, cutting his gaze away. "Christian's the only one who gives me anything. Everyone else only wants something from me."

"I'm sorry that's how it feels, Eli, but please, listen to me. Christian is not reliable. He makes promises he doesn't keep, has no intention of keeping. You can't count on him." My voice shakes but gets stronger as I speak. "I have known him for a long time. No matter what he says, we were never, ever close. He only cares about himself."

Eli shakes his head. "You're wrong. Christian's the only person in my life who's never lied to me."

"That you know of. And if he hasn't yet, he will. I promise you, he will. And I don't break my promises to you, do I? Have I, ever?"

For a moment I think he's going to protest some more. Defy me. His expression shifts.

"No. I guess not."

I don't try to hug him again. "He's charming, but he's only out for himself. I just don't want you to get caught up in something over your head. That's all. I don't want you to get hurt."

"I'm not in over my head," Eli says, hesitates, then adds, "Why, what did he say to you about me?"

"Nothing. Is there something he should have told me?"

"No," Eli says. We look at each other. "Are you going to forbid me from hanging out with him?"

I sigh and pinch the bridge of my nose again. "Would it stop you?"

He doesn't reply.

Eli has never been a defiant child, so that non-answer tells me everything I need to know. I sigh again, trying to fill my lungs with enough air to stop me feeling as though I'm drowning. I can't.

"You're not weird," I say finally.

His laugh is broken. "If you're the weird kid in elementary school, you're the weird kid forever. People remember the bad stuff."

*You were a real stoner, back in the day.* Lisa's words to me echo in my head. I'd poked Beth about her disordered eating. My son is right. People remember the bad stuff.

"High school," I tell him, "is not forever. You're going to graduate. Go off to school. Move away from here. You're going to live your life, Eli, and it's going to be amazing."

After a moment, he nods. "But Mom . . . what about you?"

I think of a bank account with a balance big enough to take care of everything. No more financial worries. No more unhappy housewife. All it will take is a little more working on Christian and an unfortunate accident.

"Don't you worry about me. I'm going to live my life too."

# 28

I WAKE UP WHEN the body slides into bed behind me. I try a scream, but all that comes out is a puff of air. I fight against the blankets. I'm soaking wet. Terrified.

"Jewel," my husband says. "It's just me."

I twist around in the tangle of my sheets to face him. He's naked. Wet. He must've come right from the shower. He smells of soap and toothpaste and mouthwash, but there's something beneath all of those scents. Musky sweat. Something sour. It's the smell of the air before a storm. Thick, oppressive, full of threat.

"I didn't mean to scare you. I was trying not to wake you up. Go back to sleep." He gathers me close, my face pressed to his chest. My nose is squished.

I turn my face to the side, mouth open to take in a breath. I won't be able to go back to sleep tucked up against him this way, not with my ears still throbbing from the pressure of my heart pounding. Not with the odor swirling around him. I push at his chest until he releases me. The covers are still snarled around me, too tight. Moving is a struggle.

When I'm on my back at last, I pull the blankets to my chin. "Why did you come home in the middle of the night?"

He's silent except for the slight whistle of his in-out breathing. I know he's not asleep. I roll toward him, my knee nudging his.

"Ken," I say sharply. I draw in breath after breath, smelling him, seeking proof that he wears the stink of another woman on him, no matter how hard he tried to wash it away. There's no perfume, but there is . . . still . . . something.

He gathers me close again, crushing me against his bare, damp chest. One of my arms is trapped between us. I put the other around him, my fingers stroking over his back. Feeling for what? The marks of fingernails? I don't know. Something.

Ken buries his face against the side of my neck. Nothing about this position is comfortable. My body aches, twisted and held too tightly. I can't breathe. I can't move.

"I needed to come home," he says.

A decade ago, his confession to me that he'd "strayed" had started out much like this, with clinging desperation. My heart kicks into another round of pounding. I tighten my arm over his back as I try to shift and give myself some small relief.

"You know I'd never do anything to hurt you," he says.

I don't want to hear this. "Shh."

"No." Ken pushes me away from him, twists and turns to switch on the lamp. He sits up bed. "Listen, baby. I want us to get out of here."

I sit too, blinking in the bright light. My heartbeat slows. "Get out of where?"

"This place. This house. This town. I want us to just . . . get out. Go someplace new. Get a fresh start." Ken sounds eager. His eyes are bright. His grin stretches wide.

I try to choose my words carefully, but they feel like marbles in my mouth, rolling and tumbling, clattering against my teeth. "I don't understand."

"I want out."

"Of . . ."

"This house," Ken says. "This town."

"What about this marriage? Is that what you're really saying?" Those marbles plunk, one by one, from between numbed lips.

We stare at each other.

"I don't want a divorce," Ken says finally.

"I'm just . . . bored," Ken says.

"I'm just . . . looking for something new," Ken says.

"I'm just . . . trying to live my life," Ken says.

Outside, dawn tickles the sky. I am grainy eyed. My stomach is upset. We sit next to each other, backs against the headboard, and every time he moves to brush against me, I shift so we no longer touch.

"Where do you even want to go?" I ask him.

"Anywhere," Ken says. A pause. "Wisconsin."

I close my eyes and press my fingertips to the lids. "What's in Wisconsin you suddenly can't live without?

"The only thing I can't live without is my family."

I twist to face him. "Is that us? Me and Eli?"

"Of course. Who else would it be? You know I have nobody else. Nothing else."

I have never seen my husband cry. Watching him break down now, I feel too distant to immediately offer him comfort. In fact, the idea of soothing him revolts me. He buries his face first in his hands as he rocks with sobs, then against my neck as he clutches me. Reluctantly, I hold him while he weeps, but my own tears won't come.

"Tell me you love me," he demands, his face wet against me. His mouth works on my skin.

I'm repulsed, but I don't push him away. I pull him closer, and I can't be sure, any longer, if my answer is truth or a lie. "I love you."

"Tell me everything will be all right."

"Everything will be all right," I finally soothe in a whisper, stroking his hair. My voice is calm. My lips pull back, baring my teeth.

"Tell me," Ken says over and over, "I'm not a bad person. Tell me I'm not a bad person. Tell me, Jewelann, that I'm not a bad person."

"You're not a bad person."

Again, as with my declaration of love, I don't know if this is the truth. I say it, though, because it is what he wants to hear, and because I don't know what else to say.

"I swear to you, Jewelann, I'm going to take care of you and Eli. And you're going to take care of me. Right? That's how it'll be."

"Of course I'll take care of you."

He burrows deeper, his breathing slowing, and I wonder how he could possibly fall asleep in the midst of all this drama. Then he snores, and I push him gently away from me so I can turn on my side with my back to him.

I'm going to take care of him all right.

* * *

"The money will be there later this week," Ken told me when I asked him again about the direct deposit that hasn't shown up. Again. "I'm on it, honey. Trust me."

I'm not sure I can.

He's home for two days before he tells me he's going back out on the road. We fight in low whispers about calling a plumber again to fix the drains that backed up again after Ken did several loads of laundry in a row, although I'd warned him not to. The basement stinks. The dryer thump-thumps with his clothes in it. There's still a load in the washer.

"The last guy said it was probably tree roots growing into them," I tell him.

"So hire someone to yank them out. Dig up the whole stupid system back there." Ken puts his hands on his hips. I see Christian in that stance. "Call the city, find out what it takes to get hooked up to the city sewer, for the love of Pete, Jewelann."

"With what? You haven't been paid in two months!" I shoot back at him. I'm no longer worried about mollifying him. Shit, as they say, has been getting real. Literally.

"My bonus—"

"They want fifteen grand to hook us up," I cut in, voice flat. "Anyway, the bonus is almost gone. You *need* to get your paycheck."

His eyes narrow. "What happened to it?"

"A giant television set." My phone catches in my jeans pocket, but I tug it free. I pull up the credit card app and bring up the most recent charges. I hold up the phone to face him. "Going to corn mazes? Pumpkin patches? Haunted hayrides? With who, Ken? If you're supposed to be on the road, traveling, who are you taking to all these places?"

His look of utter disdain is meant to knock me back, put me in my place, but I won't let it.

"All of those places need point-of-sale systems, Jewelann. They need someone who knows how to set them up and maintain them, just like any other business." He shakes his head, eyes sad, lower lip almost trembling. "To think you didn't have faith in me. Your husband. I told you I'd always take care of you and Eli. Didn't I?"

I let him embrace me, although my body stays stiff and unyielding. "But you're not taking care of us."

A long silence fills the space between us as Ken stares at me. Slowly at his sides, his fingers curl and press into his palms, making fists. He draws in a breath.

"How fucking dare you," Ken says. "All I've ever done is take care of you. All those days you were a drooling mess, I'd come home and find you passed out on the couch. All these years I worked to keep a roof over your head, and look at this shithole, you barely keep it clean, every damn thing is breaking down while you're out shopping and spending. I work my goddamned fingers to the bone . . . You really think I never knew? I'm not an idiot!"

But *I* am. That's the unspoken insult. It's always been there, and I have always pretended I didn't hear it.

"I know what you keep in there," Ken says.

"What?" But I know what he means.

His shoulders move with every breath as he pants, in and out, up and down, as his fists open and close. "I know. What you keep. In there. That storage unit. I *know*. And you've never told me about *that*, so how fucking dare you ride my ass about one single fucking thing. Ever."

Ken grits out the words through clenched jaws. The veins in his forehead bulge as his face turns a shade of crimson that scares me. He's always been so fit in the past, but he's put on weight over the past few months. He's getting older, past fifty now. Maybe I won't need that ladder and an accomplice.

"Ken—"

"I do everything for you, Jewelann! I do everything for this fucking family! Do you think I like being on the road all the time? Staying in shitty motels, eating shitty food? Do you?"

"I think you might," I reply without shouting, although my voice does tremble.

"I'd just looooove to stay at home all day doing fucking nothing. Just like you. Just like my *mother*. She was a slattern, too." He yanks my hand upward, shaking it. "Neither one of you deserved a ring like this."

Ken had only ever spoken of his mother in the same tone you'd use for a saint. I try to pull out of his grip, and he grabs again for the ring, which is stuck on my knuckle and won't come free. I cry out as the prongs scrape me, and he lets my hand drop.

"You want to change places with me? Huh?" He pokes at the air between us, but I have no doubt he'd be stabbing that finger into me, if I were close enough. "You want that, Jewelann? You want to go out and get a fucking job so I can stay home and keep house?"

"You're scaring me. Please, calm down."

He turns away, huffing and puffing and scraping both hands through his hair so that it stands on end. His shoulders hunch. He's muttering. More curses. Words I can't make out.

I think I'm watching my husband lose his mind.

"Let's talk about this," I plead.

Without turning, he says, "I want out."

Imagining this doesn't make it easier to hear. I draw in a breath. "Ken. Please."

"I want out," he says again. "Out of this house. Away from this fucking asspucker of a town. I need to get away from here. Don't you get it? I wanted to get you and Eli out of this place. Broaden your horizons. But you'll never go for it. You're embedded in this house like a goddamned tick."

I have no idea who this man is. His face twists, mouth slick with spittle and even some froth at the corners of his lips. I try to back away from him, but he grabs my wrist. He's strong.

"You're hurting me, Ken."

He releases me, instantly apologetic. "I'm sorry. I've just been under a lot of stress. You have to understand that, right? I'm out there busting my hump to do right by this family, and I come home to find out it's all going down the drain."

"Nothing's going down the drain." My attempt at humor falls flat.

This is where I would hug him, tell him it's all going to be okay. Rub his shoulders. Take him upstairs. The thought of that curdles my stomach.

I reach for him. When I touch his shoulder, Ken whirls, throwing off my attempted embrace. His open hand catches me in a slap that sends me stumbling back.

"You leave her alone!" Eli's shout turns Ken toward him.

My son launches himself at his father, fists flailing. Ken puts up his hands in defense. Eli's attack falls short. Ken grabs him by the neck. Squeezes. Eli fights but can't even speak.

I can't believe this is happening. "Let him go!"

Ken shoves Eli away from him. Eli falls to the kitchen floor. Ken spits a gobbet of saliva next to his head. "He attacked me. Are you proud of your son, Jewelann?"

"He's your son, too," I whisper. My hands shake.

For a moment, my husband looks as though he means to hit me again, but he changes his mind. Steps back, hands up. Face grim.

"Fuck this," he says. "I'm out."

Then I'm on the floor next to Eli, helping him up, while Ken disappears upstairs. Eli isn't crying, but his face is red and he's breathing hard. I push his hair off his forehead.

"Did he hurt you?" he asks.

"I'm fine." I look at his throat. "Are you okay?"

"Yeah."

We stare at each other. When he hugs me, hard, I put my arms around him and hold him tight. We stand that way for a few seconds before he finally moves away.

Thumps from upstairs have us both looking at the ceiling. Ken's feet pound on the stairs. He comes back into the kitchen and doesn't look at either one of us, but we both move away from him as he flings open the basement door. More pounding footsteps on the stairs. Then, quiet.

"Is he leaving?"

"I don't know. Look, why don't you go upstairs? Let me talk to Dad. We just . . . we just had a fight. That's all." I put on a brave face, but my son sees right through it.

"I'm not leaving you alone with him."

Ken appears in the doorway with a duffel bag slung over his shoulder. He looks at us both. His expression is completely blank. He is a stranger.

"Where are you going?" I ask.

Without answering, he turns and goes out, down the front hallway. The door slams behind him. Eli goes to the kitchen window and looks out.

"He *is* leaving," he says. "Good."

My teeth chatter, so I clamp my jaw. I can't let my son see me break down about this. But what am I going to do now?

"Are you okay, Mom?"

"Yes. It was a fight. It'll be okay. Let your dad blow off some steam, that's all. He's under a lot of stress."

Eli's lip curls. "He hit you."

"I'll be fine. Really."

"You're bleeding," he says quietly.

I touch my face, but he shakes his head and takes my hand gently, turning it palm up. The diamond no longer glitters, coated in a smear of red. The wound stings, but it will close quickly. Wincing, I tug the ring hard enough to get it over my knuckle. The blood makes it slippery enough to come free quickly. I close my fingers around the ring.

He hugs me again.

"I can give you money." He pulls out a roll of bills from his pocket and fans it toward me.

I see a five, a ten, a twenty. "Where did you get that?"

"It's my birthday money and stuff. And Christian gave me some for helping him."

I close my hand over his, pushing the roll of money toward him.

"I don't need you to do that. Okay?" I grip his shoulders and look into his eyes. "I'll take care of us."

Whatever it takes.

CHAPTER

29

THE WOMAN BEHIND the jeweler's counter smiled at me when I came in, but she's not looking quite as cheerful now. Her gaze is soft and sympathetic. She places my engagement ring on a soft velvet pillow and rests both hands on the glass countertop on either side.

"This is a lovely piece, but I'm afraid it's not a diamond."

I wish I was surprised, but I'm only resigned. "What is it? Cubic zirconium?"

"It's white sapphire," she says. "Quite lovely, as I said."

"But not worth as much."

She shakes her head. "I'm afraid not. And we couldn't sell it here. You could try a pawn shop?"

My diamond earrings, at least, are real, although it turns out they're not worth much, either. The pawn shop gives me couple hundred bucks cash for them and another few for the ring. I leave the store with my hand feeling light and my heart heavy.

I need more.

Determination gets me to the storage unit's parking lot without running my car off the road. I'm not sobbing, but my vision blurs with tears that slip down my cheeks and drop off my chin to leave dark circles of wet on my jeans. I pull into a spot and pound the steering wheel, cursing first under my breath. Then louder. I let my head rest on the wheel. My heart pounds as though I've run a marathon, and chill sweat wends its way down the channel of my spine.

When I'm finally able to force myself out of the car, the November temperatures have dropped enough that my teeth chatter. I turn on the lights inside the unit, which is not climate-controlled. In the center of the space, I sit on a chair. Shelving units stacked with boxes, bins, and bags surround me. My breath puffs out in a long plume of silver.

I sit.

I close my eyes and think about all the hours I spent sorting through other people's castoffs, finding my own treasures. The thrill of finding a new piece to add to my collection was always its own kind of high. I told myself I'd flip this stuff, but once it was mine, I could not make myself get rid of it. *I'm going to do it.* That's what I'd said to Lisa, but it was a lie to her, and worse, to myself. This stuff, my *things.* It was never about spending the money; it was about having the stuff.

At last, a sob works its way out of me. Then another. I don't try to hold them back. I bend forward, my face in my hands, and permit myself to give in to the shame that floods me. I traded one addiction for another, but I got myself off the pills. Why can't I get myself off this too?

My vision still blurs as I force myself to my feet. The closest shelf contains clear shoebox bins of costume jewelry. Flower brooches, long strands of beads, oversized cocktail rings. I'd been buying it all by the bag from estate sales, promising myself I would sort through it and resell the individual pieces, or no, make a craft from them, or no, no, actually wear them to create my own vintage style, except I never had any place to go all dressed up in the jewelry of dead women. I rifle through it now, sorting the pieces with my fingers. A pinback pricks my finger, drawing blood.

I suck on it, hating the coppery taste but forcing myself to do it anyway. I put the lid back on the bin and heft it. There's got to be several pounds of assorted jewelry in this container alone. I count how many I have.

Five.

Five effing bins of costume jewelry I've never actually sorted through. I could have something worth real money in here, or it could all be worthless. I will never know unless I make myself find out. If I can't afford to pay the monthly storage unit fees, I will lose all of this. If I keep the storage unit and all of the stuff inside it, I could lose my house.

I don't care so much about the end of my marriage, but if I lose my house, I lose safety for me and my son. If I lose that, I lose my entire life.

Quickly, working fast so I can't stop myself, I dump the bins onto the floor. I kneel on the hard concrete. I sort.

Rings. Necklaces. Pins. Bracelets. Chains. One bin for each type of jewelry. My fingers blacken with dust and from rubbing old metal. Some of the pieces fall apart when I sort them. I toss the broken pieces into a cardboard box.

An hour passes.

My body cramps. My knees begin to scream. Sobbing, I sort.

Why did I ever buy all of this? What good does it do me for it all to sit in boxes in a storage unit, year after year? What is wrong with me? Why can't I just stop trying to fill my empty space with stuff that doesn't matter, can never matter?

By the time the jewelry is all divided up, my entire body aches as though I've been beaten. I can barely get to my feet. Everything creaks and cracks. My fingers barely have the strength to grip the first bin I lift. It starts to fall, but I manage to clutch it to my chest.

My own sweat stink hangs in the air. I cradle that bin like a baby. I close my eyes. It could go right back on the shelf, couldn't it? I did the hard work of sorting it all out; that was an accomplishment, wasn't it? Surely that was enough for today. I can come back tomorrow. Tomorrow, I can take the bins to the local vintage consignment store and see what they'll give me for it . . .

"No." I say this out loud, harsh and firm, as though I'm warning a naughty dog to get out of the garbage. "Not tomorrow. Now."

I have a duffel bag large enough to fit all five boxes, because of course I do. I got this one at a thrift store and couldn't pass it up because it had a pattern of honeybees on it, because for a while I collected everything that had bees on it. I told myself I liked the bright yellow sunshine optimism of bees and flowers. Because I could. Because every time I found a new piece in "my pattern" it was a shock straight to the pleasure center of my brain.

The truth is, I don't give a single fuck about bees.

I shove the boxes in the duffel and zip it up. It's heavy, but I can manage it. I wrestle it out to the car and shove it in the back seat, then go back inside the storage unit and find the box with all the bee stuff in it. I really don't have time to sort it right now, so I take the whole thing.

My heart races, my palms sweat, I'm having what feels like a panic attack, but I close up the storage unit and get back behind the wheel.

Today will only be the second time in ten years that Eli has come home from school to an empty house, but I need to get these boxes out of my car. If I take them home, even if it's only into the garage, I will persuade myself to leave them there. I *have* to do this now. I text him, though, to make sure he doesn't freak out. Dad gone. Mom gone, too? I wouldn't do that to him.

The woman behind the counter at the consignment shop greets me by name and a smile. She ought to. I've spent thousands of dollars in this store over the years.

"We haven't seen you in a while," she says. "You look great. I have some new pieces that just came in that I know you'll love."

"Actually, Marlene, I've got some things to drop off for you." I clear my throat, hoping my voice doesn't shake. "You know, just a few things I've picked up here and there, but I just don't use."

She looks surprised. "Oh. Well, I usually require an appointment to look over things customers bring in."

"Please," I say with as much dignity as I can maintain. "I've already brought it all in."

For a moment, I think she's going to deny me, but there must be something in my face that changes her mind. Desperation, I guess. She frowns a little but gestures for me to come forward.

My hands shake as I lift the first bin onto the glass countertop. Her frown deepens. She takes off the lid.

"Oh, wow. This is quite a collection. I don't even know if I could move some of these things, Jewelann, I'm sorry. I have to be honest with you. I'd really need to catalog all of this."

I don't even take out the other bins. "Sure, I understand."

"Did you bring in something else?"

I open the bee box to show her what's inside. "This."

She leans over the counter, then comes around the side to look it over. "Oh, these are so cute. But I don't really do housewares. I can take this dress. Oh, and the capri pants, too. And I can sort out the jewelry and let you know what I'll be able to take, if you can give me a few days?"

"Of course. That'll be fine. Do you know who might be interested in the housewares?"

She names a few other shops in town and gives me a business card for an estate sale company that might be interested. I already know that company, since, as I've done in Marlene's shop, I've spent thousands of dollars with them over the years.

"You could try selling in bulk lots online," she offers, her voice doubtful. "But unless you're prepared to really put in an effort and deal with the packing and shipping stuff, it can be a really daunting prospect. And you really need to have an eye for things. You can't just . . . I mean, not everything sells. I'm sorry."

"I understand." I should have changed my clothes before I came here, I realize now. I'm grungy.

Dress for the job you want, not the one you have. Dress to impress. Dress so you don't look like you're on your way to an utter breakdown.

"You know what? I can take the whole lot." Marlene waves off my attempted rebuttal. "No, no worries. I've been thinking about expanding into housewares, and this whole collection of bee stuff is a ready-made display. I'll consider it an experiment. How about that?"

"You don't have to do that," I begin, but I'm already handing over the box and the duffel with the boxes of costume jewelry as fast as I can.

She types quickly into her computer and prints out a receipt for me. "I'll put together a more specific inventory as soon as I have a chance, but whatever sells, I'll send you a check at the end of the month, okay?"

Stupidly, I blink at the paper. I don't know why I thought I'd walk out of here with cash in hand, but I can hardly take all the stuff back from her now, can I? What would I even do with it? She's watching me carefully as I fold up the paper and tuck it into my wallet to make sure it doesn't get lost.

"Jewelann, is everything all right?"

I find a smile. "Absolutely. Just, you know, hoping to get a little spare cash as soon as possible. Is there any way to maybe find out before the end of the month if anything's sold?"

"I get it. Christmas shopping, am I right?" Marlene laughs.

I don't shop for Christmas, but I don't bother to correct her. "Please."

"I'll do what I can. But . . ." She clears her throat a little uncomfortably. She makes a small gesture at the Etienne Aigner wallet I've set on the counter while we spoke. "If you're willing to part with that piece, I've been looking for one like it to match a handbag I already have. I'll buy it from you right now."

This wallet was meant for me. I found a hundred dollar bill in it. I was going to flip it, but I kept it, because it was supposed to be mine, it is *mine*.

My hands shake as I empty out the contents of the wallet and dump them straight into my bag. Photos, credit cards, a five dollar bill, a couple of quarters I save for when I go to the cheap grocery store that makes you pay to rent a cart.

She offers me thirty dollars.

I take it.

I shove the bills, a crisp twenty and a soft, worn ten, into my pocket, since I no longer have a wallet to put it in. I leave her shop with empty hands, the first time I've ever done that. Stepping out into the dimming gray sky, I blink upward at the soft drift of fat snowflakes. First snow.

I wait to feel unburdened, or at least proud of myself, but my chest hurts. When I look at myself in the rearview mirror, I'm startled to see the bloom of black-and-blue around my eye and a small cut high on my cheekbone that is also bruising. No wonder Marlene took pity on me. I'm pathetic, but I'm not going to let myself stay this way.

I used to fear Ken leaving me, but now he's done exactly what I always worried about. Instead of terror, sharp relief cuts through me. I have hit the bottom. The only way out from here now is up.

# 30

K EN'S BEEN GONE for three days, not a word from him in all that time. I haven't tried to get in touch with him, either. As far as I'm concerned, Eli and I are on our own.

I got the paperwork for the life insurance, not that it will do me much good if he never comes home. I'm searching through Ken's dresser for anything of value that I can sell, when my phone rings. I ignore it. I'm not interested in dealing with anyone trying to talk to me about my car's extended warranty. The call shunts to voice mail. A text buzzes through. It's from Lisa.

**Hey, I just heard something I think you need to know. Call me?**

How could I have gone from spending hours on the phone back in high school to physically cringing at the idea of actually talking to someone live, in real time, with their live, real voice? Still, if you want to make a friend, you should be a friend. I swipe to dial her number.

"What's up?" I close the dresser drawer with a thud.

"You sound pretty calm. I guess you haven't heard? I thought the school would've called you or something. Ugh, maybe *they* don't know. Probably too focused on dress-coding girls for bare shoulders instead of paying attention to actual—Forget I said anything."

"Actual what?" I sit on the edge of the bed, the phone cradled to my ear in a way that'll make my neck hurt if I'm not careful.

"Ugh," she repeats. "One of those disappearing pictures circulated around of Eli selling some pills to some of the kids at school."

Ice fills me. "You saw this?"

"No. And I don't know what kind of pills they were supposed to be. But Brianna told me a friend of hers saw it. Or a friend of the friend's friend, you know how it goes. She keeps in touch with a couple of the kids that haven't graduated yet."

"I haven't heard anything about it. Certainly not from the school." I swallow hard. "Look, I know my kid's not popular. But he's a good kid. I don't have any evidence that he's even taking drugs, much less selling them."

"It could just be one of those stories that gets passed around. You know, people hear things, and they get exaggerated. If someone heard that Eli's mom used to have a pill problem, then . . ." Lisa coughs.

"I quit all of that years ago. So he couldn't be getting them from me—" I stop myself short, almost clipping my tongue between my teeth.

There was that morning I'd thought he was high. And before I'd flushed it all away, some of my old stash had gone missing, but a few pills here and there? That can't be enough for him to be actually selling anything. Could it?

*Scotty's not my friend. He just came over to get something from me. Christian's the only one who gives me anything. Everyone else only wants something from me.*

That asshole. Everything inside me crumples, a fist crushing a sheet of paper. He's been using my son.

"Ugh. I'm sorry, Jewelann. If you didn't hear anything from the school, that probably means it's nothing to worry about. You know how they are over there. Jumping on the least little thing. Back when we were kids, man, you could show up to school totally baked and nobody said a word. The girls' basketball coach was sleeping with one of his players, nothing was ever done about it. I'm sure this thing with Eli is just a dumb rumor. For all we know he could've been handing out breath mints."

"Thanks for letting me know," I tell her.

Lisa sounds relieved. "Hey. If it was my kid, I'd want to know."

"If you hear anything else, tell me right away. And I'll talk to Eli," I tell her.

I barely give her the chance to say goodbye before I'm disconnecting the call. Down the hall in Eli's room, I shove open his door and start my search. My skin crawls at this invasion of his privacy, but fuck that. If my mother had searched my room just once, who knows, I might not have become someone who makes terrible choices over and over again.

My son, like his mother, has a lot of stuff. Old toys, books, schoolwork spread out on a bookshelf that had once been mine. His closet overflows with clothes he's outgrown. I shove aside hangers and reach toward the back, run my hands along the top of a shelf so high I have to push up onto my toes to reach it.

No drugs.

His laptop is closed on his desk, but I leave that alone. I sweep a hand under the edges of his mattress, tensing for the expectation of the stiff, glossy pages of a skin mag, but I guess kids these days get all they need from the internet. His bed is made, and I'm sure to check under the pillow. I look under the base of his lamp, which had been my favorite hiding place. I find only a few spider egg sacs.

Relief tries to fill me, but I won't let it. Lisa had done her best to make me feel better, but I know something's going on. Eli is tangled up in it, and Christian is the cause of it. Still, I know better than to confront my son without proof. Kids lie, even good ones.

I search the room again. Slower this time. I find no baggies, no bottles, not even a crumpled envelope filled with bitter dust. I almost find nothing, until one final sweep of his bookshelf sends a small square of paper fluttering to the carpet.

It's a prescription, made out to Elijah Jordan, and it's been signed by Dr. Christian Campbell.

I spend two hours on the internet, trying to figure out how to unlink my kid from all of this. I haven't been able to find much. I can't even find a way to discover if he's filled that prescription or one like it, even though he's a minor. HIPAA laws are complicated. Finally, I call the hospital directly to see if I can get some kind of confirmation, but since I don't have a direct line to the surgical center, I first get the runaround. And then I get an answer.

Dr. Christian Campbell does not exist.

# CHAPTER

# 31

NOT AT KETTERING Medical, anyway.

I spend another hour doing other research. I'm sweating. Grim-faced. When the doorbell rings, I ignore it. It rings again. Someone knocks. Irritated, I swing open the front door, ready to tell someone off, half expecting to see a smug and grinning C.C., but it's Lisa.

She looks terrible. Dark circles under her eyes. Smudged lipstick. "Beth is missing."

"What? Come in." I usher her into my kitchen, where we sit at the table across from each other.

"She wasn't answering my messages. I thought maybe she was mad at me because I'd texted her to use her good sense and stay the hell away from C.C., but finally I just called her. Steve answered her phone. Said she hasn't been home in almost a week."

"Wow."

"Yeah. He said they had a fight, and he thought she'd gone to her sister's, but when he called Tammy to find out when Beth was coming home, Tammy said she wasn't there, and she hadn't seen her. Or heard from her."

"That's messed up."

Lisa drops her face into her hands for a few seconds, rubbing at her temples. "I need a drink."

I don't point out that it's barely noon. I find a bottle of wine and pour us both glasses. She drains hers and shoves the empty glass across the table.

"Do you have any vodka?"

"I might." I check in the cabinet next to the fridge, way in the back, where my parents used to keep their booze. The bottle I pull out isn't that old, but it is dusty. I put it, along with a carton of orange juice, on the table and get her a glass.

She fixes herself a drink while I watch. She lifts it toward me, sips, returns it to the table with a grimace. "She's done this before. Steve, in case you haven't guessed, is kind of an asshole, and he didn't bother to follow up for a few days. When Tammy said she hadn't seen her, he called the police. That's what he told me, anyway."

"Wow," I say again, like a loser.

"I'm seriously freaked out. Even if she went off someplace without telling me, she wouldn't go anywhere without her *phone*," Lisa says. "He asked me if I knew whether or not she was sleeping with Christian. I said as far as I knew, they were just friends."

"*Lisa.*"

"She's my friend," Lisa says. "And as far as I *do* know, they weren't sleeping together."

We stare at each other for few seconds.

"What night did you see her with C.C.?" Lisa asks at last.

"I don't remember the exact day. I'd have to look at my calendar."

Lisa gives me a grim look. "I haven't been able to stop thinking about what you said about Jen Tillis. That you thought maybe Christian was the reason why she killed herself. I don't know. Shit, Jewelann. Do you think C.C. *could* have hurt her? Not just her feelings. *Her.* Could he?"

She sounds desperate.

*Long rolls of carpet in the back of Christian's SUV.*

*Beth does not come out of the carriage house.*

*Beth's earring, broken, on the floor.*

*It's not easy to kill someone, Jewelann.*

*It's always the boyfriend.*

I drain my glass of wine and get up to look out through the sliding glass doors. His car isn't in the driveway, but I saw lights on over there last night when I got up to use the bathroom, so I know he was there. But had he been alone? "Why would Christian have any reason to hurt Beth?"

Do *I* think he hurt Beth?

"Why does any man need a reason to hurt a woman?" Lisa asks darkly, each word jagged and icy.

More silence. It stands out to me that neither one of us has dared to say the word "kill" aloud. "Nobody's saying she's dead, Lisa."

"Maybe she and C.C. ran off together—" Lisa begins.

"No." I cut her off, razor-sharp. "He . . . no."

Not after what happened between us, after I let him back in. It's one thing to know he was with me after being with Beth, but I can't bear to imagine him being with her after being with *me*. What about murdering her, though? Can I bear to think he's capable of doing that? I did, after all, ask him to help me kick a ladder out from underneath my husband.

Still, we can't go down this bumpy, winding road simply out of hysteria. I don't like Beth, and I don't trust Christian, but something about all of this feels off. I remember Beth slurring, weaving, stoned. He didn't have to kill her to be involved in her going missing. Accidents happen. And if he was responsible, he'd have hidden that, wouldn't he?

He would.

Anyone would.

"Oh, God." Lisa rocks back and forth, squeaking the chair. "This is really messed up. Should we go to the police?"

"If Steve thought Christian was involved, he'd have told the police that. We don't need to complicate anything." And I don't want the police to have any reason to come around, not until I can be sure Eli won't get caught up in this.

Lisa nods but looks skeptical.

"People have fights, they need time to cool off. I mean, look at me." I hold up my bare-fingered hand. "Ken and I had a fight a few days ago. He told me wanted out. He left. I haven't heard from him since then."

"So he's missing, too?"

"I don't think he's *missing*," I say, after a pause. Lisa stares with the concentrated focus of someone trying very hard to see only one of me. "He's just gone."

Lisa helps herself to another healthy glug of vodka, thinning the orange juice to a pale gold. She swirls it and sips with a grimace. Another heavy sigh. I sip wine while she drinks my vodka, and soon she's heading toward being smashed.

She takes a long drink and sets the glass down with a heavy sigh. "So . . . maybe Beth is just gone for a while, and she'll come back?"

"I'm sure she will." I'm not any more certain of that than I am about Ken, and I care about as much. I care about not giving the police any reason to come around.

"Are you okay?" she asks.

"Have you ever been afraid of something bad happening for so long that when it finally does, you can't even worry about it? That's kind of where I am."

Lisa nods. "I'm sorry. I know you weren't happy, but it must suck to be left without warning. You'll be okay, though. You're strong."

I don't argue with her. "Thanks."

"Thank you," she says with the bleary sincerity of the intoxicated. "For making me feel better about Beth. I'm sure you're right, and it's all going to be fine."

We sit together for a few minutes after that before Lisa hauls herself upright and leaves for home. I rinse out her glass and put the much emptier bottle of vodka away. I look across the yard to see Christian's SUV in the driveway, and my hands shake so much I drop the glass. It shatters in the sink.

I know exactly what reason Christian would have for making sure Beth disappeared.

# 32

CHRISTIAN TAKES.

Christian does not give, he will always take and take, and I should not be hurt by this, I cannot be wounded, and yet here I am, pounding on the door to the carriage house so hard I bruise my knuckles. The door is locked, no surprise. My key doesn't work, and that is.

I pound harder, slapping my palm against the metal door. When he doesn't answer the door, I call him. It dumps straight into voice mail. I call again. Again. Pounding. Calling. Texting. He's going to answer this door and answer my questions, or—

"Jesus, what are you trying to do, break it down? Chill out, Jewelann," Christian says after he yanks open the door.

His hair is rumpled, face crumpled with sleep. He wears only a pair of boxers that hide nothing. Why is he always almost naked? The way he stands opens the flap so I could see inside, if I looked.

I don't look. I push past him and into the living room. I scan for signs of . . . what, I'm not sure, but all I see is destruction. The kitchen cabinets are still missing. The floor, swept clean but bare concrete. The new furniture has been rearranged, but that's not proof of anything. The faint odor of cleanser hangs in the air, and it's not proof, either.

"Where is Beth?"

Christian shrugs and closes the door behind me. "No idea. I haven't seen her lately."

"That would be a trick if you did. She's been missing for days." I advance on him, stabbing a finger in his direction. I feel wild-eyed. Deranged, like I'm daring him to come at me, give me an excuse to fight back. I could launch myself at him and rake his face open with the blunt tips of my nails, if I had to. "Her earring was on your bathroom floor. Broken."

"What does that have to do with me? Oh, no way." His eyebrows go up. "You think I did something to her?"

"The day after I saw her here, you were leaving with big rolls of carpet. Big enough to hide a body. And you told me 'killing someone isn't easy.' How would you know that?"

"It was an *assumption*," Christian says. "I never fucking killed anyone, are you out of your mind?"

I think I might be.

"What did you do to Jen Tillis?" I am proud of the way my voice doesn't shake when I demand this answer.

Christian's brow knits. "What do you mean?"

"She killed herself. Or did she?"

"What the actual fuck are you trying to say, Jewelann? That I killed her *and* Beth? I mean . . . that's ludicrous. That's beyond messed up." He puts a hand over his heart as though I've actually hurt him.

Good. I want to hurt him. "She overdosed. That's what her mother told mine, and what my mother told me. Overdosed on tranquilizers."

Soft laughter hisses out of him. "You think I gave her pills?"

"You gave *me* pills," I remind him.

"I wasn't even seeing her anymore. I broke it off with her when we went off to school. She kept trying to get back together with me, she'd send me letters, call me all the time. She showed up at my parents' house to get them on her side. She even showed up at my dorm once. I might have broken her heart, but I did not *kill* her."

"Might have?" I laugh, short and sharp and hard.

"Fine. I broke her heart. And Beth's too, I guess. Just like I broke yours. Is that what you want me to say?"

I ignore that question. "You gave Beth drugs. And now she's missing. And I think you *do* know something about it. Something you're covering up."

I am surprised to see that this seems to affect him. With a sullen expression, he puts his hands on his hips. Unlike all the other times, the posture doesn't send me a single tingle.

Christian scrubs his hand through his hair, then over his face with a small groan before fixing his gaze on mine. "We partied. She wanted to stay the night, but I told her she couldn't. I don't know how she lost the earring, but I'm surprised she didn't lose anything else. She was wasted. You saw that, right? As far as I know, she stumbled off home to her hubby. If she overdosed, she didn't do it here, and I sure as shit didn't roll her up in a damned carpet. If you're really that worried about it, go to the police. I have nothing to hide."

"That isn't true."

His smile is brittle. Fixed. Eyes, bright. "No?"

"Where did you say you went to med school?"

He pushes past me to grab two wineglasses and a bottle from the counter. He pops off the decorative stopper and pours quickly while I watch. I refuse the glass he tries to hand me. "It's a school in the Caribbean called St. George's."

"I looked up St. George's. They have a great alumni resource center. Turns out, though, there's no way to get in touch with you through it. I wonder why that is?"

For the first time, Christian seems taken aback. He swallows the gulp of wine he took. "You looked me up?"

"You might've started at St. George's, but you didn't graduate from there. I called Kettering Medical, too. Guess what? They don't have a record of any Dr. Campbell, intern or resident or anything else. There was a Christian Campbell listed in the staff directory, and guess where he works? Maintenance."

Christian does not refute this. He looks faintly surprised, eyebrows raised. He crosses his arms over his bare chest. Stares.

"Told you I was handy," he says.

"You're not a doctor."

"Yet," Christian says, a finger in the air. "I am not a doctor *yet*."

"But you're writing prescriptions like you are. Is that why you did something to Beth? Because you wrote her a fake prescription, and something happened to her?"

"What makes you think—?"

"I found one in Eli's room. I *know* you're having my son sell pills for you."

"Cheers, Nancy Drew. Now if only it wasn't for those meddling kids." He puts his glass on the countertop. "Look, Jewelann. We all do what we have to in order to get by. Right? I do it. You do it. So I'm not sure where you get off judging me for anything."

"You wreck everyone who's ever cared about you, and that includes my son. I've sacrificed too much, tolerated too much, done too much, to let you ruin his life. You will never again ask him to sell drugs for you. You will take back whatever drugs you gave him. You will not involve him in any way with that business. Do you understand me?"

He looks . . . wary. This thrills me. I feel my own wicked grin spreading across my expression, my own Joker's grimace.

If I look insane, so what? Let him be afraid of me, for a
change.

I move past him, into the kitchen area. Things are worse
on this side of the island. No drawers. No cabinet doors. A
few pots and pans, some plates, some cleaning supplies. No
signs of struggle. Just a bachelor's mess.

My knees buckle, and I almost go to them. "You have
ruined this place. Ruined!"

"It's not ruined," he says.

I throw out my arms. "Look at it!"

"It's being *renovated*," Christian tells me.

"You're not doing shit over here but tearing it apart,
breaking the plumbing—"

"I'm not doing a damn thing with the plumbing. I told
you that. Hey. Calm down, okay?" He moves toward me, but
I hold up a hand to stop him.

"I want you to pack up your shit and get out of here,
today."

Christian grins smugly. "You can't kick me out. I have rights."

"We don't have a lease."

He shrugs. "That doesn't matter. First of all, you have
to give me three days' notice to vacate, and it needs to be in
writing."

My laugh burns my throat. "I should've guessed you'd
know the laws and how to get around them."

"Second of all," he says, still infuriatingly calm, "you
don't really need to do this. Okay? We can work it out. No
need to get the police involved."

"I thought you didn't care if I talked to the police. You
have nothing to hide, right?"

He chuckles. Shrugs. Give me an "oh, garsh" look that
used to charm the panties off me and still would, if I let it.

"I guess we all have something to hide, don't we?" he
says.

"Yeah. Like a body."

"A *body*? How do you know she's even missing? You two aren't close."

"Lisa told me she was calling Beth's phone, and her husband answered. Said she'd been missing for a few days."

Christian stares at me, first without saying a word. Then he laughs. Louder, louder, his guffaw becomes a whistling hiss. His face turns red. He has to wipe away tears. I stare, appalled.

"Her hus . . . he . . . her hus . . . sorry," he gasps out. "Shit. Sorry. Hang on."

He gets himself under control and gives me a sympathetic look. "Jewelann. If I killed Beth and rolled her up in a fucking carpet, how did her husband get her *phone*? Did I sneak into her house and leave it on his side of the bed?"

Had Beth been carrying her phone the night I saw her here? I wrack my brain but can't remember for sure. But why wouldn't she have? Like Lisa said, she wouldn't go anywhere without her phone. I wilt.

"I told you, the last time I saw her, she was messed up but alive. If you want to go pointing a finger at anyone, it should be the husband. Don't you know it's always the husband? Or I guess, sometimes, it's the wife."

"You told me it was always the boyfriend." I don't return his grin.

He says with a hint of humor, "I'm not her boyfriend."

"You are a vile, awful person, Christian."

"What are you going to do? Turn me in? Will that really make you feel better?"

Everything is upside down. I don't know where Beth is, and nobody will ever be sure about what happened with Jen. The only thing I know for certain is the same thing I have always known. I'm a terrible person, and I make terrible choices, but nothing matters more than protecting my son.

I shake my head. "No. I'm not turning you in. I'm not even going to kick you out. Live in this hovel, if that's what you want. Take all the time in the world to remodel it into something livable. I don't give a shit. And keep selling your pills, too. You're going to need the money. Because you're going to leave my son out of it, and start giving the money to me."

His laugh, at first, is bemused. It fades at the look on my face. His eyebrows raise.

"You're serious."

"Dead."

Christian gives me a grudging smile. "And what if I don't? What if I just walk away?"

"I'll go to the police and tell them you were the last person to see Beth alive. I'll tell them about the prescriptions, and I'll make them guarantee Eli stays out of it." I won't. Of course I won't. But the look on his face says he believes I might.

"But I wasn't."

"They'll come after you anyway."

"I'll tell them that you offered me money to shove your husband off a ladder."

"You can't prove it," I tell him. "Not even having a life insurance policy proves it. I told the agent it was because he traveled all the time, and he does. Money never crossed hands. I can't be convicted of thinking, but I bet you can go to prison for writing prescriptions without a medical license."

"What we have here seems to be a little case of mutually assured destruction," Christian says. "But fine, it's a deal. And only because you're so fucking sexy right now. Do you know that?"

I do know it. I feel sexy. Powerful, strong. For the first time in a long, long time, I don't feel afraid.

When he kisses me, I slap him in the face. The swing goes a little wild, but tears make it hard for me to focus. The blow clips his chin. Sends him back. He rubs it, but his expression is of grudging respect.

"You're lucky it was with an open hand, not a fist," I tell him. "Don't you ever touch me like that again."

Christian snorts soft laughter. "You can pretend all you want, but you wanted that more than I did."

My voice crackles, all sharp edges. I try not to speak, but I do anyway.

"I loved you," I tell him, at last. At first. I've never said it before, not once, not in all these years. "So much. Don't you understand that? I *loved* you. I needed you, and you were never there for me. Never."

For the first time, Christian looks taken aback. His lips part, but all that comes out is a sigh. His eyes widen, then narrow. I have revealed myself too deeply.

My fists clench at my sides. Tears slip, burning, down my cheeks. "You'll never understand that, because the only person you could ever love is yourself."

He says my name, slowly, under his breath, and turns away. I haven't moved him to some kind of tender emotion; he doesn't have it in him. Still, his shoulders hunch for a second or so before he looks back at me.

"Is it true? The rumors from back then?" He moves away from me, his turn to pace.

"You know it wasn't a rumor."

He turns back. "We were kids, Jewelann. What was I supposed to do? Marry you? We were still in high school, for fuck's sake. I had my whole future ahead of me."

"And look what a great job you did with it." My voice runs thick with sarcasm.

He has the grace to look chastised. "You never even told me."

"I would have told you, but you wouldn't see me. Wouldn't answer my calls. I had to go by myself to get it taken care of. And you . . ." My voice breaks again, shredding. "You just went on with your life, like I didn't matter. Like I'd never mattered."

"I don't know what you want me to say about it. That I'm sorry? Okay, fine. I'm sorry I was an asshole to you back then, but I'm not sorry we didn't have a baby together before we were even old enough to vote. I'm not." His shrug is huge and exaggerated. "If that makes me a bad person, I guess I'll live with that, too. But why do you think I've been hanging around here? The real reason? Why do you think I've been spending so much time with Eli—"

"Shut up! You shut up." I draw out the words, a long hush of sibilance cut off with a snap of my teeth. "You stay away from my son. You understand me? I don't want you messing with him."

*A different dim room, another bottle of wine, another open-mouthed kiss and hands on me. More secrets. More regrets.*

"I remember that night, Jewelann, and yeah, I flunked out of med school, but I still know how to count. Alllll the way up to sixteen."

"Shut your mouth," I whisper.

Christian moves toward me. "I can't regret that you got rid of the first baby we made together, but I'm here so I can get to know the one you kept."

"Eli is not yours. I know my son," I spit, "and he is *nothing* like you."

"You sure about that?"

I swallow bitter tears, but none slip from my eyes. I know my son, all right, better than anyone else ever could. I know him, and love him, and I will do whatever it takes to keep him healthy, happy, and safe. I am not, however, entirely certain of the exact night he was, or was not, conceived. And wasn't that why I'd had the baby in the first place? A possible second chance to have a piece of the man I loved and hated and loved, over and over again?

"One hundred percent," I tell him.

"He has my eyes." Christian's smirk infuriates me.

"He has his father's eyes, and his father looks a lot like you. I've been told I have a *type*." I sneer the last word. "It's not proof of anything."

We stare at each other for a few seconds before Christian, with a heavy, burdened sigh, flops onto the couch. He leans back, both hands over his eyes. "What if I want proof?"

"Why? Why would you—"

"I like the kid, even if he's not mine," he says. "But if he was mine, that would change everything, wouldn't it?"

There's a split molecule of a second in which I allow myself to entertain the idea that maybe he's being sincere. That after all this time, there might truly be something real between us. I blink, though, and it passes.

"Nothing with you ever changes, Christian."

"It's going to hurt his feelings if I cut him off cold. Might mess him up even more than he already is," he warns.

"You're good at cutting people off. I'm sure you'll manage."

He puts a hand over his heart. "You're cold, Jewelann. You know that?"

I'm unruffled.

"You want to try and pretend to me that you were getting closer to him because you thought he was yours? Don't tell me you think I'm smart out of one side of your mouth and use the other side to spew that kind of bullshit."

"I thought you liked what I used my mouth for," he says.

The knock at the door turns us both toward it. He looks as surprised as I feel. I'm the one who crosses to the door. I don't recognize either the man or the woman on the front step.

"Can I help you?"

They look at each other. The woman steps forward, not quite pushing her way through the doorway but close to it. She shows me a badge. I don't have time to read it before she's speaking.

"Mrs. Jordan?"

Behind me, I feel the warmth of Christian's body as he looks out the front door. I nudge him away. "Yes. Can I help you?"

Detective . . . I didn't catch her name, but I did see that much, looks past me. "Is this your husband?"

"No. This is my tenant. Can I—"

"Can we come in?" This comes from her partner, who also flashes his badge so quickly I'm not able to catch a name.

"What is this regarding?" I'm proud of sounding calm but wary.

They're here for Christian. But why? Did Steve tell them he'd been fooling around with Beth? What if they're here about the falsified prescriptions? Either way, I'm going to lose the edge I have on him.

I will lie, I think. I'll lie to protect Eli. But not Christian. And if he tries to throw my son under the bus, I'll—

"Your husband is Kenneth Paul Jordan? Is that correct?"

Ice centers in my guts. "Is he okay?"

"Mrs. Jordan," the woman says, "would it be all right if we came inside?"

Christian nudges me forward. "The place is a wreck right now. Remodeling. I'm in the middle of something that needs my attention. Could you talk up at the main house, maybe?"

"That would be fine. If it's all right with you?" the man says.

If they don't want Christian, what do they want?

Is it . . . me?

"Sure. All right. Fine. Follow me." Their eyes bore into my back as I lead them across the yard.

Inside my kitchen, I offer them mugs of coffee, but it's gone cold in the pot. "I can heat it up."

"No, thanks. I could use your powder room, though, if that's all right?" the man asks politely.

"I'm sorry, I didn't catch your names. Could I look at your badges again?"

They share a glance, but both show me their badges. Detective Anderson is the woman, about my height, short dark hair, piercing blue eyes enhanced by eyeliner and mascara. Detective Phipps is the man, six foot or so, broad-shouldered, with gingery hair and chocolate-brown eyes. A faint spray of freckles across his nose gives him a very Ron Weasley vibe that I suspect he uses to his advantage. Like right now.

"Sure. It's down the hall. But, umm . . . just be careful with the flush. We're having some trouble with the plumbing."

They exchange another of those looks I can't interpret. I heat up a mug of coffee for myself in the microwave. Anderson declines one again. She looks at me patiently.

"Where's your husband, Mrs. Jordan?"

Motion in the backyard catches my eye through the window over the kitchen sink. "He's on a business trip. And he hasn't been home for a while."

"When do you expect him back?"

If I go around to the sliders I can see the driveway. A truck has pulled up into it. Two men are walking around the backyard, poking the ground with a long pole.

"Mrs. Jordan?"

I half turn. "Sorry, there's someone in my yard."

"It's pretty important that I speak to your husband. Can you tell me if he was on a business trip . . ." She pauses, then sounds as though she's reading some dates off her phone.

I'm barely paying attention. I put down my mug and open the slider to step out onto the deck. "Hey! What are you doing?"

The men turn. One strides toward me. He doesn't offer a hand to shake.

"Here to inspect the septic tank. Got a call you were having some issues with it?"

"I didn't call anyone."

From behind me, "Mrs. Jordan?"

"From your husband, then," the septic guy says. "And I can tell you, ma'am, just from my first impression, you definitely have a failure on your hands."

"Hold on. Stop whatever it is you're doing, poking around out there. Okay? Just give me a minute." I hold up a finger. I turn back inside to Detective Anderson. "I'm sorry. I have to deal with this."

She stands and looks out the window. When she faces me, her gaze is assessing. "What's going on?"

"We've been having some issues with the plumbing. We got a tenant a few months ago, and the extra use has been . . . anyway, I'll take care of it."

Detective Phipps appears in the kitchen, adjusting his belt. "It didn't overflow, but it did take a long time to flush."

"Yeah, someone's here about it. I really need to—" I step out onto the deck again.

The two men have pulled a long hose from the tanker truck, and there's now some kind of odd piece of equipment on the grass. No signs of Christian, that asshole, he's probably hiding away in the carriage house. I hope he's sick with anxiety that the detectives are here for him. I can't focus on that now.

"Hey! I said don't do anything until I can talk to you!"

The men give me conciliatory waves. I turn back to the detectives, both of whom have now joined me on the back deck. Phipps shades his eyes to look across the yard. Anderson doesn't take her eyes off of me.

"When do you expect your husband to come home?" she asks.

I give her a level look. I'm trying to stay calm, but it's hard. Those men with the tanker truck are tromping back and forth across the yard. One has gone into my garden, crushing the horseradish leaves and the freshly planted garlic I plan to harvest in the spring.

"He travels a lot. To be honest, I'm sorry, I'm not sure. A few days? He checks in with me. Usually."

"Can you maybe check your messages? See if you have one from him?"

"Is he all right?" I demand. "Was there an accident? Is he missing?"

"No, not that we know of," she says. "Why? Do you expect him to be missing?"

Déjà vu.

I have no idea how to answer her that won't sound suspicious, but I give it my best. "Of course not. But when two detectives show up at my door and start asking questions, what am I supposed to think it's about?"

"Why don't you tell me?" Detective Anderson gives a pointed look toward the carriage house. Without looking at me, she asks, "How long has your tenant been living with you? A few months, you say?"

"Yes." I want to shout again at the men tramping through my garden, but I hold back.

"Was he a friend of your husband's?" This comes from Detective Phipps.

I shake my head. "Christian and I went to high school together. He needed a place to stay, and we needed some work done on the apartment, so we're . . . it's all working out for us."

"I bet. That sounds convenient," Anderson says.

My shoulders square. "I'm not sure what you're getting at?"

"Not getting at anything." Her smile is meant to reassure me, but it doesn't. She pulls a card from her wallet. "If your husband gets in touch with you, would you let me know when he'll be home? I have a few questions for him about an ongoing investigation. That's all."

"What kind of investigation?"

She looks again at the carriage house. Christian has now come out to look at the men with the tanker truck. She waves at him. After a second, he waves back.

"You're not here for Christian?"

She faces me with a small frown. "Should I be?"

"I don't know," I say after a moment. "I guess it depends on what you're investigating."

We stare at each other in silence, until she smiles.

"We'll be in touch. Hope your plumbing issue gets fixed. Have a great day."

The pair of them take their leave before I can say anything more, not that I had anything to say. I head for the men in the backyard. Christian has gone back inside.

"I told you to stop. I don't want you messing around back here." I turn on the guy in my garden. "Get out of there, you're ruining it."

He looks apologetic, but it's the other guy who speaks.

"Sorry. A Ken Jordan called us, said you were having issues with the plumbing backing up, slow flushing, slow draining. He asked us to come out and pump the tank, but also to inspect it. But if you really want us to leave—"

"Will pumping it help?"

The guy shrugs. "It might? It should. But not if the tank itself is failing. To be honest, ma'am, we don't see many septic tanks in this plat anymore. Most everyone's hooked up to the city sewer line. Have you considered that?"

So much money.

"I can't afford that right now." I can't afford the fee to have them pump the tank, much less anything else. "Do I have to pay you today for pumping it?"

"We can send you a bill. But honestly, ma'am," he says, apologetic, "it's only a short-term fix. You really need to get a new tank or hook up to the city."

I pull my phone from my pocket. No messages from Ken, so there's nothing to send to the detectives, and for the first time since they showed up, I have a second or two to allow myself to wonder what they want with him. I check my bank app. No withdrawals, but also, no deposit.

Stabbing the screen with my fingertips, I call Ken's home office. I'm expecting to get the voice mail, but a female voice answers. I'm so stunned that at first, I don't even speak.

"Hello?"

"Sorry. I'm trying to get in touch with Ken Jordan." I step back from the men. One goes back toward the truck.

"Who's calling?"

"This is his wife."

The man has a shovel. He pokes it into a spot at the end of the patch, turning up the earth there. I see a white garlic clove come to the surface. I take the phone away from my face.

"What are you doing?"

"We need to find the access cover."

"Not in my garlic you won't! Get out of there!" Into the phone I say, "Sorry, there are some men here trying to dig up my garden."

"I'm sorry, did you say you were Ken Jordan's wife?"

The men are out of the garden, hands on their hips, shaking their heads. I can see them thinking I'm a crazy woman. I feel like one.

"Yes. And I have a question about his paycheck. He said there'd been a changeover with the accounting system, but this is the third time his check hasn't come in on time. I'm just trying to figure it out." My laugh is fake. I'm gesturing at the men to get out of the garden.

"Mrs. Jordan . . ." A sigh.

I turn away from the septic guys. I close my eyes. I focus. "I really just need to be sure his check is going to be deposited soon. Can you please find out about it for me?"

"I'm sorry to tell you this, but Ken doesn't work for us anymore. He was let go."

I stagger forward a step or two and almost drop the phone. "What? When?"

"Right before Labor Day."

# 34

"I DON'T UNDERSTAND."

"During the restructuring, I guess there were some performance reviews and . . . look, it's not my place to say. You should really talk to Kenny about this."

*Kenny.* So casual, so intimate. I've never even called him that, but let's face it, she seems to know more about my husband than I do.

I disconnect without even thanking her. I shove the phone into my pocket. I turn toward the septic guys.

"Change of plans. You're going to have to leave. I'm not authorizing you to do this." I sound calmer than I feel.

They look at each other. Shrug. They don't care, and why should they? It's just a job to them. They probably get paid by the hour, not whether they pump the tank. They trundle their equipment back to the truck and leave.

I call Ken.

Ken does not answer.

Eli will be home from school in a couple of hours. I need to get myself together before he does. Christian is going to abandon him, and I know all too well how devastating that can be. I'll need to be there for my son with my own head on straight, and how will I manage to do that?

One thing at a time.

There's a pale, gauzy haze around everything I see, and a faint whooshing in my ears that covers up the pounding of my heart. I blink rapidly and focus on my breathing, in and out, until I stop feeling like I'm going to keel over.

First, I check my garden. Boot prints stamp the dirt. A few horseradish leaves are bent and broken, but horseradish is notoriously hardy. I pat the plants back into place. They'll survive. Several garlic bulbs have been brought up to the surface, so I tuck them back into the dirt.

I sit back on my heels with my fingers going numb in the freezing soil. This garden . . . it has made all the difference in my life. This garden has literally saved my family. I've hated it, the work it takes, the person it has made me, but I can't deny that without it, we would have fallen apart long ago.

Weeping, I let my face fall into my hands. I don't care about the dirt on them. It will stain my face. I'll wash it off. I'll wash it all away.

"Jewelann?"

"Fuck off, Christian."

"What did you tell them? The detectives?" He crouches next to me, his hand on my shoulder.

I jerk my entire body away from his touch. "Leave me alone. They weren't even asking about you. They wanted to ask Ken some questions about some kind of investigation."

"Shit," he says.

Frowning, I look him over. "Do you know something about it?"

"No. Of course not. I mean . . . he got some stuff from me." He stands.

I stand, too, thinking of the night Ken snuck across the yard. "Ken got 'stuff' from you? But he never, he doesn't . . ."

"Hey, I don't ask what anyone wants it for. I just supply it." He shakes his hands in front of me as he backs away. "Just forget about it, okay?"

"Ken does not take drugs."

Christian snorts. "Baby, I bet there's a lot of stuff your hubby does that you don't know about."

I don't want to believe this, but my heart says it's true. "Yeah, like losing his job and not telling me. Back in September."

"Oh. Shit."

"Yeah," I say. "That. I called his office to finally get an answer about why his paychecks aren't being deposited, and the receptionist told me."

"When's he coming home?"

"I don't think he is. He left last week after a fight, saying how he wanted to get out of this town. He was ranting. I'd never seen him act that way. I haven't heard from him since. And then these guys show up without warning, telling me he called them—"

"About that," Christian says. He rubs his hands over his bare arms. He has, at least, put on a T-shirt and jeans instead of standing around in his boxers. "It's freezing out here. Come back inside with me."

Hands on his hips, fingers pointing down, framing that dick that has gotten him so far in life. I hate how much he looks like my husband when he does that. And there's that charming smile, too, the bad boy next door.

"What do you mean, 'about that'?"

"I'm the one who called them. I told them I was Ken. Jewelann," he interjects before I can speak. "I had to. I couldn't deal with it backing up. You should thank me. Where'd they go, anyway?"

His foot squelches as he shifts his stance. We are standing on the literal failure of what is meant to keep my life's shit contained. If that's not an accurate representation of what's been going on, I don't know what is.

"I sent them away. I don't have the money for it."

He sighs. "Fine. I'll pay for the tank pumping. Come back inside. You're not even wearing a coat. Your hands are dirty. C'mon, let's get you cleaned up."

He takes me by the elbow and leads me to my own house, where he runs the water in the sink. While I wash my hands, Christian helps himself to mugs from my cupboard. He puts the kettle on. Sets out milk and sugar. I study what he's laid out, all very homey. Of all the times Christian has done something to make me cry, this one feels the most wholesome.

"Where do you keep your teabags?" Christian asks.

"I don't have any."

He stares. Shakes his head. Sits at the table. "Well, look at me trying to be the nice guy. See where it got me."

What would it feel like to believe him? I let Christian take my hand and brush a kiss across the back of it, while he smiles at me all dewy-eyed and soft. As though we are lovers. *In* love.

"Does Ken know you've involved Eli in your business?" I ask him.

"I don't think so. Your hubby doesn't know very much about his son at all, does he?"

"If the police are trying to ask Ken questions about fake prescriptions, they're going to find out about you pretty quick."

"And Eli," he says. "We'll all be screwed, huh?"

We're both silent. The breath I draw in shakes, but I let it out slowly, one puff at a time. He takes my hand. I let him hold it, but I don't return the squeeze of his fingers.

"I don't think they're asking about Ken because of anything to do with that, though. Why wouldn't they talk to me? I was right there. And whether you want to believe it or not, I'm not even under suspicion of having anything to do with Beth, or they'd have asked me about that. Don't you think?"

"Are you trying to convince me, or yourself?" I ask.

His fingers squeeze mine again, gently, and although I wish it wasn't, the warmth of his hand on mine is nice. "I'm just trying to make you feel a little better. It's going to be okay. Hey. Look at me. I'm here for you. I promise."

He's lying again. I can tell by the crinkle at the corner of his left eye. The soft, barely discernible dip in his tone. I wish I could let myself sink into it, though. That lie. All of it.

"Stay away from my son, Christian. I mean it."

An expression flickers across his face, but he nods. "Fine."

This time, I believe him.

*　*　*

The temp place only has openings right now for jobs I'm not qualified for, so I have to figure out something else. I haven't had a job since before Eli was born, but I waited tables at a local Mexican place all through high school. The restaurant has new owners now, an updated menu and décor, but they hire me right away. So many places need help now, they don't seem to care that my serving skills are rusty. They'll even let me take the lunch shifts so I can be home to spend the evenings with Eli.

The job starts next week. I'm getting my feet under me. I spoke with the mortgage company and explained the situation so I could ask for an extension on the payments. They're working on it. Marlene sent me a check for the entire bee collection without waiting for the end of the month, and I don't care if it was from pity or convenience, because the amount is enough to cover the rest of the monthly bills. Serving tables might not be enough to make ends meet, but for the moment, we're going to be okay.

One thing at a time.

Flashing lights line my street as I pull up to my house. I can't get into my driveway because of the police cars. There's also an ambulance. Panicked, I call Eli's name as I burst through the front door, but he doesn't answer me.

Detective Anderson does. She greets me in my own kitchen, where she's standing next to my sink and looking out over the backyard. Eli's at the table, his face drawn and eyes hollow.

"What's going on?"

I will lie for him. I will tell them the drugs are mine. I was the one working with Christian. Not my son.

"Jewelann . . . do you mind if I call you that?" she asks.

"It's my name."

The smile she flashes me is oddly sympathetic. "You might want to take a seat there with Eli."

"I'm fine standing. What's going on?"

She sighs. Eli looks stricken. He's shaking a little. I put both my hands on his shoulders, squeezing gently, and feel him settle.

"Have you heard from your husband?"

"I have not." My chin goes up. "To be honest, I believe he's left us. I'm not sure I expect to hear from him again."

The detective sighs again and presses a fingertip between her closed eyes. "Mrs. Jordan—"

"They found a body," Eli cuts in. "Bones. They found a skeleton in the backyard."

CHAPTER

# 35

"JEWELANN? FRED, GET one of those ammonia capsules. No, don't bother with the EMTs yet, I think she just . . . hey," the detective says as I swim back up out of the darkness that had hit me over the head. "Hey, there. You okay?"

I shake my head, quelling a gag. I don't remember her sitting me onto the kitchen chair or pushing my head between my knees. Everything became a red, hazy blur, and now I'm staring at this woman in my kitchen while my son sobs quietly across the table from me, but I don't know how I got there or what's going on.

"They found a body?" I manage to say.

"Apparently, your husband contracted a company to excavate and remediate that failing septic tank. They're the ones that discovered the remains." Her face is kind, but her eyes pin mine.

"Christian did it."

"Christian Campbell," Detective Anderson says after a second. "Your tenant. He buried the body in the yard?"

For a moment I consider agreeing with her. It won't stick, of course, but I could seriously mess up his life for a while. That would spill over onto Eli, though, so I can't do it.

"No . . . oh, no, I mean he called the septic people. He was working on fixing up the carriage house and he said he was going to have them come out because I didn't have the money . . . because we were bartering services for rent . . ."

"I see. You had no idea the men were coming to excavate and replace the tank?"

"No. Did they dig up my garden?" I shake my head. My mind races, whirls. It's all I can think about, the ruin of the plants I tended so carefully. "They dug up my garden, didn't they? It'll all be ruined . . ."

Detective Anderson bends in front of me so her face is level with mine. "Jewelann. I need you to focus for me, okay? I know this is a shock. If you know where your husband is, I need you to tell me. You might want to protect him, but—"

"I don't," I say. "I don't want to protect him."

"Can I get some water?" Eli asks.

Detective Anderson nods and gestures at someone else in the room. Oh, it's the other detective, the man who'd been with her the other day. I can't recall his name. He brings two glasses of water from the tap. Eli drinks his greedily, but I can't bear to even sip mine.

"I don't know where Ken is. We had an argument, and he packed some things and left. I haven't heard from him since then." I watch water droplets slide down the side of the glass. They'll make a puddle on the kitchen table. Someone should get a towel.

"What did you fight about?"

"Money," I answer honestly. "I was questioning him about why his paychecks weren't arriving. I didn't know at that time that he'd been fired."

Eli grunts. "Mom. What?"

"It'll be okay." I reach for his hand and squeeze it. His fingers are cold. To the detective I say, "I really don't know where he is."

"He lost his job?" She pulls a small spiral-bound notepad from her pocket and tugs the pen free of the coils. She jots something down and looks at me again. "When?"

I tell her the whole story. Ken's company being restructured. Him being let go but not telling me. His "bonus" that was really severance pay, and the paychecks he pretended were simply late. How he kept traveling, and I had no idea that he wasn't actually working.

"How long has this been going on?"

"Since Labor Day, I guess," I tell her. My mouth is dry, lips sticking together, tongue cleaving to the roof of my mouth. I swallow what feels like razor blades. Still, I can't bring myself to try and drink, too afraid I will vomit it all over the floor.

"Could you tell me some of the places you know he's been?"

"I could tell you where he told me he was going, but at least once, I know for sure he was someplace other than where he said he'd be. Wisconsin, once. He went to the Dells."

"Asshole," Eli barks out. "He promised to take me and never did!"

She nods, scribbling something. "Do you have any proof that he was in those locations on the dates? Credit card charges? Anything?"

"Mom, should you be waiting for a lawyer?"

I squeeze Eli's hand again and address the detective. "I don't know. Should I?"

"You're not under any investigation or charges, Jewelann."

"But Ken is?" One plus one plus one is sometimes something other than three. It's falling into place for me, now. "You're asking me all of this because of what they found in the backyard."

"Yes. We haven't made a positive identification yet, but the size of the remains indicates that it was a child."

Eli moans. He buries his face in his hands and puts his head on the kitchen table. I get out of my seat to wrap my arms around him as best I can.

"Billy Peak went missing in this neighborhood about ten years ago. He was a friend of yours, Eli?" Her eyes are bright and sharp, and her voice retains some of the kindness, but it's also pointed. Direct.

"It's Billy," Eli says. "The bones are Billy's."

"We don't know that for sure," she begins.

I cut her off. "Could Eli be excused? I'll be happy to talk to you about whatever you want, but he doesn't need to sit here, does he?"

"I want to hear," Eli says.

He's not crying anymore, and although his face is still pale, he sits up straight. He doesn't shrug off my hands, but I can feel his shoulders tensing as though he'd like to. I step back from him. Take my own seat again. His gaze meets mine. His lips press together. He gives me a tiny, almost indiscernible nod.

"I'm okay, Mom. I need to hear."

The detective takes a seat between us. "Detective Phipps and I have been investigating a series of murders that have taken place over the past twelve years. All of the victims have fit the same profile. Male children between the ages of five and ten. Blond hair. Blue or gray eyes."

That describes Billy Peak, all right.

"And you think my dad killed them? You think my dad's a serial killer?" Eli's voice goes high and scratchy.

She nods. I like her, how she treats my son. She has compassion, but I can tell she's also determined to do her job. To catch a murderer.

"Were they all killed the same way? Could it be a terrible coincidence?" Of course I would like this to be true. It can't take away the horror and trauma the parents of those boys must be feeling, but it might be better for them to have died by accident, rather than a murderer's hand.

"Were they strangled? Drugged and strangled? You think my dad's the Playground Killer." Eli's voice shakes, but he clears his throat to add, "The stories and theories have been all over Reddit."

*I can't help it. I get sucked in and have to read all the updates.* I suppose now I know at least one thing my son's been reading all those hours alone in his room.

Detective Anderson nods. "There are similarities in each of the cases that lead us to believe it is the work of the same person. I can't comment on the nickname some internet groups have given the perpetrator. All I can tell you is that we have strong evidence to place your husband in at least one of the locations where a child went missing. Anything you can do to help us find Ken would be extremely helpful."

"Serial killers always use the same methods, right?" Eli asks.

She hesitates. "Usually, yes. But I can't really comment on more than that, we don't have any proof—"

Eli jumps in. "You know if it's a serial killer, though. You have to be working with cops in other states, maybe even the FBI since he's been crossing state lines. If you have enough evidence to tie it to a single person, you're convinced. They were all killed the same way, no real variations. It's how you know you're looking for one guy. How you know it's not just random happenstance. Right?"

"You seem to have done your homework," she says.

The other detective, the one who's been silent this entire time, at last pops in with, "You listen to a lot of true crime podcasts, do you?"

"How do you know whose . . . the bones . . ." My voice scrapes at the air.

"Like I said, we don't know for sure, but almost eleven years ago, Billy Peak went missing. Some clothes identified as his were found by the river in downtown Dayton a few miles away. The assumption was that he either drowned or was placed in the water, but no body was ever recovered. He fits the profile and lived in this neighborhood, and he was known to be a playmate of your son's."

"I remember." I could never forget.

"Dental records should be able to help us identify him. Give his parents some peace." She says this last part firmly, as though it's the most important part, and I suppose she's right about that.

"If he was drugged and strangled, how would you be able to find that out from a skeleton?"

"Jewelann," she says gently, "how he died is irrelevant, to be honest. The fact he was disinterred from your yard tells us something bad happened to him."

"You really believe Ken killed Billy?" I cannot laugh out loud at this. I cannot clap my hands over my mouth to hold back a burst of hysterics. My eyes sting and burn with tears she'd understand better, but my body wants to scream and guffaw and sob all at the same time.

Detective Anderson is too smart to say anything that could come back to haunt her. "If you could provide some evidence of where he's been traveling over the past six months, longer if you know it, that would be really helpful to this investigation, Jewelann. I really can't say more than that right now. And if you do know where he is—"

"I don't. I truly don't."

She nods. "Okay. I believe you."

"But I can give you the credit card statements for the past few months." I think of the charges for the corn maze, the water park, the candy shop. Learning the truth about my husband is a fever, and I can't tell if I'm burning up or frozen to the bone.

Detective Anderson looks faintly surprised, as though she was not expecting my cooperation. She looks at Eli, whose head hangs.

"That would be helpful. Yes."

"And the cell phone bills? Would that be useful? I don't know anything about towers or pinging—"

"Anything that you'd be willing to let us have would be great. Thank you." She pauses, looking at Eli. "Are you going to be all right?"

"I'm fine." He looks up at her. "Like my mom said, it'll all be okay."

She nods and gets to her feet. "Listen, Jewelann . . . if there's anything you'd like to share with us about . . . well. Sometimes, in situations like this, it turns out that the family isn't surprised. Not really."

"You think we knew all along?"

We stare at each other, her eyes searching mine. I'm being interrogated without even a word. She won't see what she's looking for, no matter what she thinks. How could I have known? The man who insisted on family dinners and keeping traditions, who never indulged in intoxicants, who never even swore or raised his voice in anger, how could he be any kind of killer, much less one who preyed on children?

"I never in a million years would have thought Ken could be capable of doing anything like that," I tell her, and it's the truth.

She nods again, maybe not convinced, but willing for the moment to let it pass. "Can you get me those statements right now?"

"I have some older ones in my file drawer. I'll get them. But I'll have to print out the more recent ones. That could take some time."

"Are you going to arrest my dad?"

Detective Anderson looks at Eli. "I'll be honest with you, Eli. I hope so."

"Me too," he says.

He excuses himself to go upstairs, and I pause with him in the hallway. "Don't read the forums, Eli. Not right now. Promise me? Don't do that to yourself right now."

He nods. I hug him, tight. I grab my laptop from my bedroom and take it downstairs to the kitchen, where the detectives are waiting.

"I can log in with this, but the printer is in Ken's office. I guess you probably want to see it, anyway."

"I'll check it out with you. Sure." Phipps follows me into the basement.

I print out as many statements as I can before I run out of paper, but Detective Phipps says it's enough for now. He takes a look around the office without touching much and tells me not to do anything in here. They're going to have to come back, I guess, with some kind of legal documentation.

They leave, promising me they'll return tomorrow.

I wait until all the cars are gone before I go out the back sliders and across the dug-up mess of my backyard. I need to talk to Christian. I need something from him. Something to take the edge off. Bitter candy.

His car isn't in the driveway. When I get to the carriage house, the door stands open. I call his name anyway, pushing inside. The place is gutted, basically. In the bedroom, all of his clothes are gone. Nothing personal in the bathroom, either. Standing in the ruin of the kitchen, I have to cover my mouth with both my hands to hold in my sobs.

He's gone.

# 36

I WANT TO BE stoned right now. I want to lose myself in the dim, the shroud, the veil. I want to sink into the warm, deep waters of oblivion, not giving one single fuck about anything that's going on. But, like my grandma's pendant lamps and the kitchen cabinets, like every promise he ever made me, Christian has taken it all away.

He's left nothing. I search every drawer, every shelf. The fridge, the freezer, the inside of the washer and dryer, inside the toilet tank. Nothing. The more I search, the uglier and more ruined the carriage house looks. The small improvements he did make only make the rest of it look even worse. I wanted him gone, but now that he is, I am desperate to have him back.

I don't feel the same way about Ken.

My heart breaks for the parents of the children he abducted and killed. I don't need proof from any detectives that he did it. I would never have guessed he would do anything like that, but now, without question, I *know* he did.

My relationship with God is not transactional. No "If I do X, will you give me Y?" Jews don't kneel to pray, but my legs are giving out under me, and I end up on my knees anyway. The bare concrete is chilly and rough against my skin. I don't pray. I think.

The need to get high doesn't fade away. That's not how it works. I shove it away, though. Hard. I take a few deep breaths and fight the urge. I need to focus, now. I still have a son to protect and provide for.

I can do this. I got a job, and if I need to, I can get another one. I can get my hustle on. I can do whatever I have to in order to make it work. I know what I'm capable of, and it's a lot. I just have to get started.

My phone buzzes.

**Beth's in rehab!**

Lisa's text is followed by another of a shocked emoji face. I call her. "What's going on?"

"Girl. Beth is in *rehab*. Apparently, she didn't want anyone to know about it, so she told Steve to tell people she was *missing*. Or maybe he just said that to me to save face or make her look like an asshole, I don't know. Hey, at least she's not dead, right? But what a bitch."

I know better than to believe Lisa really thinks that Beth is a bitch, so I don't murmur my agreement. "I'm glad she's okay."

"I guess she will be?" Lisa makes it a question. "It'll get her off the downers, anyway. She's going to the police about where she got the drugs. She's suuuuper pissed off at Christian for giving her those prescriptions, and look, she's my bestie and all that, but she can also be a mean, mean bitch. Don't tell him anything, okay?"

"He's gone," I look around the empty apartment again, unsure if I want to laugh or cry.

"Where'd he go?"

"I don't know," I say. "But he took all of his stuff and ran."

Lisa is silent for a second or so. "Shit. That's good, though, isn't it? That must feel like a relief?"

Nothing feels like a relief right now. Detective Anderson asked me and Eli not to tell anyone about their investigation or their suspicions, but even if she hadn't, this isn't something to share with Lisa over the phone. It can only be a matter of a few hours before she hears about it anyway. It's going to be all over the news. There won't be any hiding it from the world . . . and that, I think, is all right. I mumble an excuse about needing to get off the phone and disconnect before I can break down.

It seems impossible that either one of us could be hungry, but when I get back to the house, Eli is rummaging in the cupboard for crackers, and my stomach rumbles. The two of us haven't yet spoken about the possibility that Ken might be what they say. We sit across from each other at the table with his empty chair between us and devour the pizza I have delivered. The small, square slices stain my fingertips with red sauce because the inner pieces don't have any crust to hold them by. Eli has a hearty appetite and polishes off nearly half of the pizza himself.

"What's going to happen to Dad once they find him? They will find him, won't they?" Eli asks.

"I don't know. I guess it depends how hard he's trying to hide. He might have no idea anyone's looking for him, so it might be really easy for them. They'll arrest him, I guess. Put him on trial."

"Will we have to get him a lawyer?"

I lean forward to look into his eyes. "I'm not getting *anything* for him."

"Good." Eli nods. His expression has gone grim and determined. "I hope he rots in prison. I hate him."

"Eli . . . All of this is really hard to process. Do you need me to make an appointment for you to see someone so you can talk about it? Nobody would judge you for having a hard time," I tell him. "You don't have to go to school tomorrow, or for as long as you want. I'll tell them you have the flu."

"Okay." He hesitates but meets my gaze. "Someone on the forum said they knew there was a named suspect."

"I thought I told you not to look at that stuff," I say with a sigh. "Did they name your dad?"

"No," Eli says. "They just said that there was a break in the investigation."

"Was there anything about what they found in the yard?"

"Not yet. But there will be. It's only been a few hours. It's all going to hit soon, though. The news, those forums. People are going to know it was Dad who killed all those other kids," Eli says. "Does Christian know?"

"Honey . . ." Quickly, I tell him about the empty carriage house. No note, no word. No idea where he went. "He was afraid the police were here about him. He could be anywhere. You know why he'd be afraid of that, don't you? You know what he was doing."

"Yeah," he says after a moment. "I know."

"You know that you could get into major trouble if anyone connected you to what he was doing."

"I know."

We are both silent.

"I wanted to help you," he says in a burst of words, breathless. "I knew you needed money, and Christian told me it would be an easy way for me to do that."

I swallow my emotions. "He should never have gotten you involved with that, no matter what."

"You warned me that he'd let me down, Mom. You were right. He hasn't answered any of my texts. He just *left*."

"I know," I say. "Believe me, honey. I know. But we're going to be okay. I don't want you to worry about anything. I'll take care of us."

"I know you will. You always have."

"We will get through this."

He nods and draws in a long, deep breath. "It's going to suck."

"Yeah. A lot," I tell him, but there is a lightness in the house that hasn't been here in, if I'm going to be truthful with myself, years.

After dinner, he heads upstairs to sequester himself in his room again. I don't bother telling him not to read the forums. I finish cleaning up the kitchen. I hop on to my laptop and log in to my Connex account. My page fills with updates from people I never speak to in real life. On a whim, I search for Beth's name and find her profile, but it hasn't been updated in weeks. She posted a lot of selfies with duck lips, pictures of her with her daughters, hardly any mention, ever, of her husband. Lisa's profile has a lot going on, memes and recipes and photos of her and her kids. Her life, according to social media, is happy, fulfilled, and totally without a care.

Why does everyone lie so much?

I check out the forums Eli had been reading, the ones talking about the Playground Killer. Some of them call him the Candyman because he allegedly lures the kids with the promise of candy that turns out to be drugs, and when they pass out he . . .

I don't want to read any more of the details.

I close the lid of my laptop and sit back in my chair. I'm nauseated. Detective Anderson didn't tell me not to try to text or call Ken, she only said that if he got in touch with me, I should let her know. I don't know if they're able to track Eli's or my cell phones without our permission, but she didn't ask for it. It doesn't really matter. I'm not going to try to get in touch with him, and if he tries to contact me, I'm not going to protect him.

Ken is gone, and I no longer have to hide anything from him or anyone else.

CHAPTER

# 37

THE WOMAN ON the phone sounds tired and irritated. "You really should have done this years ago. Didn't you get the literature they sent out when the project started? Everyone was supposed to be fully informed about the costs and options."

"It was my parents' house. I don't know if they were ever told about it." The lie slips easily out of my mouth. My parents haven't been responsible for the house for almost two decades.

"Well, now you can download it from the site. There's a couple of forms to fill out for the authorization for the work, your application for the grant to cover the cost, all of that. Do you need the link?"

I'd gone to the link first, of course, who doesn't go right to the website first these days? "The page had an error."

She mutters and sighs and grumbles. "I'll mail it to you. What's the name and address?"

I give it to her and wait for a gasp of recognition. We've been all over the news for the past week. She simply repeats the number and street name. Asks me if there's anything else she can do for me in a tone that indicates she hopes I say no. She disconnects the call almost before I'm finished answering.

The floor creaks overhead. Eli's been doing school from home, taking advantage of protocols that were put in place during the pandemic, so at least he's not going to fall behind in class.

Through the window over my sink, I see a bunch of people in coveralls mingling around the dug-up portion of my lawn. Some have shovels. One has a clipboard. Before I have the chance to go out and ask them what the hell they're doing now, my front doorbell rings.

"Can I come in?" Detective Anderson doesn't try to push or look past me this time. She looks me in the face, her expression solemn.

I let her in and take her to the kitchen. "Coffee?"

"Sure. The men in the backyard are there to begin an investigative excavation. I have the paperwork."

I pour us both mugs of coffee. I spot Detective Phipps in the back, overseeing the people using stakes and rope to mark off sections of the yard. I give Anderson her mug and take a seat at the table.

"You think you're going to find other bodies."

She sits, too. "We have to check. Do you have someplace you can go while this is going on? It could be unpleasant. At the very least, it's going to affect your septic tank. You won't be able to use the plumbing at all."

"Fuck."

She looks startled for a second, then grins. "Ah, there it is. I was hoping I'd get to see the real Jewelann Jordan."

"Whatever that means." I wrap my hands around the mug. "How long will we need to be gone?"

"I don't know. It depends on what they find, if anything. And how long it takes to get the city in here to hook you up to the main line. You *are* going to have that done, aren't you?"

"Apparently, there's a hardship grant I can apply for. I definitely think we qualify, don't we? I don't know how I'll pay for a hotel room for more than a few nights, though."

"Do you have anyone you can stay with?"

"I'll see what I can do." Jonathan and Eve might take us in. Maybe Lisa.

She studies me. "I have other news."

"You've found him." I wait to feel something. Fear. Anger. Anxiety. Sorrow. I'm a blank slate. Numb.

"He was arrested in a town outside of Chicago yesterday afternoon. We got a tip from someone who says he was caught trying to talk to her son outside of the library, where he was waiting to get picked up. Fortunately, the kid ran inside and was able to give the police there a good description of the car. They found Ken in a motel a few miles away."

I stare into my mug. If I look into her eyes, I'm not sure what she'll see in them, so I keep them cast down. "What happens next?"

"He's been tied to cases in several states, including here in Ohio. There's going to be some back-and-forth before it gets settled. For now, he's being held in Illinois. Jewelann," she prompts so I look at her. "You're going to get a *lot* of attention for this. Eli, too. Reporters. Looky-loos. I wouldn't be surprised if those true crime assholes aren't all over this. You don't have to talk to anyone, you understand? Don't let them promise you anything."

"You think someone's going to want to what, pay me? To talk about Ken?"

"They might. I'd get the money up front, if they do." she sighs, rubbing at the bridge of her nose. She looks tired. "I wish you wouldn't, though. I can't stop you from it, but I hope you're careful. Something like this can really mess up your life."

"I think that already happened, Detective. Didn't it?"

Her smile is thin, but genuine. I like her. I'm glad I'm not the target of her attention, though. I have a feeling Detective Anderson has a high success rate at getting what she goes after.

"Has he admitted to any of the crimes?"

"He's made no admissions, no. He's waiting for his lawyer," she says.

It's my turn to rub my face. My go-to point is between my eyes. I press my thumb and index finger at the ends of each brow, making small circles. It doesn't ease my rising headache, but it gives me an excuse not to look at her.

"We don't have the money for that."

"He'll be appointed one. He's made some kind of contact with his sister—"

My hand jerks, knocking my mug. Coffee sloshes, but Detective Anderson is quick. She catches the mug before it can fall off the table.

"You didn't know," she says, but it's clear she expected that.

I get up from the table to get a kitchen towel. I move in twitching, lurching steps, a robot with faulty batteries. I have to grip the edge of the sink to keep myself from falling over. My heart pounds, and my breath is thick in my throat.

"He told me he was an only child. That his parents died in a house fire when he was eighteen. I've never heard of a sister." I concentrate on steadying my breathing. I can't quite manage it. I pull out a glass and fill it with water from the tap, remembering too late that the sink won't drain.

"She lives in Wisconsin. Married, two kids, both girls. Apparently she was much younger than him and was put into foster care after the fire. She claims she's had nothing to do with him until recently. I don't have all the information, but it does seem true that the parents died. It's possible that . . ." She trails off.

She has compassion, that's clear, and it's appreciated. But I also think she's testing me to see what I really do know, or don't know. Or maybe just what I suspect.

Looking out the window at the growing insanity in my backyard, I say, "You think he killed his parents?"

"It's possible."

"That's outside of what his . . . he's been . . ." My throat closes. I shake, shoulders hunching, hands gripping the rim of the sink hard enough to turn my fingers numb.

"It's not his M.O., no, but sometimes killers get started with something else first, before they settle into their habit."

"Ken killed his parents, left his sister alive, got back in touch with her after all these years, and I never knew it." Something that tries to be a laugh slips out of me. "You must think I'm the biggest kind of idiot."

"No, Jewelann. I just want you to be prepared that more information might come out, and it could have the potential to really upend everything you thought you knew about your life." She pauses. "The skeleton we found in your yard had a nail in the middle of its skull. They're still working on it, but they're pretty sure that was the cause of death."

"Not strangulation." My shaky laugh is out of place, and I clamp my lips shut over it.

"No. We don't have a definitive answer yet if the body was strangled beforehand, but the head wound is most likely what killed him."

"And it's Billy Peak," I whisper.

Detective Anderson nods. "Yes. Dental records have confirmed that. We think it was probably a crime of opportunity, not quite like the others. Ken was probably still establishing his . . . habits. Billy was here, Ken saw a chance, maybe he wasn't able to fight a compulsion. He panicked."

"Did he say all that?"

"He's been saying a lot of things, Jewelann."

"Worse than what you just told me?"

I wait.

She sighs. "We're digging up your backyard because we have to make sure that he hasn't buried any other victims there. Ken's adamant we won't find any."

"Wouldn't that make you want to look all the more?" I glance out through the sliders but can't see more than motion.

"Yeah. Absolutely. We have to be sure."

I face her. She stands, almost as if she means to hug me, but thankfully she does not. She puts her hands on her hips, instead. I think she doesn't know how intimidating this makes her look, or maybe she does.

"He says that not only will we not find any other bodies in the yard, he is insisting that he did not bury the body we found." Detective Anderson frowns. "He's saying that you did it."

The tiny laugh that burbled out of me a minute ago becomes a cackle, a guffaw, a short, sharp startlement of shocked hilarity. I cough it out of me, ratta-tat-tat, machine gun fire. To my surprise, Detective Anderson joins me in it, although her laughter is more melodious. Less strained. We laugh together. I have to put a hand on my stomach against the pain of tensing muscles. I wipe my eyes once, and then again, as the laughter becomes a strangled, garbled sob.

"If he thought I buried a body in the backyard, why would he have told me to have the septic tank dug up?"

"He says he thought you had it in a storage unit."

*I know. What you keep. In there. That storage unit. I know.*

*I know you know what I did, Jewelann. You have to forgive me. If you forgive me, if you support me, I promise you, I'll be better. I'll never do it again. I swear to you.*

I'd thought he'd been talking about another woman. I'd promised, and I'd kept my promise, but Ken had not. Another bout of hissing laughter rips out of me.

"I have a storage unit, that's true. But it's full of stuff I bought," I tell her. "I have kind of a shopping problem. But there aren't any *bodies* in there. You can look, if you want."

"I'll have to do that," she says, apologetically, just in case, but I'm not worried about it, because I know what I told her is true. She won't find any bodies in my storage unit.

"I'm sorry," she says. "I know that has to feel like a real betrayal to hear. But don't worry. We've got him, we're going to keep him, and we're going to convict him. You and your son are going to be all right."

She tells me more, but the words honestly go in one ear, right out the other, and I retain next to nothing. She squeezes my shoulders as she says goodbye, promising to check in with me. Asks me to let her know where we'll be staying, so she can be sure to keep in touch, let me know of any updates. She warns me again about trusting anyone trying to get information out of me.

When I close the front door behind her, I lock it. I have to sit on the steps and put my head between my knees. I keep laughing, laughing, until I choke again on a sob.

I feel betrayed for many things my husband has done, but not by him blaming me for burying that child in the garden.

After all, I *am* the one who did it.

CHAPTER

# 38

NOBODY ADMITS OUT loud how hard it can be to stay at home with your kid. Yeah, there were mommy groups, but none of those women had been my friends in high school. Why would I want to spend time with any of them simply because we had kids the same age? They were all still cliquey. I didn't fit in. I didn't really want to.

I tried the crunchy thing. Reading storybooks instead of plopping the kid in front of the television. All meals made from scratch, nothing from a box or pouch or, heaven forbid, a fast-food place. I made my own laundry detergent. I hung my sheets out to dry.

Being a housewife had never been in my life's plan, but there I was, on call twenty-four-seven. That was my career. That was my life. Being someone's everything was all so much. Too much.

Who could blame me for being a little down? Hey, the Rolling Stones had it right when they talked about Mother's Little Helper. I wasn't old, not yet, but it was still a drag, and I needed . . . something . . . sometimes.

Ken had been gone for a week, which meant he could be home at any moment. He might not expect me in an apron, but he would expect me to put on a smile. Our happy family needed to be happy, and didn't I want that too? Of course I did. I wanted to feel good. Content with the choices I'd made. Satisfied, even.

When the doorbell rang, I expected a kid selling cookies or magazines or wrapping paper. I knew Billy Peak. He lived two streets over. I used to see him on the playground next to their house, when I took Eli there. Sometimes, his mother was there, looking even more tired than I usually felt. A lot of times, he was by himself while she stayed inside. Sleeping, the little boy had told me once, pronouncing it without the "l."

"Mama is sweeping," he'd said. "I'm not apposed to wake her up."

So I'd given him a sandwich and some Goldfish crackers, and he and Eli had played together very nicely. Over time, he'd started following us home on occasion. The boys would play, I'd feed them an early dinner and drive the kid home . . . or walk him, if I was too stoned to get behind the wheel. I always meant to get his mother's number, but I never managed it, and she clearly never got mine. Never even noticed her kid was at someone else's house for hours.

Taking care of Billy always made me feel like I, at least, could not be the shittiest mother in town.

That day, the kid looked more unkempt than usual. Hair a little too long in places, too short in others, as though he'd taken the scissors to it himself. Mismatched clothes. To be fair, if Eli dressed himself, he'd also have worn something rumpled that didn't go together . . . but he didn't have to, because at six years old, he still got help from Mama.

Eli was happy to see Billy. I was happy to have a respite from entertaining, educating, being "on." With the boys playing together in the basement, I didn't have to smile. I didn't even have to pay attention. They were safer there than left alone to wander the streets, right? I was the good mother, the one who set them up with games and toys and snacks.

I deserved a little break.

Didn't I?

I don't know what shook me awake. A sound, probably. A scream? I wasn't sure. I found the boys in the basement, but not in the rec room, where they'd been told they could play.

They were in Ken's office, which had once been my father's workshop, where they'd been expressly forbidden to go.

Billy, on the floor. Eli, my precious boy, standing over him with the heavy nail gun dangling from his two small hands, so heavy, how could he even have lifted it?

The wound in Billy's head was very small. Almost no blood. If not for the way his small body was so limp, his face so blank, I might have thought he was pretending.

"What did you do?" My words fell from my lips like the toads and snakes in a fairy tale story, words from a cursed woman's mouth. I fell to my knees in front of my son. Grabbed his shoulders. I took the nail gun from his hands and put it on the concrete floor. "What did you do?"

My son was gone. Nothing in his eyes but blankness. I gathered him to me. His body softened against mine. He stirred. Moved. I pulled him away from the sight of his friend.

"Go upstairs. I'll take care of this. Mama will take care of you. Nothing bad will happen to you. Go upstairs, Eli."

An accident could still ruin a life. I could not allow my son's life to be set on that course. And what about mine? A mother out of her mind on pills, too messed up to know her son was playing with something so dangerous? Another child, killed? It might not have been my fault, but I would've been held responsible. They would have taken my son away from me. It would be the end of everything. So I took care of it, my own mind still hazy, my fingers fumbling. But I took care of it, to protect my son.

To protect myself, too.

I'd never had a garden before. It would be the perfect time to start one. A small plot, far back in the yard.

Later, but so much later, days later, we heard about the missing boy from two streets over. His mother came to our house finally, for the first and last time, to ask us if we'd seen her son. I didn't tell her he'd been with us many times when she had no idea where he was. She didn't ask. I told her what I'd told the police, that he'd walked home from our house on his own, and she went away with the rest of her posters clutched in her hands.

I heard she and her husband—who knew she even had one?—had moved away. The pain of their loss too much to bear. I understood that. They left the place where they'd lost their son.

And I . . . well, I'd made my choice, and I had to remain in the place where I'd made sure he would stay.

ELI BURSTS INTO tears when I tell him that they found Ken, that he's in custody. When I tell him what Detective Anderson said about Ken's claims, Eli's sobs taper off. We sit side by side on his bed. I take his hand and hold it.

"You told me you'd take care of it, and that nobody would ever know what I'd done." Eli raises his wet face to mine.

My hands cup his cheeks. I use my thumbs to wipe away the tears there. "I did take care of it, honey. Your father killed a lot of little boys, and now he's going to be punished for what he did. Nobody will ever know what really happened, and we never need to have anything to do with him, ever again. We can sell this house. Go someplace new. Start all over. We're all right."

Eli's eyelids flutter, and he closes them tight for a second or so before opening them. He pulls slightly away. I let go of him. His voice is hoarse, but his tears are drying. "And we can be with my *real* dad."

His words hit me like a punch to the gut. "What?"

"Christian," Eli says. "I know you're in love with him, Mom. And I know I gave you a hard time about it, but I was being a dick. But he told me all about it, how you guys were together since you were my age. And now that Dad's in jail, Christian can come back."

"Oh, no, honey. No. That's not going to happen." I shake my head, as much to emphasize this negative answer as to throw out any hopeful thoughts my son's idea has put into my head.

Eli scowls. In his fury, he looks more like Ken than he does me. I can see his father, his real father, in the lines of his furrowed brow, the parentheses at the corners of his mouth. My son might wish he wasn't related to Ken, but the truth is written all over his face.

"Fine, then. You don't have to be with him, if you don't want to. But I'm going to go live with him, then. He said I could!"

I am slapped back by this. The horror of it rakes me up and down with jealous claws. I am rent open with it.

"You can't go and live with him, Eli. He's a stranger. And he's not your father. I'm sorry if he told you something different. And I know it sucks to think that you're related to your dad. But he *is* your father. Not Christian."

"Why do you want me to think *he's* lying to me?" Eli cries and stands, pushing me back not with his fists but his words.

I stand my ground. "Because it's what he does!"

Softening a bit, I add, "Anything Christian told you was for his own reasons, Eli. I already told him you were not his child. And I can tell you that I am a hundred percent sure that even if he does believe you're his kid, he has no intention of being a real part of your life. If he did, he'd be here, wouldn't he?"

"He promised he was coming back to talk to you."

"He texted you?"

"I texted him," Eli says. "But this time, he replied."

We both go quiet, breathing hard. I swallow carefully to form my next sentence. My heart is breaking, and I am livid with rage once more at the man who'd decided he could swan in and out of my life for so many years. At how he's messed with my son.

"Christian lies, Eli. He's always lied to get his own way, and he lies to get people to do what he wants them to do. He manipulates people who care about him, and he always will. He's not even a real surgeon. He flunked out of med school. He didn't leave because I chased him off. He ran away because he was afraid he was going to get caught for selling those pills. He ran away because that's what he does. He lies, and he lets you down. I'm sorry." My breath hitches on a sob I hate myself for.

Eli's head hangs. His shoulders droop. "You're wrong about him, Mom. I know you're mad at him, and yeah, the pill thing isn't cool either, but Christian really does want to be a part of my life. He told me. And he's going to talk to you about it when he gets here."

Now I do take a step back. Every time I think my life can't get any more fucked up, something new hits me over the head. I try to breathe in deep, but my throat is closing.

"When will he be here?"

"In a little bit. You need to talk to him, Mom," Eli pleads. "Get it all straight. You don't have to be with him if you don't love him, but you can't deny me the chance to have a real, true father who loves me. You *can't*."

"When he gets here, I'm going to need some time to talk to him. *Alone*," I emphasize.

Eli nods. "Okay. But promise me you'll listen to him. Give him a chance. Please."

* * *

I set the scene with wine. Glasses. Cheese and crackers on a plate, although my stomach is twisted into such a knot, there's no way I'm going to be able to eat or drink anything.

For the first time in a long time, I don't crave the soft cotton comfort of being wrapped in a pill's haze.

My mind is sharp. Clear. I am ready for whatever comes next.

"Jewelann," Christian says when I open the front door to find him leaning in the doorway. He's brought . . . roses?

What an asshole.

I take the flowers with a deceptively happy murmur. Years of practice. I step aside to let him in. I take him to the kitchen and put the flowers on the counter.

"You should put those in some water," he says.

I face him. "Wine? Snacks?"

His gaze takes in the table I've set. "No candles?"

"What do you want, Christian? Why are you here?" How many times have I had to ask him the same question over the past few months? Too many. But this time, I am determined to get an answer out of him.

"Eli asked me to come over and talk to you. Where is he, by the way?"

"Upstairs, in his room. I told him I wanted to see you privately." I pour the wine and hand him a glass. My first sip goes down nice and smooth. I already feel drunk with anticipation.

Christian eyes me, suspicions clear on his face. Can't trick a trickster, I guess. He looks at the glass.

"You spit in this?" He laughs as he says it but lifts and swirls it with the light behind it.

"I didn't put anything in it." I lift my glass.

He clinks his to mine and sips, his gaze never leaving mine. He runs his tongue over his lips when he takes the glass away. His small smile, smug, makes me want to laugh. He totally thinks I'm trying to seduce him.

"Aren't you going to invite me to sit down someplace more comfortable?" Christian asks.

"Maybe later." I gesture at the table. "Have a snack."

He pulls out the chair and sits, but not without a sideways glance at me. "Okay, let's just get all of this out of the way. Eli told you he invited me over, right? And he told you why."

"He says you told him you're his real father, and that you're willing to let him come to live with you." I set my glass between us and put my hands flat on the table.

Christian's low chuckle raises the hairs on the back of my neck. "Yeeaaaah. About that."

"About that? That's what you've got to say to me? You've been filling my son's head with garbage for months. You get him involved in a bunch of bullshit that could get him into long-lasting trouble. Then you up and disappear, only to keep teasing him into thinking he's got some kind of relationship with you? The kid's father is going to prison for being a child predator, Christian," I hiss. "He's grasping at anything that will distance him from that. You preyed on that. As far as I'm concerned, that makes you no better than Ken."

Christian grimaces and holds up a hand. "Wow. Whoa. Hold on there. You can't compare anything I've ever done in my entire damned life to what that sick piece of shit did. It just makes you look irrational and hyperbolic, Jewelann. Get real."

"Oh, I'm getting real. I want you to tell Eli the truth. You have no intention of being any kind of father to him. Then you leave us alone. You stay far away. You don't involve him with any of this bullshit you've got going on with the pills—"

"Ah, yes. The pills. Well, I do need to talk to him about those," Christian says, "since, as it turns out, he's still got most of my stash."

I didn't know this, but it explains why he's back. "I hate you. You know that?"

"You *wish* you could hate me," Christian says.

I lean back in my seat. "So, he gives you back the pills. You leave us alone."

Christian gets up from the table to go to the sink, where he pours the wine down the drain. "You have shitty taste in vino, Jewelann. Cheap."

His words sting, because he says them so sincerely. Not even like an insult, just a truth he feels compelled to share. Something he wants me to learn from. He turns around.

"I hate cheap wine more than I hate cheap women," he says. "So here's how this is going to go. I'm not taking back my stash. You and the kid are going to help me move it. You've got connections with all your lady lunch friends, and he can get it in front of . . . well, not *his* friends, because let's face it, that kid's never going to have any. You're going to let me live for free in the carriage house for as long as I want. Yeah, it's kind of a dump, but if the sewage isn't backing up into it, I can deal."

"For how long?"

"As long as I want," he says. "As it turns out, flunking out of med school costs the same as if you graduate, so I need to pay back those loans. I also plan to go back to school. I *will* become a surgeon, Jewelann. It's all I ever wanted, and I'm going to make it."

"I was going to sell the house," I say, my voice faint.

Christian rolls his eyes. "Good luck. There was a dead kid buried in the backyard for a decade, and your husband did God knows what to other kids here. The place is in shit shape, even if you get the plumbing fixed. Who's going to buy it from you?"

I crumble. I sag. He has a point, but that doesn't mean he's right.

I straighten. "Look, with Ken gone, Eli and I have no reason to stay here. The bank can take the house. I don't care. I'll figure out something, and it doesn't include getting caught up in your drug dealing. We're out of here, and I want you out of my life, and my son's. You have nothing to hold over us."

"Oh, I think I might. See, I know the truth about who really killed that kid and who really buried him." Christian slides his tongue along his grin-bared teeth.

"You don't know anything."

He shakes his head, moving toward me. His expression is faux-sympathetic. He clucks his tongue. "I know everything. Eli told me all about it. The nail gun. The workshop. How you buried his little buddy in the yard and never told anyone about what happened to him, not even when his parents came to the house wailing and gnashing their teeth. He says you told him you'd protect him. Ken's out there telling everyone he didn't bury that kid, and turns out, he's telling the truth, huh? What do you think will happen if I tell the police?"

"Christian?"

We both turn. Eli stands in the kitchen doorway. He frowns.

"You swore you'd never tell anyone about that," Eli says.

Christian shrugs. "Just trying to make sure your mom understands what's going on."

"She was there that day. She already knows. But you said *you* wouldn't tell. I trusted you." Eli's expression ripples. Anger. Disappointment. Sorrow.

"Look, kid—"

His words are cut off when Eli rushes at him. The punch lands soft, clipping Christian's jaw without enough force to do more than send him back a step. Christian rubs the spot where Eli's fist connected.

"Watch it," Christian warns.

Eli is breathing hard. Both fists clenched. "You promised. But I guess my mom's right. You're nothing but a liar.

I guess you were lying about wanting to be with us? Being a family?"

Christian's laughter is harsh and barking. He sneers. "I had a vasectomy when I was twenty, long before you were conceived."

"What?" I blurt.

"After you," he says, "I wanted to be sure there was no way I was ever going to . . . that I could never . . ."

It is perhaps the most honest confession I have ever heard from him.

"Anyway, Eli, there's literally no way you're my kid. Thank God."

"That's enough, Christian." I can't stand here and watch him break my son's heart. It's enough that he's always broken mine.

There must be enough warning in my voice to stop him, because Christian flicks a glance at me. His lips press together in a thin grimace. He is so handsome, but the harsh overhead light is not flattering. Or maybe it's that I can see him with clear eyes for the first time. He frowns at whatever my face is showing him and turns back toward Eli.

"I promise not to tell anyone else. How about that? So long as you and your mom help me out." Christian holds out his hands, fingers spread. Trying to charm.

Failing.

"I don't want to sell the pills for you," Eli says.

Christian's amiable expression sours. "Tough shit, kid. You're going to help me, or I'm going to tell the police the truth, just like you told me. Could be enough to cast doubt on Daddy Dearest's crimes, you know what I mean? If he's telling the truth about not killing and burying that kid, he might be telling the truth about not doing any of the others—"

"No! No, you can't! He can't get out, not ever!"

It's clear Christian is not expecting Eli to hit him again. This time, the blow rocks him back a full step. Both his hands go up to block the flurry of Eli's punches. My son screams, a high, hoarse sound that hurts my ears. There are words in it, but I can't make them out. I can only hear the fear in them, and the fury.

Christian grabs one of his arms. Holds it. Bends back Eli's thumb while my son cries out in pain. Christian doesn't shout, he mutters a stream of low, hard invectives, and finally says out loud, "Cut it out, you fucking little psycho."

They fall away from each other. Eli cradles his hand against his body. His eyes are bright. Chest, heaving. Crimson spots paint his cheeks, and his hair is sweaty, stuck to his forehead.

"Both of you fuckos listen to me," Christian begins, but I don't let him finish.

I've had enough of listening to men who think they know what's best for me.

I stab him in the chest.

# 40

T HE KNIFE FROM the dish drainer slices through Christian's shirt and into his skin, no problem, but it takes a bit of a shove to get it in all the way to the hilt. I put my weight into it. His mouth opens, gaping like a fish's. When he starts falling, I step out of the way. He hits the kitchen floor with a horrible crunch that could be his nose breaking or the knife punching through his entire body.

There's blood, a lot of it. It pools on the floor. I stand over him, watching to see if he tries to get up.

He doesn't.

"Mom," Eli says after a few seconds pass in silence.

I find my voice. "He was wrong. It isn't hard at all."

I stagger, then. Eli helps me to the kitchen table. He tosses some hand towels onto the spreading mess on the floor. He gives me a glass of water I can't manage to sip without choking on it. He sits across from me and takes my hand. He rubs my back as I cough and spit.

"He was never going to leave us alone. He was going to hold us hostage to get what he wanted. He was going to tell people about . . . you. About what you did." I gulp in air but still feel as though I can't breathe.

"Mom . . ."

"I promised you, Eli!" I say this fiercely. My voice is stronger than I feel, but I want him to know I mean it.

A sob bursts out of him. "I'm sorry, Mom! I'm sorry!"

"You don't have to be sorry, honey." I squeeze the hand I was already holding. "I promised you I would never let anyone find out what happened to Billy. I meant it."

Eli shudders. His eyes close. He rocks in his chair, pulling his hand from mine. "I told Christian what you told me, but . . . that's not what really happened. It's what you told me happened, and I was just a little kid, I didn't remember, so I believed you when you said I did it. I could have done it. I could never remember anything about it, so I might have done it, right?"

Desperately, he shoves back from the table and stands, but if he wants to pace, Christian's body prevents him. He stares down at the sprawled limbs, the spreading blood. Then at me.

"I told him what you told me, when we were talking about what scares us. But when they took Dad away, I thought . . . I think . . ."

"Just talk to me, Eli. Please." If getting on my knees to beg him would work, I would do it.

Instead, I watch my son, my bright and shining star, crumple in front of me. Gasping, he chokes, fighting for breath and to find the words he needs to speak. I grab him. Hold him. He doesn't fight me. Eli buries his face against the side of my neck.

"Mom, Mom," he moans. "Oh . . ."

And then, at last, here it is, the thing we have kept a secret for all these years. The poison that's infected us both. Truth bubbles up and out of him, lava from a pit. It burns us both right to the bone.

"Wait," I tell him. "Slow down. I don't understand."

I hold my son's face in my hands and hope my touch gives him strength. He shakes. I expect tears, but his eyes are wide, staring, dry. Small cracks in his lips bleed from where he has chewed them.

"Dad made me do it," Eli says the same words I didn't understand the first time. "Dad made me hurt Billy."

*   *   *

Two little boys, venturing where they were not supposed to go.

"We're not allowed to go in there," Eli said, but the door was open, and Billy pushed it even wider so they could both peek inside.

Toys, all the coolest ones, lined the shelves inside. The action figures Eli had requested for Hanukkah and his birthday but hadn't received. Games. Train sets, packs of crayons.

Candy.

Boxes of it, full-sized bars and bags of treats Eli was rarely allowed to have. His mouth watered. Billy looked at him, eyes wide.

"Is this Santa's workshop?" Billy asked.

Eli shook his head, remembering at the last moment that Mom had told him never to tell Billy the truth about Santa Claus, because that would be really, really mean. "No, it's my Dad's. He sure isn't Santa."

Before Eli could stop him, Billy had gone through the door. He was reaching for the nearest box of chocolate bars when Eli's dad came out of the back part of the workshop. He was rubbing his hands with a cloth that he tucked into his back pocket when he saw the boys.

"Sorry, Dad! Sorry!" Eli cried out hastily.

Dad frowned. He looked mad. Eli was afraid of Dad when his face did that crunching up thing. "You boys know you're not supposed to be in here."

A bad taste in Eli's mouth. He blinked. Billy was taking something from Dad's hand.

"Candy," Dad said. "You like candy, don't you, Billy?"

A blink.

Billy was crying.

A blink.

"Stop it, you little fucker!" Dad's whisper was worse than a scream. He waved a hand bright with blood from where Billy bit him.

Dad hit Billy. Billy hit the floor. A blink. Dad's hands were around Billy's throat. Billy kicked. Billy tried to scream.

A blink.

Dad had the nail gun in one hand. He looked at Eli. He still looked scary. Mad. Like a monster.

"Hold this. In your hands. Hold it, you little shit!"

A click. A thunk. A blink.

Eli stood over Billy with the nail gun in his hands. It was too heavy. He tried to drop it but was afraid it would hit Billy. Billy's eyes were open. His mouth was open. A red spot of blood was in the middle of his forehead. Dad was gone.

"Eli?" Mom's voice came around the corner of the basement. Footsteps came closer, toward the workshop.

"What did you do?" Mom asked. "Oh, baby boy, what did you do?"

Blink.

Blink.

Dark.

* * *

"I'm sorry, Mom. I'm so sorry."

We hold each other for a few moments more before we each step back.

"You do not have to be sorry. Do you hear me? What your father did was horrible. It was wrong. He's a sick man. He deserves to be locked up. He deserves worse than that."

"If I'd told you back then, he would never have been able to hurt anyone else!"

"Shh. None of that is your fault. He did it. Only him."

Eli swipes at his face. "I looked again, you know, years later. I remembered the toys and the candy and stuff, like it was a dream. I looked in there, but he never kept anything like that there again. So I told myself it had never been there at all."

"You can't blame yourself, Eli."

We both look at Christian. He hasn't moved since he fell over. The blood is no longer spreading.

The low, long sound of mourning that issues out of my throat does not sound like my own voice, but I can feel it tearing up from my chest and out of my lips. I keen, rocking back and forth over Christian's body. I can't touch him, I won't touch him, so my hands hover over his back and lower, down to his ankles, where at last I put my hands on the filthy kitchen floor between his splayed feet. I hunch over, fighting the sobs.

"Mom, please, don't."

"I loved him." My voice is a raw whisper. "I loved him, and I killed him. What are we going to do?"

Eli moves around the body to look out the sliding glass doors and the hole in the backyard. The septic company is coming in two days to crush the tank, fill the space with concrete and cover it all over. With the house hooked up to the city sewer, there will never be any reason for anyone to dig up the decommissioned tank.

"We bury him."

# EPILOGUE

"**I**'M HEADING OUT for that meeting, but I'm going to grab food on the way back. Do you want me to bring you something?" Lisa's cream suit sets off her dark skin and hair, but it's the light in her eyes that really showcases her beauty.

The small shop front we share is golden with sunlight and green with plants. My half features shelves displaying collections of items I have for sale, while hers is set up more like an office space for consulting with the clients who need her help staging their home for sale. In addition to the shop, I have a thriving online business. I still buy things at estate sales and thrift stores, but I hardly ever keep anything for myself.

"I'm closing up early today to meet Eli after school. He has some college applications to go over, and we're going to my brother's to see my niece's play after that. Thanks, though."

"Have fun! Oh, hey," she adds, "are we still on for that spa day next week?"

"We're definitely still on," I tell her. I'm looking forward to a mani-pedi and a massage. Not so much the part where Beth joins us, but . . . one thing at a time.

It took six months of lean times, but the house finally sold during a huge housing boom. Having the sewage hooked up to the main line and a mostly renovated carriage house got us twenty thousand dollars over asking price, and the buyers didn't ask us to do a single other repair.

The remnants of the blood spill in the kitchen they found during the forensic investigation was a point of contention— too fresh to belong to Billy, but still possible proof that Ken had hurt someone there. The blood type was O positive, the same as Billy's, and also Ken's. It's the most common blood type in the world and could have belonged to almost anyone. Even so, the jury seemed to think it meant Ken was guilty as charged.

He went to prison still insisting that he never buried Billy Peak. He claimed he thought I'd hidden the body in my storage unit and left the boy's clothes by the water so everyone would think he had drowned. He said he thought I'd done it to protect him.

Only one of those three statements was true.

In the apartment I share with my son, we toasted the news of Ken's conviction with sparkling water. Eli's thriving in his new school. He belongs to several clubs. He has friends. He even has a girlfriend. Here in this new town, this new life, Eli and I are trying our best to be happy, and for the first time, maybe ever, I am.

When the bell jingles overhead, I look up from where I was shutting down my computer. I recognize the young woman right away from her pictures on her blog, but I pretend I don't. She makes a show of looking at the collection of Merry Mushroom kitchenware I have set up near the front of the store.

"Can I help you?"

"Are you Jewelann Jordan?"

"Kahan," I tell her smoothly.

"Right. I was wondering if you'd be willing to talk to me for my podcast?" She hands me her card.

I knew it was only a matter of time.

I stand and walk around my desk, taking her gently by the elbow to lead her toward the door. "I don't discuss what happened. I'm sure you can understand."

She's outside on the pavement before I think she knows it, and I lock the door before she can try to get back in. I smile and wave at her, though. No hard feelings. She'll be back anyway, or someone like her, digging around for an inside scoop. That's all right.

I'm very good at keeping secrets.

# ACKNOWLEDGMENTS

WRITING IS A solitary adventure, but nevertheless, books don't get published without the help of a team. I want to thank the entire Crooked Lane Books crew, especially Melissa Rechter for her eyes on the page. She guided me toward a much better book than I wrote on my own. Thanks also to Nicole Lecht for a cover as off-kilter and subtly detailed as I hope the book turned out to be.

Thanks to my agent, Lynnette Novak, for her unflagging enthusiasm. It's a lot easier to be excited about writing something when someone else tells you how wonderful your ideas are!

Gratitude to my writing friends: Lauren Dane, Jaci Burton, Shannon Stacey, HelenKay Dimon (aka Darby Kane), Sarah Wendell, Vivian Arend, Misty Simon, Dorothy F. Shaw, and Brenda Murphy . . . nobody knows a writer's pains like another writer. Thank you for listening to me vent, offering suggestions, pushing me to get the words out.

Finally, everlasting thanks to my husband, Rob E. Boley. My first reader, my most patient feedback giver, my best brainstorming partner. For two people who laugh together as much as we do, we sure come up with some twisted story ideas.

Read an excerpt from

# LIKE
# A MOTHER

the next

## THRILLER

by MINA HARDY

available soon in hardcover from
Crooked Lane Books

NEW YORK

# CHAPTER

# 1

S ADNESS AND GRIEF are not the same.
Compared to grief, sadness is as shallow as a puddle. Grief is an ocean, fathomless. Grief is insurmountable. Sadness fades, but grief goes on and on.

"Excuse me, but I need some fresh air," Sarah Granatt said to the kind-faced woman whose name she did not know and could not be bothered to learn. A coworker of Adam's, she thought. It didn't matter.

Ignoring the woman's murmur of concern, Sarah walked steadily but double speed out of the crowded kitchen, where she'd been trying to get a glass of cold water. Through the dining room, past the table groaning with platters and trays of food she had not provided and had not been able to eat. Through the living room and the line of low chairs the funeral home had set up. Past the shrouded mirrors and the front door, unlocked and open to allow those paying their respects to enter without knocking.

By the time she got to the top of the stairs, she didn't think she'd make it to the bathroom in time. She lurched through the overwhelming mess of her bedroom and into the small en suite. The cool tiles pressed into her knees as she folded onto them. Bile surged upward in her throat, acrid and foul, and she spat into the toilet bowl, helpless to do anything but wait for the sickness to overtake her. She heaved, stomach muscles aching, but nothing more came up. The nausea remained, relentless and brutal.

Minutes ticked past until at last Sarah pushed herself to her feet. She splashed her face with tepid water from the dripping faucet Adam had promised he would fix. He never had. He never would.

She found no anger, no matter how hard she searched for it. Only this vast and depthless mourning doing its best to drown her, but although Sarah wished she could let herself succumb to the pull and simply sink, down and down, she had to fight it. She had Ellie to think about, and there was also this baby inside her, the one she and Adam had tried so hard to create. The last piece of him she would ever have. She could not bury herself next to her husband, even if that was the only place she wanted to be.

Emerging from the bathroom, she didn't expect to be greeted with a glass of chilled ginger ale and a small plate of saltine crackers, but she gratefully took them both and gave Ava Morgan a small smile.

"Oh, Sarah, are you okay? Maybe you should lie down." Ava's deep-brown eyes shone with empathy as she watched Sarah ease herself onto the edge of the unmade bed. She kept a few steps' distance, one arm folded across the front of her classic black dress. Her other hand toyed with her jade pendant necklace.

Sarah didn't want to lie down, didn't want to close her eyes, did not, especially, want to sleep. If she slept, she would dream, and if she dreamed, she would wake up, and when she did, Adam would still be dead, but, terribly, she would have had some brief moments in which she wasn't aware of that loss. Better to stay awake than lose him all over again.

So instead, she squared her shoulders and took a cautious sip of ginger ale. It stayed in her stomach, but fresh nausea burbled and she set the glass on her nightstand, next to the plate of crackers she could not force herself to look at, much less nibble.

She settled both feet firmly on the floor. It had worked in college for the spins after a night of too much drinking, and in the times when her mind tried to separate itself from her body and float away. Maybe it would help now too. "Where's Ellie?"

"Graham's reading her a story." Brackets carved the corners of Ava's mouth. "What can I do to help you? You've had a lot of stress. You look . . ."

"I know how I look." Hollow cheeks, dark-circled eyes. Like a grieving widow.

"Why don't you take a little rest up here, where it's quiet," Ava urged. "You don't need to worry about anything going on downstairs. Ellie's fine with Graham. I can tell people you're sleeping if they ask."

"We're sitting shiva. You're not supposed to ask things like that."

Ava took a step closer. "Well, if they do, I'll take care of it. Do you want to . . . talk?"

Nobody was supposed to ask things like that either.

Graham Morgan and Adam had been friends since college and business partners for almost as long as that, but he and Ava had been married for only about a year and a half. Sarah and Ava had formed a friendship, but they'd never become as close as their husbands had been. Still, Ava had helped with childcare, rides to and from the hospital, dropping off groceries when Sarah'd been run ragged and didn't have time to shop. Ava had always been kind, but she'd never really known Adam when he was healthy. *Her* husband was hale and hearty. She couldn't begin to know what Sarah was going through.

"At least try to rest a little bit. Eat something," Ava urged when Sarah stayed silent. "I hear it helps with morning sickness . . . ?"

Her voice trailed off into the question. Instinctively, Sarah placed both palms on her stomach, still rounded from being pregnant with just-turned-three-year-old Ellie. She was twenty weeks along, but the morning sickness had been more like all-day nausea. She'd barely gained even ten pounds. She and Adam hadn't told anyone yet.

At least Sarah hadn't.

"I need to check on Ellie," Sarah said.

Ava tucked a strand of her sleek auburn bob behind one ear. "You need to take care of yourself."

"I'm fine. I appreciate your concern."

This was a lie, but Sarah sold it as best she could. In the past year of Adam's illness and decline, she'd learned how many people wanted to help . . . and how often that help came with expectations. Gratitude, of course, but also a certain entitlement or a patting of themselves on the back.

Ava's frown deepened, but her tone became more soothing. "I told you, she's with Graham. You know how she loves Graham."

"She loves me too. I'm her mother. I should be with her." Sarah stood, her legs still a little unsteady. For a moment, it seemed as though Ava was going to physically step in her way to keep her from getting to the door, but Sarah pushed past her.

"Sarah!" Ava's voice turned her before she could get to the doorway. "Wait. Before you go downstairs, I wanted to talk to you about something private."

The doorbell rang. Sarah stiffened. Nobody should be ringing the bell right now, and nobody should be asking her to talk about anything, private or otherwise. No ringing bells, no forced conversations—you were supposed to give the mourners space and time for their grief, not infringe on it. Her fingernails dug into the meat of her palm. People, she thought grimly, did not understand the etiquette of sitting shiva.

"This isn't the time, Ava."

Sarah cringed at another jangle of the doorbell. Her teeth felt bared, her eyes open too wide to help her hold back tears. Her palms stung. She willed herself not to rush downstairs to scream at whoever was ringing and ringing.

"Sarah. Wait," Ava repeated. "This is important."

When it became clear Sarah was still heading for the door, Ava actually did take a few quick steps to get in the way. Sarah's brows rose. So did her gorge. It would serve Ava right if Sarah puked all over her.

"I wanted to make sure you were . . . you know. On board. With the paperwork," Ava said.

"What paperwork?"

"The guardianship paperwork? For Ellie. In case something happens to you." Ava spoke quickly, sharply, her eyes skating over Sarah's face and lower, over her stomach. "Adam asked me and Graham to adopt her."

Blinking rapidly, Sarah moved away from her. "He asked you to do what?"

"He was worried about her. And you, of course," Ava said hastily. When Sarah didn't answer, Ava moved toward her, hands out as though she were soothing a skittish colt. "He wanted to make sure Ellie would be taken care of."

"I'm taking care of her. I'm her mother," Sarah repeated, this time through numb lips.

"Of course, of course. This would just be in the event of . . . well, a tragedy. Or something you couldn't handle. You don't really have anyone else, and they were so close—"

Sarah took another step toward the door. "I can't discuss this with you right now. I'm going downstairs."

This time, Ava spoke more boldly. Her gaze flashed as she blocked Sarah's path. "Please don't disrespect your husband's dying wishes."

The utter gall of those words stopped Sarah as hard as if she'd slammed herself into a wall. The bright-penny taste of copper flooded her mouth as she bit her tongue, trying to sound civil. "If I decide to sign any guardianship paperwork about my child, I'll let you know, all right?"

"We want to adopt your baby," Ava cried in a clipped, ragged voice that shook the same way her hands were shaking, still held out in front of her as though she'd grab Sarah if she had to.

Frozen in place, Sarah let out a soft noise of dismay. At last the anger came, and if she couldn't channel any rage about her husband's death, she sure could find it for this delusional bitch in front of her.

"Get out of my way, and then get out of my house," Sarah said.

Ava didn't move. "I know you don't really want it, Sarah. You *can't* want to raise a baby all on your own, not when you already have a toddler who still needs so much of your attention. I know you thought it was the right thing, trying to get pregnant even though Adam was sick, but —"

"If you do not get out of my way, I will get you out of it," Sarah said in a voice so full of gravel and grit she barely recognized it as her own. "How dare you? How dare you *ever*, but especially right now? What is wrong with you? Are you insane, or just incredibly awful?"

Ava blanched. The glint in her gaze turned steely. "We're only trying to help you. We've been trying so hard for a child—we have so much love in our hearts for a baby. And *you* already have a child—"

"Get out of my way, or I will punch you in the mouth." Sarah's throat worked as she fought against the splash of bile at the back of it. She clapped a hand over her lips. The last and only time she'd ever hit someone was in the self-defense class she'd taken in college.

Ava didn't move. Her voice went from soothing to scolding. "You are in no position to be having another child. You're going to have to get a job, and is that what you want for your baby? To be raised by strangers in a day care?"

Breathing in through her nose and out through her mouth, Sarah stared Ava down. She wanted to feel her knuckles split on the woman's teeth. Her expression contorted into something that must've been horrific, based on the way Ava's gaze sheared away from it. Finally, Ava stepped out of the way.

"Just trying to help," she called after Sarah, who didn't turn.

She needed to find her daughter, make sure she was safe. To bury her face in the mess of dark tangled curls so much like Sarah's own. To hold the small, solid body, to look into the little girl's eyes that were so much like her father's. She needed her daughter, *her* daughter, she thought almost frantically as she scanned the living room for any sight of her. She spotted Graham talking with one of the neighbors, but Ellie wasn't with him.

Her heart wrenched. The room was too full, overflowing with bodies, too much heat. Too much noise. She tried to get to the kitchen but stubbed her toe on one of the folding chairs taking up so much space. Everyone was staring at her. Solemn faces. She couldn't stand it.

For a moment, the world wavered as though she looked at it through a lace curtain. Voices slowed like a record on a player unplugged during the middle of a song. She knew she wasn't moving, but her toes still seemed like her only anchor to the floor while the rest of her drifted up toward the ceiling. If she wasn't careful, she was going to fly away.

The first time Sarah had dissociated from her surround-ings had been in elementary school during a classroom dis-cussion about what each student's father did for a living. Her dad had been "gone" only a couple of weeks. She hadn't yet understood that "gone" meant dead, but she'd known something was very wrong at home by the way her mother was acting. When the teacher called on Sarah to share her father's profession, she'd looked at the pencil in her hand and thought both the pencil and her hand belonged to some-one else. Words had come out of her in someone else's voice. Nobody else seemed to notice.

The last moments of Adam's life had been that way, his hand in hers, the sound of his breathing getting sharper, des-perate and finally, in the end, choking into silence. She'd sat still as stone and loved him into whatever waited for him after he took that final gasp, but she'd done it from a dis-tance. Floating. Watching, but not really there.

In grade school, she'd quickly figured out that not every-one's mother paced the house at night, determined to con-front imaginary intruders she fended off with mountains of old magazines. Sarah was in high school when she real-ized that not everyone sometimes stood outside themselves, watching themselves as though they were viewing a movie. In college, her Intro to Psychology course taught her there were terms for what she experienced—depersonalization and derealization—but Sarah had taught herself how to navigate through it. How to bring herself out of it and back to herself.

Another grind of her nails into her palms centered her, here and now. Through the dining room window, she could see Ellie on the swing set they'd bought for her first birth-day, long before she was big enough to play on it by herself. A woman Sarah didn't know was pushing Ellie so high the little girl's curls blew back from her face as she crowed with laughter Sarah could not hear.

She pushed her way out the dining room's sliding glass doors and onto the deck. More people gathered out here, plates of food in hand, chitchatting with each other like this was some kind of party. Sarah moved around them, down the few steps into the too-long grass. The San Gabriel Mountains rose in the distance, so different than the shores of Brigantine, New Jersey, where she'd grown up. She'd lived in California since she was eighteen, but today its beauty didn't move her. Maybe it never would again.

"Underdog, underdog!" the stranger cried in a shrieking, gleeful voice as she gave the swing an enormous push before running beneath it.

Ellie's giggling squeals sounded a lot like screams. Breathing hard, Sarah tried to call out, but she might as well have stuffed her mouth with grass and dirt.

The woman saw her and casually caught the swing with both hands on the chains, slowing and then stopping its rise and fall. Ellie protested, but at the sight of her mother, she waved one small hand. Sarah barked out a warning cry as she watched the little girl start to topple off the narrow rubber seat, but the woman who'd been pushing her held her up as easily as she'd stopped the swing.

Hefting Ellie onto one hip, the stranger smiled with crimson-painted lips as she walked toward Sarah. Her black blouse matched a black skirt and set off her blonde French twist. Diamonds gleamed in her earlobes. She looked familiar, like a celebrity Sarah couldn't place, an actress who'd once been a star but hadn't had a role in a long time. A client of Adam's?

"She's okay, Mommy," the woman said cheerfully. "We were just playing."

Sarah reached for her daughter, who practically leaped into her arms. The force of the sudden weight had Sarah tottering for a moment, but she found her balance and buried her face against Ellie's neck. She squeezed. Tears burned in her eyes and down her cheeks.

"Mama sad," Ellie whispered, her brow creasing. She wiped Sarah's cheeks.

The woman watched them, her grin softening. She tilted her head, looking them both up and down. "Other than the hair, she's his little carbon copy, isn't she? But all that wild hair. That's all yours."

"I'm sorry, who are you?" Sarah shifted Ellie's weight. Her heartbeat was slowing, but she still felt woozy. Untethered. Lost.

"I'm Henry's mother," the woman said.

"Whose mother?"

The woman frowned. "*Henry's* mother."

"I don't know anyone named Henry."

"Of course you do," the woman said. "He was your husband."

# 2

"My husband's name—"

"Was Henry. Adam was his middle name," the stranger added. Two deep grooves crinkled her forehead as Sarah took a few steps away from her. "He must have talked about me."

"He didn't." Sarah's reply was as unyielding as a concrete slab.

The woman's chin lifted, and her lips trembled. "But . . . I'm his *mother*!"

They stared at each other. This stranger had said Ellie was the image of her father, and that was true, but Sarah was stunned to see that the same slope of brow, the same blue eyes she'd so adored in both her husband and her daughter were also present in this interloper's face. She had Adam's pale hair and complexion too. Her heavy foundation covered up any freckles but couldn't shield the high, rosy color flooding into her cheeks. Adam had never been able to keep a secret; those cheeks had always given him away.

Or maybe not.

"I don't understand," the woman said as her hands flapped themselves into birds trying to escape a cage. "I know we had our differences—"

"How did you know to come here today?"

The woman's blank expression was disturbingly, eerily familiar, Adam's face overlaid on hers like a vintage movie special effect. A metamorphosis. Her eyes skated over Sarah's without landing. "I wanted to come to the funeral, but you'd already had it. He's already in the ground. I didn't even get to see him, to say goodbye."

"But I mean . . . *how* did you know?"

She finally met Sarah's gaze, her own sharp and glittering with tears. "If your child was dead, wouldn't you know it?"

"Mama, I hungry." Ellie pressed both her chubby hands onto Sarah's cheeks, again forcing her mother to look at her.

Sarah used her free hand to carefully peel away Ellie's grip from her face. "Okay, let's get you a snack. I'm sorry—"

But she hadn't asked for or been given the woman's name, and so her words stammered to a halt. She wasn't even sure what she meant to say or do. Offer an invitation to come inside? Shout at the stranger to get off her lawn? Neither choice seemed appropriate.

As it turned out, Sarah didn't need to decide, because without another word or a look in her direction, the woman claiming to be her mother-in-law turned on her heel and stalked toward the house. Her shoes left a divot in the grass where she'd spun. She went inside.

"Mamamamamama . . ."

"Yes, ketzeleh, meow meow, meow. Let's get you a snack. How about a nice little kitty treat?"

Ellie giggled and shook her head at the suggestion. Sarah took her to the kitchen. With shaking hands, she sat Ellie on one of the barstools at the island and took a paper plate from the stack on the counter. A little tuna salad, some egg salad, a few apple slices . . . the plate dipped and swayed in her grip. When it hit the floor at her feet, splashing food across the toes of her black flats, Sarah gasped aloud but could not make herself bend to pick it up. If she went to the floor, she wouldn't get up.

"Here, hon. Let me. Bex, can you get the little one something to eat? Sarah, come on upstairs with me."

Sarah looked into the woman's kind blue eyes. Linda Ruttenberg had been the first to welcome them to Temple Beth Or when they'd joined four years ago. She'd always been there to greet them for a Friday night service, or on Sunday mornings when they dropped off Ellie for the preschool program. She'd been a shomeret, one of the people who sit with the dead during the twenty-four hours between death and burial, and she'd also stepped up to arrange the shiva so Sarah didn't have to.

"Ellie," Sarah whispered.

Linda put an arm around Sarah's shoulders. "Bex will take care of her. June's here too. Ellie knows both of them from Kindertime. She'll be okay."

"I shouldn't leave her," Sarah protested under her breath, her cheeks hot, too aware of everyone looking at her. A spring of shame bubbled inside her about the scene she'd made. Her gaze darted around the room and through the doorway, but she didn't see Ava anywhere, or the blonde stranger. Her palms throbbed where her nails had cut into the skin.

Linda smiled. "Whatever you want, honey."

If the older woman had insisted, Sarah would've kept protesting, but in the face of that solid compassion, she broke. Not strong. Not competent. Grateful, though, to be taken upstairs and settled into the bentwood rocking chair Adam had bought at a flea market so she'd have a place to rock their babies. Grateful too for the blanket Linda tucked over her lap and the cardigan she pulled from Sarah's closet to wrap over her shoulders. It was an old one of

Adam's, but she didn't care that it was too big as she drew it around her.

*Adam*, she thought. Or was it Henry?

* * *

"Hi. I'm Adam."

Wide smile, charmingly crooked teeth. Sarah had been instantly wary of him. Too tall, too blond, not as handsome as he thought he was, she'd thought. He had the fresh-scrubbed audacity of someone who'd always been told he was something special and had never been given any reason to believe otherwise.

Before she could move to a new seat, the professor slapped a heavy book down on the podium, sending a rumble throughout the classroom. Adam jumped and gave a little laugh.

"I'd say he scared me out of my wits, but that would mean I had some wits to be scared out of," he said.

And Sarah . . . was . . . smitten.

The class itself turned out to be reasonably interesting—reading the Bible as creative fiction rather than faith-based inspiration had set some of her classmates' heads figuratively on fire. The professor, a shambling, gray-bearded man with wild eyebrows, never once revealed his own religious practices but took great glee in probing into those of his students, trying to get them to think outside the often narrow boxes in which they'd been raised. Adam had been one of those who'd debated with him. Sarah, comfortable and confident in her own beliefs, never felt the need.

Three weeks into the semester, Adam asked Sarah out for coffee after class.

A week after that, he kissed her for the first time under a full moon with a hint of frost in the air.

Five weeks after that day in the classroom, she took him to bed for the first time. After they'd made love, he confessed that she had been his first.

They'd been inseparable ever since. It had never mattered to either one of them that she was a senior while he was a freshman, or that she dreamed of creative pursuits while Adam was focused on the tech world. They'd simply fallen into each other, cream in coffee, sprinkles on a sundae, applesauce on latkes. Sarah and Adam just *went* together.

A perfect match, a perfect little family. At the touch of Linda's hand on her shoulder, Sarah shook away the memories. Perfect like a peach with a rotten spot in the center.

Linda rubbed Sarah's shoulder and pressed a bottle of water into her hand. Sarah cracked the bottle open and dared a sip, hoping her stomach wouldn't revolt. Her hunger rushed to life, and she thought with longing of the platters and trays of food downstairs.

"I'm desperate for a bagel with cream cheese and lox right now."

"I'll text Barry to bring one up. You want everything on it?"

"Everything." Sarah bowed her head to hold back a rush of tears. A sudden terror gripped her. "Can you ask him to check on Ellie?"

"Of course." Linda typed out a quick message on her phone and held it up to show Sarah the reply that came a second or so later. It included a picture of Ellie with Linda's daughters. "She's playing with Bex and June in her room. She's fine."

"I want to make sure Ava isn't anywhere near her. She's got dark-red hair and a black dress with a big green pendant necklace. Or her husband Graham. Tall, dark hair, navy suit?"

Linda's expression scrunched in thought. "I saw them both hustling out the front door while you were in the yard. Not friends of yours, I take it?"

"Graham's Adam's business partner. They've been friends since college. But after what his wife said to me . . ." Sarah swallowed what felt like a handful of razor blades.

"You don't have to talk about it if you don't want to," Linda said.

Sarah took another slow sip of water. A quick rap on the door revealed a solemn-faced Barry, who brought in a paper plate laden with a bagel dressed in all the trimmings. He gave Sarah a small smile and ducked back out without saying anything. Sarah settled the plate on her lap and tucked a stray caper into the gooey cream cheese. She sighed. *Did* she want to talk about it?

"Everyone must think I've lost my mind."

Linda tutted. "Nobody thinks any such thing."

"I *thought* they were friends," Sarah whispered around the lump in her throat. She looked at Linda. "But Ava said they wanted to adopt my baby."

Too late, Sarah remembered that she and Adam hadn't announced the pregnancy yet. Linda's gaze dropped to her belly, then met Sarah's eyes. If the news shocked her, Linda didn't show it.

"Adam must've told them about the baby when he knew he was . . ." Sarah trailed off and bit into the bagel. Cream cheese and salmon flooded her mouth. She chewed and swallowed, chewed and swallowed.

Linda leaned against the dresser. "Why would she think you wanted to give your baby away?"

"Apparently being a widow means I don't want to take care of my children. Or that I'm not capable of it."

"I'm so sorry, honey. I'll have Barry at the door tomorrow evening, if you want. To make sure they don't come in."

Linda's expression twisted in distaste. "No wonder you're so upset."

"There was a woman outside. With Ellie. Pushing her on the swings." Sarah choked out the words one at a time like coins clinking into a tzedakah box. She looked up at Linda, who bore a gentle, concerned expression. "She said she was Adam's mother."

Linda went at once to the windows overlooking the back yard and twitched back the curtain. "Is she still there?"

Sarah drew in a slow breath and shook her head. "She came inside, but I didn't see her after that. Maybe she left."

Linda turned back toward Sarah. Frowning, she said, "What do you mean, she *said* she was Adam's mother? Hadn't you ever met her?"

"I couldn't have," Sarah said. "He always told me she was dead."

# 3

B Y THE TIME Sarah finished her bagel, the shiva hours were over. Barry and Linda, true mensches, both of them, stayed behind to clean up the kitchen and put all the perishables away. Bex and June had read Ellie to sleep with as many stories as she'd asked for. The Ruttenbergs made sure the doors were all locked before they left, and Linda confirmed that Sarah had her phone number programmed into her favorites list.

"If you need anything, you call me. My ringer will be on. Are you sure you don't want me to stay?" Linda's brows knitted with concern.

"I'm okay. Really."

"Try to get some rest. We'll see you tomorrow, late afternoon. We'll make sure nobody comes in that you don't want to be here." Barry gently punched a fist into the opposite palm.

There'd be nothing like sleep for Sarah tonight; she knew that already. She nodded anyway and accepted another hug from Linda and one from Barry too. She shut the door behind them and turned the dead bolt.

In the quiet house, she moved room by room, cataloging all the places where Adam had once taken up space. The couch where they'd snuggled to watch scary movies, their fingers linked as his thumb-stroked the back of her hand. The kitchen where he'd made French toast with sugar and cinnamon and they'd danced to the music pouring from the speaker connected to his phone. He'd loved pop music that was popular in his teenage years, when he'd been forbidden to listen to it.

She went into the dining room table, where she had lit the Shabbat candles and Adam had sung "Eishet Chayil" to her every week. *A woman of valor, who can find? Her price is above rubies.* He'd learned that song of praise for her. He'd learned everything about their life for her.

At last she went to the bedroom and the bed in which they'd made love and babies. His pillow no longer carried the scent of him, even though she'd refused to wash the sheets since the day he'd gone into the hospital for the last time. Sarah sat on his side of the bed and looked at the glass of water on Adam's nightstand. A thin film of dust covered the water's surface. If she lifted it now and pressed her lips to the place where his had rested, she wouldn't even be able to taste him.

He was gone.

It would have been easier if she could weep, but instead Sarah sat with dry eyes and a tight throat, staring at the windows overlooking the backyard. She hadn't spent a night alone in this bed for years, and then all at once, she'd been in it by herself forever. Her fingers stroked the comforter, and she closed her eyes, imagining the rise of his legs beneath it. His body, firm and athletic, not wasted away from the cancer that had taken his life. Her eyes shut tighter and tighter until she gave herself a headache and red swirls infiltrated her vision, but she didn't want to open them and see the empty place where her husband had once been.

The faint sound of Ellie's cry pushed Sarah to her feet. She was down the hall almost without conscious effort, her feet taking her faster than her mind was able to process the fact that the sound had come from outside. A cat, probably. Not her daughter, who slept peacefully, a thumb in her mouth and her favorite stuffed bear tucked up close to her. Sarah hovered for a moment, debating if a kiss would wake her. Ellie had always been difficult to get down and almost impossible to get back to sleep if she was woken.

Deciding she didn't dare risk it for something that would only be a comfort to her, Sarah backed slowly and silently out of the room. At the door, she turned off the light switch operating the small, dim-bulbed lamp near the window.

A bright flash slashed through the glass, lighting up the room as quick as a lightning strike. Sarah froze. The past few days had been warm and bright, with cloudless blue skies. No storms predicted. She waited for the sound of thunder but heard only Ellie's soft snore-whistle.

There. It happened again, not so bright this time but a definite, deliberate sweep of light outside. Sarah went for the windows. Halfway there, her toe connected with a discarded toy, something soft that still managed to make a lot of noise as she kicked it across the room. Ellie let out a whimper, and Sarah froze. From here, she could see through the glass and out to the cul-de-sac.

Had it been a car? The Durwoods to her right had a college-aged son who was home for spring break and sometimes stayed out late. The Forsters to the left both worked early shifts and went to bed early.

Sarah crept to the window and looked down. Their neighborhood didn't have streetlights, but the three houses here at the cul-de-sac all had dusk-to-dawn lamps at the ends of their driveways. Hers wasn't lit—someone must've turned off the switch by the door, disabling the auto function. Behind her, Ellie turned over in her sleep, murmuring wordlessly.

Nothing was out there. The light must have come from a car turning around in the dead end. It might have been a single freak streak of lightning. Or someone using a flashlight while walking their dog, Sarah told herself as her eyes strained to see into the darkness.

Around her lamppost, the orange lilies waved in a night breeze. Their shadows flickered. From this vantage point, the tall red maple blocked out most of her view. Something shone dimly for a moment. A reflection?

A phone screen.

Not a bright flash this time, and maybe it was just a trick her eyes were playing, but . . . was that a person standing beneath the tree? Pressing against it? Dressed in black so as not to be seen?

Sarah held her breath. Watching. Her heartbeat filled her ears, blocking out Ellie's faint sleep noises. Sarah opened her eyes wide, not wanting to look away for even a second, but no matter how much she tried, she couldn't be sure if she was really seeing something . . . someone . . . or if it was only her imagination.

There was one way for her to be sure. Sarah took the stairs carefully, hand on the railing, well aware of how easy it would be for her to lose her balance and fall. She'd always been a little klutzy, but pregnancy made her even more so. She stubbed her toe on the newel post at the bottom and hopped, hissing, for a few seconds before she was able to steady herself.

She'd left a light on in the kitchen, but the living room was dark. Sarah went to the living room and looked out the front windows. One, then the other. They offered an even more limited view than she'd had from upstairs.

She flipped up the switch by the door, and the driveway lamppost came on but went off a few seconds later. Trying to remember how to get it to stay on instead of remaining in the motion activation setting, she turned it off, then on again, in rapid succession. This time, the golden glow spread out over the bottom of the driveway and revealed the end of the driveway and part of the curb.

It did not show anyone lurking beneath her maple tree. Sarah stepped through the front door and tugged Adam's cardigan tighter over her chest. In late March the days were warm but the nights still chilly. She went to the edge of the porch, her toes curling over the rounded concrete ridge. The urge to shout *Hey!* rose inside her, but she clamped her lips shut.

Four houses down the street, a shadow passed in front of the lamp at the end of the driveway. Quick, shapeless, ducking through the small circle of light and into the darkness between the houses, where it disappeared. Another faint cry drifted to Sarah on the breeze, but it was too far away for her to tell where it had come from.

"Hey." The word squeaked out of her. Nobody replied, but someone *had* been there.

She was sure of it.